THE NO.1 BESTSELLING SENSATION
NICOLA MAY

RAINBOWS END
in FERRY LANE
MARKET

HODDER

First published in Great Britain in 2022 by Hodder & Stoughton
An Hachette UK company

1

A CIP catalogue record for this title is available from the British Library

Paperback ISBN 978 1 529 34651 0
eBook ISBN 978 1 529 34652 7

Typeset in Plantin Light by Palimpsest Book Production Limited,
Falkirk, Stirlingshire
Printed and bound in Great Britain by Clays Ltd, Elcograf S.p.A.

Hodder & Stoughton policy is to use papers that are natural, renewable
and recyclable products and made from wood grown in sustainable forests.
The logging and manufacturing processes are expected to conform to the
environmental regulations of the country of origin.

Hodder & Stoughton Ltd
Carmelite House
50 Victoria Embankment
London EC4Y 0DZ

www.hodder.co.uk

Also by Nicola May

Welcome to Ferry Lane Market
Starry Skies in Ferry Lane Market

For Rita May, my beautiful mum,
whose young and vibrant spirit lives on in my heart
and breathes through my writing

'I would rather die of passion than of boredom.'
Vincent van Gogh

Chapter 1

'To be honest, I'd rather celebrate with a mariachi band and burgers down the front at Frank's Café.'

'What – you'd prefer that over a marquee in my beautiful grounds with caterers and a four-piece string quartet? Glanna, *really*?' Penelope Pascoe tapped her freshly manicured nails on the handset.

'Yes, *really*, Mum.'

'Well, you're only 40 once, dear, that's all I'm saying, and the Penhaligons at Crowsbridge Hall are expecting to attend a big event.'

'Good to know that your posh neighbours are on the guest list for *my* party. Thanks for that.' Glanna Pascoe blew out an exaggerated breath then, checking herself in her hall mirror, ran her hands through her expensively highlighted blonde crop and wiped a smudge of mascara from her eyelid.

Penelope Pascoe tutted down the line. Then she said wistfully, 'It would be lovely to have you back home for your birthday. Plus, if the predicted Indian summer bestows itself upon us, the pool should still be warm too.'

Glanna didn't allow the familiar manipulation to get to her. 'My home is here in Hartmouth, not at Riversway with you, Mum.' She glanced at her watch. 'I've got to go; I'm meeting someone at six.'

'Ooh, a date?' Penny asked excitedly. 'I always hoped that when you hit the big four zero, you'd grow up, find love, have a family and live happily ever after.'

'Bingo! All your dreams coming true, just like that.' Glanna couldn't help but smile through her sarcasm. 'I can see it now. Middle-class utopia.' She became staccato in her delivery. 'Two children – a boy and a girl, of course – Mind*less* Chef deliveries four times a week, and a couple pretending that monogamy is what they both want and should abide to.'

Her mother sniffed. 'You're a stroppy madam today, aren't you?'

'You've wound me up, that's why. Anyway, I don't think even you can class my very married therapist as a date.' Glanna pushed her chunky brown tortoiseshell glasses back on to the bridge of her prominent nose. 'And how many times do I have to tell you that I'm happy as I am?'

'Well, I'll bet that shrink of yours will tell you the same as me. Nobody can be happy single, darling. We all need somebody.'

'Says the woman who's exhausted every dating app in Cornwall.'

'Exactly! I'm not denying that I'm sick of rattling around this mansion with a sex drive that's off the scale for a woman of my age.'

Glanna grimaced. 'Anyway, I have Banksy. Far less

trouble than any partner.' The sleeping black whippet let out a little snore from his kitchen-based basket as if acknowledging his important role.

'You'll be a sad, lonely old spinster at this rate,' Penelope Pascoe muttered, then more loudly: 'Not everyone will hurt you like Oliver did, you know.'

'Mother! Enough! I've got to go.'

'I was thinking maybe you could pop over to Riversway for dinner this Saturday, if you fancy it?' the indomitable woman continued.

'I can't, sorry. I'm taking photos at Kara Moon's wedding.'

'Oh. That's the ferryman's daughter, isn't it? I do hope they're paying you enough.' The woman didn't stop to take a breath or to give time for Glanna to admit that she was doing it in exchange for two months' worth of fresh flower displays for the reception desk of the Hartmouth Gallery, her much-loved business where she exhibited and sold not only the works of some well-known local artists but also various pieces of her own.

'And, darling,' Penelope went on, 'if you hear from your father, I want to talk to him. He hasn't been in touch for over a week and that's so not like him.'

'OK. I'll tell him. Goodb—' Desperate to finish the call, Glanna began fidgeting.

But Penelope Pascoe always had to have the last word. 'Think about a nice grown-up party please, darling, for all our sakes,' she trilled, and hung up.

3

Chapter 2

'It annoys me that you never start the conversation.'

After she'd got that off her chest, Glanna wrinkled her nose at the soft-bellied bald man opposite her and wondered if it was a prerequisite to being a counsellor that you had to have kind eyes and an expressionless face. She also wondered if Myles Armstrong put a hint of mascara on his lashes – surely no one could flaunt such beauties without make-up.

'You know that's not the drill,' Myles said, suppressing a smile.

Glanna reached down to stroke Banksy who, having managed to stealthily poke his long snout into her handbag and finish all his treats, was now lying innocently next to her feet, eyes closed, his jewel-encrusted collar sparkling.

'Mum's pissing me off again. She's such a bloody snob.'

Saying nothing, Myles flicked a piece of fluff from his jeans and cocked his head to the side in anticipation of his feisty client's next comment.

He had liked Glanna Pascoe the minute he had met her, just under a year ago. On their first meeting, the tall willowy woman, dressed like she'd walked straight off the

Green Fields at Glastonbury, had breezed in and, without requesting whether it was OK for the black whippet trotting at her heels to stay with her, sat down and announced drolly, 'Hi. My name's Glanna, which my mother tells me means "pure" in Cornish.' The corners of her mouth had then fleetingly upturned, and she had given him the cool look he had by now become accustomed to from her huge, doe-like brown eyes.

It had taken Glanna a while to trust the 40 something professional. However, in time, the mild-mannered therapist had succeeded in gently coaxing out the information he required to start working with his new client.

Where mental health was concerned, everybody was different, but due to Glanna's brief stint in rehab and ongoing support, Myles Armstrong could tell that she had already put a lot of work into herself and was well on the way to being sorted. The truth was, she was his favourite kind of client. Troubled but intelligent. She challenged him in a good way. In fact, she reminded him of a thoroughbred racehorse, sleek and beautiful but with the ability to turn and buck him off at any second.

He was pleased with her progress and hoped that the time she had spent in therapy with him had brought her close to the stage where she would be able to form healthy relationships and make the decisions that were right for her. Plus, of course, keeping herself sober along the way.

It had been an exciting but also toxic journey that had led Glanna to be sitting here mending her mind at the age of 39 and three-quarters.

Cornish born and bred, as soon as she'd left school after her A levels, her life had consisted of travelling to far-flung places with her friend Carmel from Crowsbridge. Like Glanna, Carmel too had been bankrolled by her family, until she met and married the Earl of Newham after getting pregnant by him during his yacht party in Ibiza. She subsequently went off to live in her new husband's huge pile in Dorset, popped out two more kids and was regularly seen in four-page features in *Country Lives* magazine and the like.

Throughout her twenties, when not travelling, Glanna intermittently returned to the family home, Riversway, nestled along the banks of the River Hart and across the estuary from Hartmouth, where her gallery business was located. At Riversway, she would spend her time sketching in the wooden art studio right at the edge of the water that her dear dad had built specially for her. For pocket money she'd do the occasional shift at the cafe in the grounds of Crowsbridge Hall, the local Cornwall Trust property.

It was only after her mother's constant nagging for Glanna to do something constructive with her life that, at the age of 25, she had headed to London where she became a mature student and obtained a first-class degree in Fine Art at University College in Bloomsbury. Aided financially by Penelope Pascoe, of course.

But even with a distinct proof of education under her belt, Glanna had chosen to remain in the city and continue to live a student lifestyle, but without any of the former self-discipline that had got her the excellent degree. Let loose from the constraints of university, vodka binges, drug-taking, and a constant flow of partners of both sexes became her norm. This, combined with her irascible, unreliable personality had caused her to neglect her artistic talent and instead get hired, then fired from various jobs, including working in an exclusive boutique and as a receptionist of a casting agency.

Back in Cornwall Penelope Pascoe, who was busy focusing on her role as society hostess at Riversway, would blindly fund her troubled offspring's chaotic life, ignoring the danger that Glanna was in and prolonging the situation by bailing her out every time. Thus, through the first three years of her thirties, still supported purely by the ugly currency of money instead of love, Glanna Pascoe's cycle of addiction and indulgence began to spiral out of control.

Now, in Myles's pleasant treatment room, Glanna glanced through the open double doors to view the estuary twinkling below. It was a hot June day and its still waters reflected the deep blue of the cloud-free sky. She could just make out the yellow and red outline of the *Happy Hart* ferry landing across the quay at Crowsbridge. A few boats were making their leisurely way out of the harbour towards the ocean. This serene scenario was, Glanna knew, the relative calm before the storm. For once the kids broke up from school near the end of July, and the 'haves and have yachts' descended on Hartmouth, it would turn into a bustling hive of activity for young and old alike. Great for her gallery, not so great for getting around the town or finding a seat in one of her favourite eateries.

'Glanna, are you with us today?'

'Sorry, Myles. It's just that now I'm coming up to 40, it's making me think about my life.'

'Go on.'

'Mostly, where have my thirties gone?' She looked to the outside again and sighed. 'I've wasted so much time.'

'Time is never wasted if you've learned from it. We are all a work in progress, Glanna, whatever age.'

The woman in front of him smiled weakly. 'I keep thinking of my years at university, with everything that came after that, then meeting and living with Oliver before coming back here on my own . . . In the autumn, it will be two years that I've lived in Hartmouth and run my own business. The time's just flown by in a haze.' She reached down to stroke the whippet and made a funny little noise. Myles heard her gulp. 'And Mum's getting on my nerves too. Going on again about me settling down.' Glanna's voice turned into a whine. 'What if I don't want to settle down? What if I am happy being single and childless?'

'Well, are you happy?'

There was a lengthy pause. 'Yes! Yes, I am.'

'You took your time there, Ms Pascoe.'

'Don't go all therapist on me, please, Myles.' The sage man remained silent. 'Anyway, I don't want to talk about it now.'

'That's fine.' Myles waited.

'Oliver encouraged me to freeze those eggs,' Glanna went on in a rush. 'I wish he hadn't, it makes me feel guilty.'

'"Those eggs"?'

'OK, OK. *My* eggs.'

Myles nodded slowly. 'But guilty, for what? For whom?' This was only the second time she had mentioned this, and his trained ears homed in attentively.

'It's like there's little pieces of me sat in a fridge some-where waiting for something to happen, which isn't *going* to happen, and I don't like that. I'm angry. Angry that I've started something that's not going to be finished. Angry that Oliver managed to persuade me so readily.'

'And the feelings of guilt?' Myles pushed.

'Oh, I don't know,' Glanna said impatiently. 'For what could have been, I guess. And for today's society making women feel guilty for not wanting to be breeders. As though if we dare to not follow the sacred path to fertility, we should be banished to a life of living with twenty cats and have the word "odd" tattooed on our foreheads.'

'No one can *make* you feel anything, Glanna. You do that all by yourself.'

'Yeah, right, but when someone fires off the loaded question, "So, do you have children?" I just want to reply, "No, I bloody don't. I like my freedom. I like my peace and quiet. I like to have money. I DO NOT WANT children." Instead, I smile sweetly and just say, "No, not yet."' She scratched her head manically. 'It's not that I don't like kids. I just don't want to have the responsibility of having my own, I guess. Oh, I don't know.'

She started to fiddle with Banksy's lead, causing the sleepy whippet to let out an agitated sigh. 'I really did love Oliver, you know.' Her voice cracked. 'I get it, that he wanted a family. And who was I to stand in the way of his dream?'

'Tough stuff.' Myles nodded.

'What – to realise that me on my own wasn't enough for him, you mean?' Glanna checked her watch and stood up abruptly, causing Banksy to give a little whimper of dismay for being so rudely awoken. 'I need to go.'

'You've only been here twenty minutes.' Myles noticed the rare glisten of tears catch the light from behind his client's glasses.

'I'll pay you for the hour.'

'I didn't say it because of that.' His voice was kind. 'It's your session to do what you want with, but I've got a free slot next Wednesday at seven if you did want to come back and finish this one off.'

With an agitated bark from Banksy at the unexpected jerk on his glitzy collar, Glanna rushed for the door and without turning around, said, 'I'll let you know.'

Chapter 3

'Get your summer strawberries, ripe and juicy, just the way I like 'em, two quid a punnet, three quid for two,' Charlie Dillon bawled, his family's fruit and veg stall already in full market-day swing as Glanna walked down the hill from Monique's Café with one of her favourite takeaway coffees in hand.

A heavily pregnant Kara put down the bunches of sunflowers that she had just carried out from inside her shop then, on seeing Glanna, she beckoned her over to her bloom-filled market stall.

'Hey, Glanna. How's it going?'

'Good, good, thanks. Just grabbed one of Monique's Morning Macchiatos. They're potent enough to perk a sloth up, I reckon.'

'Tell me about it. God knows what Enrico and Breda put in them. My Billy has one and tells me he could ditch his tug and just push the ferry right across to the other side of the estuary all on his own.'

'I see how you got in that state now,' Glanna said directly, causing the pregnant woman to laugh loudly and her full breasts to shake to the happy beat.

'He's on a complete sex ban at the moment.' Kara

pointed to her stomach. 'Last thing I want to happen is for these two little bundles to be prodded out before the wedding – not that I feel in the mood anyway.'

'Twins? I didn't realise.'

'Yes, we thought it might skip a generation but alas, we have been blessed with double trouble. At least I shall only have to do this once, hopefully.'

'The wedding or the babies?' Glanna joked, taking a tiny sip of her scalding coffee.

Kara laughed and moved her hand to her ample hip. 'Saying that, if Billy has his way, Penrigan United won't have to advertise for any future players.'

'Anyway,' Glanna brusquely changed the subject, 'what time do you want me at the reception tomorrow? And still the same brief as our first chat?'

'Around six, if that's OK. And please, no formal photos. I hate them. So just some casual shots inside and outside of Frank's Café with the estuary behind us. I'd quite like some black and white ones too. If there's just a couple of good ones for me to put up in the flat and a handful for my lot and Billy's family to choose from, I'll be happy.'

'Sure, whatever you like.' Glanna glanced at the sun. 'Looks like it's going to be a scorcher tomorrow, so that's a bonus.'

Kara grimaced. 'For whom? I'll be wearing a kaftan, not the planned dress at this rate. Oh, and just shots of me from the boobs up if you can manage that.'

Glanna laughed, then said, 'You look stunning, Kara,

or maybe I should say "glowing". That's the right adjective to use for a pregnant woman, isn't it?'

'Growling, more like. I'm so bloody tetchy and knackered. We'll be home and tucked up before this fat lady sings if I have my way.'

'Best make sure your Billy doesn't have one of these coffees first, then.' Glanna put her takeaway cup on Kara's stall and picked up a long-stemmed red rose from one of the metal buckets on the ground. She pressed it to her nose and inhaled its sweet scent. 'Can I just ask why you didn't wait to do it until after the birth?'

'Why did I want to be a big fat teetotal bride, you mean?' Kara grinned.

'Well, since you've put it like that . . .' Glanna smiled back at her.

'My Billy's got a bit of an old-fashioned streak, wanted the two bubba Dillons to arrive in wedlock, and we'll just about manage it with a month to go. God knows why we didn't get hitched in the spring. The next thing is to try and agree on suitable names to go with the surname. I'm just thankful that we already have a Bob the Dog in the family, as even though it's not spelled the same, I know how my fiancé's sense of humour works.'

'Bob Dillon – ha ha! How about Doris and Dennis?' interjected the blonde and ethereal Star Murray as she walked around the front of her jewellery stall to tidy a display of necklaces and stood next to her best friend Kara. 'I can see the pair of them running around now. Two little gingers with *big* personalities.'

As she spoke, the black-haired baby with podgy bare legs hanging down from the blue and white striped papoose she was effortlessly wearing let out a blast of bubbly wind. 'Matthew Murray, have you no manners in front of the ladies?'

'Bless him.' Kara reached out and gently stroked his downy hair with one finger. 'Doris and Dennis, what's your mummy on about, eh?' She turned back to Star. 'And how do you know it's not going to be two girls or two boys, Madam Murray? Or that they might not be gingers like me but have their daddy's dark hair and colouring?'

'Sorry to interrupt you lovely ladies,' Glanna broke in, 'but this macchiato is calling and I'd better open up. I'm already late on parade this morning.' She went to put the red rose she was still holding back in the bucket.

'Keep it,' Kara told her. 'See you tomorrow. I'm having a few days off after the wedding, but I'll be sure to sort your first flower display for the week after.'

'That's kind.' Glanna looked at her rose. 'I haven't been given one of these in a while, and there's no rush for my flowers – although saying that, I do have my new show called *Seascapes in All Seasons* running from the end of next week so it would be nice to put on a bit of a display.' She had pinned up posters all around the small town of Hartmouth, and in the surrounding area, as well as advertising the show on her website. Bidding both young women goodbye, she headed off to open her shop.

Kara watched her go. 'Oh, to be so tall and willowy.'

'She always looks a bit sad to me,' Star said thoughtfully, then screwed up her face. 'Poo! I'd better get inside and change this one's nappy!'

Chapter 4

'Oh, so you're wide awake now, are you, mister?'

Glanna Pascoe stroked Banksy's soft ears as he blinked at her from the cosy dog basket under the reception desk-cum-counter of the Hartmouth Gallery. The contented canine brushed his cold nose against her hand, then yawned widely and stretched.

It was almost a year to the day when she had noticed his sweet little pointed face looking longingly at her from behind the bars of his Westmorland Whippet Trust cage. And it had taken her a mere three seconds to decide not only to rehome him, but to rename him Banksy too. After an inspection from the charitable trust, her home above the gallery at Flat 4, Ferry Lane, Hartmouth found itself with a new, sleek and handsome four-legged inhabitant. Albeit a little shy and sometimes sly where food was concerned, Banksy was a perfect companion for the recently single Glanna. He was also a blessing with regards to her physical and mental health as boy, could he run when she took him out for his regular walks up on Penrigan Moor.

'Alexa, play "Changes" by David Bowie on repeat,' Glanna ordered then, draining her coffee, she glided through to the kitchenette and cast the takeaway cup into the recycling bin. The stable-style back door led on to a small concrete yard with an outbuilding in which she stored her overflow of stock and her beloved electric-blue electric bike. Standing there, with Banksy at her side, she closed her eyes and sucked in a breath of fresh summer air, the seagulls' cries echoing above her.

Oh, how different her life was now, Glanna thought, from the one she had led in London. But that was the old Glanna, and now that the new Glanna was at last beginning to emerge and find her feet, she discovered that she actually quite liked her.

Single, with just Banksy at home for company, she could see things much more clearly these days. Could see how she'd taken a life of privilege for granted – the travelling, the freedom, her studies – all paid for without any effort on her part. She had never had to worry about money. Had never experienced hardship and poverty. Instead, she had partied the years away. She couldn't deny that the drinking, drug-taking and sexual encounters had been a whole lot of fun, most of the time. She'd enjoyed men, and even the odd woman too would light her fire, usually when she was high on cocaine and when even her inhibitions had lost *their* inhibitions. It wasn't unknown for her to wake up with two other bodies in the bed after a night of debauchery.

But before long, the drink was taking away far more than it was giving her. The hangovers and fallouts with her companions began to eclipse the good times. Her once alabaster-clear skin became blotchy, her face puffy. Her mind wasn't focused. Despite looking in the mirror and flinching at the sight, she didn't stop. With every high came a low and the lows were getting ever lower and more frequent.

It is said that everyone must hit their rock bottom in order to start climbing back up to the top. In Glanna Pascoe's case, her rock bottom came when she drove straight into the back of a parked Range Rover in the heart of Chelsea, regaining consciousness to find the emergency services cutting her out of her Alfa Romeo Spider. The doctors said the fact that she had been twice over the alcohol limit had, in fact, saved her from more serious injury, since her body was not tensed up. The physical damage consisted of two badly bruised ankles and a deep cut above her eye, where a scar remained to this day. The mental damage was much deeper. She had not driven a car since.

Standing in court, as the magistrate dished out a two-year driving ban and forty hours' community service, Glanna could still remember the sight of her mother, huge sunglasses covering all emotion, and her father with his hand on his heart trying to convey his feelings of love for her. It was only thanks to her solicitor telling the court that his client wholly regretted her actions and had already spent twenty-eight days in a dedicated addiction facility that she managed to escape a custodial sentence.

Glanna was more fazed by the community service bit than the ban. Scrubbing giant graffiti off the sides of buildings and off underpasses was sacrilege to her as she knew that the street artists who had created them would have put their heart and soul into the illegal but colourful masterpieces.

She had also had to accept the brutal realisation that once she was no longer the resident party girl and cocaine cash cow, the hangers-on had long since disappeared. Not one of her so-called 'friends' had remained to pick up the shards of her broken body or mind. And that hurt. It hurt a lot.

'Ch-ch-changes . . .' Glanna began to sing along to the iconic Bowie track that had got her through many a dark day of alcohol cravings. Where she would repeat over and over again her coping mantra: 'S.H.O.W. – Sickness, Hangover, Obesity, Waste', until the urge for a drink had gone off and she could breathe again.

Going back inside from the yard, Banksy trotting behind her, she took a duster from the cupboard under the sink, then went through to the gallery and started flicking it randomly around. Glanna found no satisfaction in either tidying or cleaning – probably because she'd never had to do it. Oliver, for some reason, loved both – and in fashionable Clapham, south-west London, it was he who had kept their flat in order. Back in Hartmouth, Glanna regularly thought about getting a cleaner, but her mother's helpers had always been so chatty and nosy, and she really couldn't do with having to make endless chitter-chatter or deal with somebody snooping around her private affairs. When she moved into her Ferry Lane apartment, she had resigned herself to being her own Mrs Mop.

The Hartmouth Gallery was very much Glanna's sanctuary. Painted bright white, the unit had a huge, curved front window in which one big, dramatic oil painting was usually displayed as a feature, with smaller oils or ceramic pieces surrounding it, often with a scattering of beach stones, flowers or other objects to create a mood and a setting to catch the eye. Inside, she had made the best of the available space. The walls of the gallery were hung with framed watercolours, acrylics and oils of varying sizes and prices – some still life pencil drawings and a variety of seascapes and portraits. Small sculptures were dotted around on shelves or on separate white plinths. Local well-known artists regularly supplied the gallery, especially with the Cornish landscapes and seascapes which were a big hit with the tourists. A stylish touch was provided in the body of the shop by the smart black easels, each holding a white-framed limited edition print.

The back of the shop, behind the gleaming new counter where Banksy sat and protected his mistress, led through to a hallway and a discreet kitchenette and toilet by the door to the yard. A steep flight of stairs had a chain across with a sign marked *Private*. It was up those stairs that Glanna and Banksy lived, and where Glanna had her own separate art studio, filled with light.

When her mother had surprised her with the keys to the shop and flat soon after her return to Hartmouth, Glanna had immediately wanted to rename the gallery 'Art & Soul'. However, on finding out that the previous owner, who was giving up the lease to retire, had created such a good business and reputation, and on the advice of the family solicitor, Glanna had kept the name as it was. And thus, a sober and somewhat green-to-business Glanna Constance Pascoe found herself the proud owner – well, more proud lessee than owner – of the Hartmouth Gallery.

It had been a shaky start, but with her passion for art, determination to show her parents – and herself – that she could do this, she had managed to turn over a small profit in the first year. This was achieved with the help of the gallery's loyal customers, a friendly accountant and the behind-the-scenes practical assistance and advice from her dad. As her confidence grew, so did the sales, which were now beginning to improve month on month.

The art part rather than the business side of things was where Glanna's strengths lay, so instead of mainly buying in catalogue artwork as the previous owner had done, she went all out to support and encourage local artists and beyond. The slight, tattooed and pierced Sadie Peach was one of her best discoveries. A second-year art student at Penrigan University, Sadie particularly loved painting the *Happy Hart*, the Hartmouth ferry, at sunrise and sunset and during all seasons. These pictures were enormously popular with locals and tourists alike. In fact, Kara's father Joe Moon had had one especially commissioned for Kara and Billy's wedding present. He had asked Sadie to paint in his late father Harry Moon, himself and his new son-in-law Billy Dillon – who was now the captain of the *Happy Hart* – in order to show the generations of the family who had worked the ferry. The painting also featured a pregnant Kara waving them off from the ferry quay. His other daughter Jen, along with Joe's beloved fiancée Pearl, could be seen as tiny figures over the other side of the water, on Crowsbridge quay.

In the gallery, each artist would be offered an area for themselves, and it was agreed that Glanna would take 35 per cent from any sales. The deal was that if, after a month, they didn't sell anything, she wouldn't charge a penny when they did finally get a sale. However, not wanting any of her artists' confidence to be weakened, Glanna would sometimes buy one of their works secretly, and then either resell it or increase her own personal hallway gallery in the flat above.

If there were any gaps in the displays, Glanna would frame and bring downstairs to the gallery more of her own artwork – often scenes with a rainbow as the central theme. Oh, how she loved to paint! The escapism of it – the feeling of freedom and peace when it all came together, when she could stand back and marvel at her work, finding it hard to believe she had created it with her own fair hand and imagination.

Glanna had found rainbows magical from when she was just five years old. Whenever one appeared, her dad would look across the estuary from Riversway and tell her that, 'Rainbows end in Ferry Lane Market, dear Glanna.' And that if she was a good girl and went to sleep straight away every night, the fairies who lived at the end of the rainbow would one day lead her to her very own pot of gold, which would not be money, but happiness.

Even back then, she had taken great joy in painting rainbows at school and at home, so much so that her dad was the first one to affectionately label her 'the Rainbow Painter'. So, when tourists had started coming into the Hartmouth Gallery specially to ask if 'the Rainbow Painter' had produced any new work, for Glanna it had brought up feelings of both nostalgia and pride. OK, they weren't asking for her by name, but she preferred it that way. Fame and fortune were not her endgame. Giving pleasure to people who appreciated her art, that was what she was after.

Glanna had once drunkenly compared her relationships to rainbows, saying some had been wonderful for a time, but most were few and far between and often very short-lived. It was so sweet that her dad and Oliver, wherever they or she might be, would text her a photo if they saw a rainbow and she would always insanely run outside, just in case by some miracle she could see it too. Weirdly, that had been one of the hardest things to bear. Missing her rainbow texts from Oliver.

When a rainbow did appear, in order to capture it in all its glory, her first act was to take a photo in case it vanished at once. A photo would never do it full justice so then, with her micro portable palette in hand to record the colours perfectly, she would mark them on her pad, along with a rough sketch of how she wished to interpret the scene before her.

An adept photographer too, she was happy to have her camera out again for Kara and Billy's wedding. Sunsets and sunrises over Hartmouth estuary were renowned for being beautiful, so she painted studies of both, in watercolours generally. She needed as much stock as possible, as the main bulk of the tourists were soon due to descend on Hartmouth, and holiday home-owners might be looking to upgrade their cottages with some new artwork or find something they liked to take back to their main residence. Her online business, which provided art for hotels, had also started to take off and these kind of mood-evoking paintings were very much sought after to grace the corridor walls or as bedroom art.

It was a juggling act to keep the gallery looking minimal but also make sure it had enough stock and income to pay the rent and bills. Especially on her insistence that she pay back every single penny that her mother had put into setting up the H*art*mouth Gallery. Glanna didn't want any more handouts as the business developed. It would have to pay its own way. It felt good to earn her own money. It felt good to be excited about the future of her very own venture. And even though the entire burden of running every part of the business fell on her, since right now there was no money for a full-time assistant, Glanna was content.

The coveted window space was shortly to be given over to the talented and exuberant ceramicist Sally Jefferson. To fit with Glanna's *Seascapes in All Seasons* show, Sally was going to drive down from her shop in Truro with a collection of her beach-inspired, hand-painted jugs and plates. To go with them, Glanna had already sourced some heavy pink and cream conch shells, plus a couple of trendy lobster-trap lamps to make the window display look gorgeous and tempt the crowds of summer visitors. A Private View had been arranged to open the exhibition, featuring an evening talk by Sally and a Q&A session, with a seat reserved for the reporter from the local paper, the *Hartmouth Echo*. Locals and holidaymakers alike seemed to love these events, when Glanna would provide a free glass of Prosecco to get bums on seats and a special discount to get hands in pockets. Sally's pieces were collectable and quite expensive, meaning that the gallery would get a decent commission.

Since setting up her business, Glanna had realised that it wasn't actors or musicians or film-makers who excited her. And it wasn't even writers, although she did love it when she found the time to bury herself in a good novel. No, it was quite simply other artists – they were on her wavelength and they really brought her alive.

And while Sally Jefferson was someone she greatly

admired, there was another, very special, Cornish artist for whom Glanna would have given up a good deal more than her window and wall space . . .

Chapter 5

Saturday evening at Frank's Café and the Dillon–Moon wedding was in full flow. While Glanna was checking the light for her next batch of shots, Billy shimmied towards her relaying tunelessly that he really did have the 'Moves Like Jagger'. Looking handsome in his smart beige linen wedding suit, he stopped singing for a moment to ask: 'How are you getting on? I can chivvy people about if you need to get some more posed shots.'

'No, I'm doing fine, thanks,' Glanna told him, knowing that the new Mrs Dillon would hate that. Thank God this was a one-off. A wedding photographer she most definitely was not.

'Doesn't my girl look a picture!' Joe Moon exclaimed in passing, while being dragged on to the makeshift dance area by Pearl who, on hearing the music switch, was itching to show off her moves to Elvis and his 'Blue Suede Shoes'.

Glanna's only other wedding photography stint had been in London a few years back when everyone, including the bride's mother, had been absolutely smashed. It was then, after having the same conversation ten times over with ten different guests and continually having to wipe spit off her face, that Glanna had realised that being a non-drinker wasn't such a bad thing, after all.

Thankfully, this celebration didn't have quite the same level of debauchery.

Memories. Funny how they suddenly caught up with you when you least expected them to. Seeing Kara looking so beautiful in her specially designed wedding dress and silk veil, hand-embroidered with summer flowers, brought thoughts of a different kind to the forefront of Glanna's mind. Namely, of Oliver Trueman and of the day she had first met him.

♡

Dear, kind, patient and loving Oliver Trueman: a handsome, six-foot-two, ebony-skinned man with a close-cropped buzz cut and a smile so wide even the *Mona Lisa* would have had to change her superior smirk to a proper full-on grin upon meeting him.

Glanna thought back to when she had first bumped into Oliver in the corridor of the rehab facility called Brightside House, which was to be her home for the next twenty-eight days.

She had joked with him, thinking he was another guest there and asking if he was Idris Elba using a pseudonym so as not to be recognised when he came out of this god-forsaken place of resurrection and reconstruction. He had beamed at her and replied casually, 'I wonder which one of us would be the happiest if that was true?' He then bade her farewell as she walked back into what she was to learn was the Activity Room. The very same room where later that evening she had found Oliver setting up the workstations and easels in his professional capacity as a freelance art teacher working for the rehabilitation centre. And the very same room where she found herself spending countless hours, to escape both herself and the outside world.

Their relationship had been a slow burner. An ex-addict himself, the gentle man didn't want to blur work boundaries. He had also wanted to make sure that she wasn't rushing into something she would regret. That she was happy in herself and ready to commit to one person. After both managing to keep the physical side at bay for almost six months, they were at his flat in Clapham scoffing a take-out pizza and garlic bread, when she caught herself staring into his melting brown eyes and felt not only trust but a deep love for him. He almost cried when she said that she was ready for the next step. The love they made that night on Oliver's huge comfy corner sofa would forever be etched in her mind.

Oliver's past allowed him to understand Glanna, warts and all. Picking her up, holding her, loving her. With honesty and communication always at the fore-front of his mind, he had openly expressed his desire for a family. Being 41 and seven years Glanna's senior he was ready to get married and do the whole kids thing. She had sneakily stayed on the pill and pretended anguish at not conceiving for three years, while Oliver took tests to show that his sperm count was normal. But then crunch time came. Oliver had taken her on holiday to a beautiful retreat where, on a mountain walk overlooking the Caribbean Sea, he had announced that he loved her dearly, time was passing, and he wanted her to be his wife and the mother of his children. It was now or never: she was nearly 37, he was 43. He had gently asked how she felt about freezing her eggs. He suggested that they could maybe try to get pregnant naturally for a further six months and then if that didn't work, as a last resort, they could consider IVF.

Reluctantly, Glanna had agreed to this invasive process. It took the pressure off until crunch time came again. And when it did, instead of communicating honestly and like an adult with him, she had monumentally fallen off the wagon in a Soho wine bar and slept with an ugly barman fifteen years her junior.

She had woken at 5 a.m. at the bloke's messy shared digs, been sick as a dog then, feeling like death on a stick, had hastily summoned an Uber.

Oliver, who had not slept a wink, had jumped up from the sofa as her key hit the lock. She had confessed everything, telling him to please leave her and her womb alone. Told him blatantly that she didn't want his babies. Told him she didn't love him, and that it was over. The dirty self-sabotage of an addict at their classic best.

Oliver had listened and listened some more. He had then taken her in his arms and rocked her like a baby, until eventually she had stopped her ranting tirade and begun sobbing uncontrollably. And what, out of all her sinful and disgraceful behaviour, had her sturdy protector cared about most? The fact that after years of sobriety, his precious, troubled and tempestuous girl had succumbed to the demon drink.

With a deep pang of regret Glanna waved back at Kara, who was now sitting on her new and somewhat tipsy husband's lap, smiling widely as he gently rubbed her huge bump. The sun was beginning to set over the estuary. Gulls were hopping around in the hope of buffet leftovers. Michael Bublé's 'Save the Last Dance for Me' was playing through Frank's top-of-the-range speakers. Friends and family were chatting, dancing and playing the fool. Love really was all around.

Glanna gulped. She had walked away from a love as tender as this. How could she have been such a bloody fool! Gorgeous, handsome and kind Oliver. He was such a good man. He had from the very beginning told her it was a dream of his to have a family and that, if you wished for something badly enough, then that dream would come true. She had flippantly dismissed his words, retorting, 'Next you're going to tell me that there really is a pot of happiness gold at the end of a rainbow, just like my dad used to tell me.'

He had been nothing but transparent with her; it was she who had been the liar. And despite her sleeping with another man and Oliver saying that, given time, they could work it out because he loved her dearly, she had still walked away.

Getting herself an ice-cold tonic water from the outside bar that was being manned by a giggly Skye Bligh and a mate, she put her camera case on the ground and propped herself against the white railings that ran along the outside area of Frank's. Yachts and dinghies effortlessly glided over the still surface of the estuary. Laughter carried across the water on the summer breeze, along with the wedding reception tunes from the cafe's big speakers. Boaters were going past, tooting their horns in congratulation at the popular local couple.

Frank and his partner Monique had done Kara and Billy proud: they had turned their cafe into the perfect wedding venue. In line with Kara's love of flowers, buntings of summer blooms adorned every structure possible, and church candles, ready to be lit at dusk, were housed in original brass ships' lanterns on each table. This was a nod to Billy being the captain of the historic *Happy Hart* ferry which had been in the Moon family for generations. Joe Moon, Kara's father, had handed over the helm to Billy so that he could retire after a lifetime's service of ferrying passengers and their vehicles over the other side of the River Hart to Crowsbridge.

The buffet had also been incredible, with this morning's market providing every kind of cold meat, wholesome fresh-baked bread, salads and local Cornish cheeses you could imagine. The wedding cake was in the shape of a huge bee in homage to Kara's grandad, Harry Moon, a keen gardener and beekeeper who had had his own hives and had lived all his life until his death at Bee Cottage, latterly with his son Joe Moon.

The sun was going down and Glanna was conscious that she mustn't miss a shot of the impending sunset. She was just about to pick up her camera to check the lighting when a woman approached her. She had a neat little figure, was sporting a silky blonde bob and wearing a figure-hugging strapless dress.

'Hey, Glanna, isn't it? I'm Jen Moon, sister of the bride and extremely happy to *always* be the bridesmaid.' She downed her wine and, taking Glanna's empty glass, placed them both on a table nearby, along with her huge Gucci sunglasses.

'I do love a cynical soul,' Glanna said, and meant it. 'And yes, I'm Glanna Pascoe, fake wedding photographer and lover of all things arty.' To her surprise, she found herself flirting. 'Kara mentioned that you were thinking of moving out of London?'

'The best of us always do, evidently.' Jen took in the stunning woman with the white-blonde crop, khaki linen jumpsuit and chunky spectacles in front of her. 'I'm backwards and forwards at the moment. I've set up an accountancy firm down here with Jack Murray

– you know Jack? He's married to Star from the crystals stall.'

'Yes, I've met him briefly.' Glanna nodded.

Jen went on, 'But I'm more of a sleeping partner until my boyfriend decides whether he can bear to move down to the depths of Cornwall. He's such a city boy, not to mention he has two kids and a bitch of a needy ex to deal with back home.'

'Ah, I see. It is quite a commute, I guess.' Glanna laughed.

'That it is.' Jen let out a little burp. 'Oops, pardon me, I'm a bit pissed, and excuse my manners. I've been sent by Kara to offer you a drink and here I am prattling on about fuck all.'

'I've just had one, thanks.'

'Go crazy. Have another. Frank got a licence specially, so how about a glass of champagne, or a little shot of tequila with me, at least?'

If this wasn't coming from such an attractive-looking woman, Glanna might have been annoyed at feeling pressured.

'I don't drink alcohol.' Glanna cleared her throat. Her voice tailed off with her reply. 'I used to. Quite a lot of it, actually.'

'Oh.'

Glanna, although used to a drinker's standard reaction to this decision, still preferred them to think that she had been a raging alcoholic, rather than assume she was a teetotaller who had never allowed an alcoholic drink to pass her lips in her entire life. That way, at least they'd think she had once been exciting.

'Doesn't that make for a boring life?' came the question.

'It makes for a full life, actually – and anyway,' Glanna went on hurriedly, 'Van Gogh said he'd rather die of passion than boredom and there's no stopping me on that front.'

Suddenly reverting to her old ways and feeling that maybe sex was the answer to distract her, Glanna played her doe-eyed look on the attractive Jenifer Moon to gauge her reaction. Which, for someone who had just mentioned a boyfriend, was far more favourable than she had hoped.

'I . . .' Jen let out a nervous laugh then bit her lip, a trait she shared with her sister, Kara, when they were unsure of what to say.

Suddenly the music was turned off and they could hear Big Frank Brady shouting in his strong Irish accent: 'Jesus, shite, what the feck? An ambulance, Monique, call a fecking ambulance! Kara has only gone and broken her babies' waters in the back kitchen!'

As Jen ran to her sibling's side, Glanna sat herself down on a bench, looked over the estuary and found herself blowing out a long, miserable breath.

The endless sky, streaked with dazzling strokes of red, pink and orange, was a sight to behold – but painting it or photographing it was the furthest thing from her mind, for the sight of the dying sun, a ball of fire gradually sinking below the horizon, felt appropriate for her confused and aching heart.

Chapter 6

Sunday evening in her flat and Glanna delighted in throwing open the balcony doors and sitting herself down on her comfy sofa. After Kara and Billy had rushed off to the hospital the night before, she had quietly crept home, but with thoughts of her past and future spinning through her mind, she had struggled to get to sleep, hence felt really tired today. Making a mental note to find out about Kara, she lay back to watch some easy TV. Banksy, delighted that he could spread himself along the sofa with her, was soon jolted awake by Glanna's gasp at the realisation of the documentary that was just about to start. Double clicking the information button on the remote, she smiled. *The Tradition of Art in Cornwall.* Her ears pricked up further when she heard the presenter introduce 'the famous artist Isaac Benson, who is promoting his upcoming exhibition at Tate St Ives in early autumn, and before that, his talk on the theme of Light at the Tate Modern gallery in London'. Staring at the screen, completely captivated by the look of the man, Glanna's desire to know more about him had accelerated tenfold.

A local art sensation for many years, prior to his worldwide appeal, 55 year old Isaac Benson at six foot six was a chunk of a man, sporting a mop of tangled dark brown curls and a matching unkempt beard. His hands were huge, she saw, and even on screen she sensed an air of mystery about him – something that in Glanna's experience only ever attached itself to highly creative and deep-thinking people. His green eyes were unreadable, she decided, and hearing him speak, she was surprised by his soft voice, which belied his giant-like stature. All this combined to make him worthy of a 'weird crush' nomination.

The part of the programme focusing on Isaac Benson was filmed solely at Kevrinek, the artist's Cornish home, located high up on the remote and rugged coastal area of Penrigan Point. This, he told the interviewer, was where he had lived, with his late parents and now his sister, all of his life. The introduction showed the artist at work in a huge studio which sat at the end of a granite farmhouse dating, they were told, from the 1800s. And what a studio it was! Glanna stared in envy. A vast skylight let in masses of natural light, and one wall was made entirely of weather-resistant glass. The room was strewn with finished and unfinished paintings leaning against walls. Two easels were set up. One was obviously a painting in progress, covered in a black silk drape; the other one was for Isaac to work on for the benefit of the programme-makers. A brown and white sheepdog lay quietly in a bed by his feet. It was obvious to see that both man and dog found the camera an intrusion, and the whole thing something of a chore.

The camera moved round to show the breath taking

view from the glass wall, revealing stone-walled fields sweeping down to craggy clifftops and the white-tipped ocean far below. When asked where he sold his work, Isaac Benson explained that, although he had an agent who organised the exhibitions and sales of his paintings in major galleries in London and abroad, he was loyal to his community, giving the occasional talk and showing smaller pieces in Cornish galleries of his choice, especially ones that might need a leg-up. His humility combined with his assertiveness was a seductive mixture, and Glanna loved that he was so erudite and well-informed. She could see he was a person of many layers with multiple stories to tell. And she really, really fancied him. He was, in her opinion, the complete definition of cerebral porn.

Glanna, completely captivated, put her hand to her heart when he spoke of never having forgotten his basic roots. His parents, now sharing the same resting place as the poet John Betjeman in the graveyard of St Enodoc's Church in Trebetherick, had done everything to allow their son to follow his dreams, he said, including paying for him to study Fine Art at a place where so many famous artists had gone before him – the Slade School within University College, London. Glanna gasped. It was where she too had studied.

Every day, he said, he felt grateful to be able to do what he loved, and above all to be surrounded by the seasonal delights of nature that being born in Cornwall had allowed him to experience and in which he could immerse himself. The fields, the restless sea, the sheer clifftops that reared up over the endless beaches and the wild creatures hereabouts all fuelling his need and passion to recreate them in his work. Isaac Benson was renowned for being fiercely protective over his private life. When asked if his commitment to his art had found its double in his love life, he frowned, then calmly quoted Pablo Picasso's comment that 'Art is the lie that enables us to realise the truth', followed by an abrupt, 'Next question?'

As the programme went to a break, Glanna walked through to the kitchen to make a cup of tea. How wonderful to see the great man in his own surroundings, she thought.

The discovery of Isaac Benson and his huge, swirling landscapes of the Cornish countryside and coastline was one thing she did have to thank her mother for. The original of *The End of the Land As We Know It* had hung in stately-home fashion above the marble fireplace in the grand dining room at Riversway for as long as Glanna could remember, ever since she was a teenager. A five by three-foot oil painting, it was the artist's impression of Cornwall's very own Penrigan Point. His vision was of a raw and natural landscape, with a lone figure standing, arms outstretched, at the very edge of a cliff, her long black hair and white gown flowing back into the wind.

Glanna saw something different in the painting every time she looked at it. She loved its tempestuous mood, the sombre colours and the bold brushstrokes depicting the storm. She could lose herself in it. But what she had always wondered was, who was that woman in bare feet standing at the edge of the cliff? And why had the artist chosen to include a figure in this painting, when all his other canvases were pure landscapes and seascapes with not a human being in view?

To Penelope Pascoe's delight, the dramatic picture had served its purpose many times over, which was to impress her guests. The sixteen-seater dining table was also a strong talking point. The story that went with it was that a huge oak tree had fallen in the grounds of Riversway during a mighty storm. A specialist tree surgeon had cut the wood into nine-foot-long planks which were carefully stored and dried out over several years. That was when Fred Gribble, Glanna's father – a teenager at the time and a gifted carpenter – had started working on the estate. Marvelling at the beauty of the oak, he had asked his new employers, the rich young couple Mr and Mrs Adams, for permission to use it, and from the wood he created a magnificent table for them, made in heartfelt gratitude for their giving him his first proper job opportunity, doing something he was born to do.

The table had been made with love, whereas the painting had cost Penelope an eye-watering sum. In Glanna's eyes, both the table and the painting were priceless masterpieces.

The programme came to an end and a yawning Glanna turned off the TV and stretched herself out noisily on the couch. She was just debating running herself a bath, when her mobile rang.

'Glanna Pascoe, is that you, darling girl?' The woman was very well-spoken.

'Yep. That's me.'

'It's Sally Jefferson here. I'm so sorry to do this to you just days before I'm supposed to be coming over to your gallery, but I've had a family bereavement. Ghastly business! My mother-in-law fell into the trench the builders had started to dig for our swimming pool and the poor woman broke her neck. I need to support my husband Christian, of course, and frankly it's all a bit much for me to get my head around at the moment, let alone organising and carting a bootful of china up to your little shop in Hartmouth.'

Glanna finished the bizarre and macabre conversation with kindness, then hung up with a frown. It was definitely too short notice to get another reputable artist in the window for next week, and she would also have to cancel the Private View and talk. Yes, the exhibition would go on: she could juggle the other show pieces around and make the gallery look great, but it was still disappointing and would mean a big hit on her projected monthly revenue.

As if feeling his owner's pain, Banksy came to her side, looked up at her quizzically and let out a tiny, uncharacteristic bark.

Glanna, patting his tiny head, smiled knowingly, for the documentary had given her food for thought for a very interesting and hopefully lucrative backup plan.

Chapter 7

'Hi.' Myles Armstrong's geeky husband greeted Glanna awkwardly as they passed on the steps of the Ferry View Apartments flat which the couple had shared for ten years. This had only ever happened once before as, due to client confidentiality, Myles usually only arranged evening sessions around his partner's job as a guitar teacher. Tonight must have been an exception and Glanna suddenly realised that she didn't even know the man's name.

A minute later, Glanna plonked herself down in front of her therapist and said immediately, 'Thanks for fitting me in tonight – and before you say it, I know I'm only here for thirty minutes to make up the session I tore out of so rudely.'

'Banksy couldn't make it tonight, then?' This was the first time Glanna had come alone.

'Even he's sick of my dark moods and I was running late so it was easier to jump on my bike.'

'What's going on with you, then?'

At that moment, the noise of two babies crying loudly whisked its way along the balconies from the Dillons' flat.

Glanna put her hand to her heart. 'Thank God. I've been so full of my own stuff that I hadn't even found out what happened. Kara went into labour at the wedding – it was mad.'

'Those babies are in fine voice, that's for sure,' Myles soothed. 'I was on my run this morning, and the happy parents waved down from their balcony. Each rocking a tiny white-blanketed bundle, with two little ginger heads on show.'

'Aw. A boy and a girl perchance?'

'I don't know,' Myles replied. 'I just called up to check they were all doing well. Why did you ask?'

'Oh, it's just Star Bligh – I mean Star Murray – and her witchy predictions.'

'Right.' Myles sat quietly.

'I'm glad they are all OK.' The crying of the babies subsided. Glanna said, 'Sally Jefferson – you know, the artist who was to be the feature of the next window display – well, she let me down.'

'That's annoying for you, sorry to hear that.'

Glanna's face twitched. 'Her mother-in-law fell in the swimming pool trench they were digging at their house, and she broke her neck. I know it's terrible, but for some reason I keep seeing the funny side.'

Myles put a hand to his mouth. 'Oh no.'

'You can laugh too, you know. You may be my therapist but you're still human . . .' She tried not to smirk. '. . . ish.'

Myles coughed to cover his laugh over the woman's sad demise.

'It's so good to laugh.' Glanna took a swig from the water bottle she had brought with her. 'I'm not unhappy but I'm not happy either, if that can be a state?' She screwed up her face. 'I don't know what's wrong with me, Myles. Saying that, I did feel a bit strange when Kara went into labour. It was like a sinking feeling, but I had been thinking about Oliver too, just before that happened.'

'Have you ever considered talking to Oliver since you left?'

'What about?'

'Do you think maybe reconnecting on a friendship level would help you make peace within yourself?'

'Hmm . . . no. That's ridiculous.' Glanna sighed. 'I don't want to relive everything again, it would hurt too much. It's been nearly two years now, anyway. He will have found someone new, got the baby or even babies he so wanted. I deleted all his socials when we split, and something stops me from looking, as although I didn't want to have his children, I know I wouldn't like it if he had a child with someone else. That makes me feel so bloody selfish. I do just want the best for him. God, I sound like that Adele song now.'

'Not selfish, just sensitive. You loved him.'

'Obviously not enough to give him what he wanted or to stay friends with him. Mind you, I couldn't believe he still wanted to *be* friends. Oh Myles, I didn't even fancy that bloke I slept with! What the hell was I thinking?' She made a face, remembering that awful morning of confrontation. 'Oliver was so hurt. God, I'm a bitch.' She pushed her glasses back up her nose. 'Bloody, bloody drink!'

'Easy to blame, isn't it?' Myles's face remained inscrutable. Then, realising he had made an instinctive and very unhelpful comment, his voice softened. 'We do what we do, Glanna, and from what you've told me, Oliver loved you very much and, turning this on its head, do you not think that maybe you were looking out for yourself, for once? It takes two to make a baby.'

'Bit of a drastic way to do it though. Most normal people would talk about it, not throw themselves under the cheating bus.'

'Whatever normal means,' Myles added.

'But compromise is what makes a relationship, isn't it?' Glanna sighed again.

'Bringing a new life into the world is a big compromise for any relationship, I'd say.'

'Myles Armstrong, you are so bloody good at what you do. You never fail to make me feel better.'

'I can't *make* you feel anything. You do that all by yourself,' Myles said, reaffirming his familiar mantra. Then: 'Why do you think you don't want children, Glanna?'

'Oh, bring me down again, will you?' she snipped sharply. 'I told you. They are noisy, smelly and drain both your soul and resources.'

'In your opinion,' Myles said calmly.

'In my mother's opinion.'

'Go on.' The therapist felt hopeful for Glanna to gain some further insight.

'She said it all the time. I don't think she ever loved me, not properly.' Wishing she'd brought Banksy as a petting distraction, Glanna looked away, then snapped, 'I don't want to talk about this any more.'

'OK, when you're ready. So . . . with Oliver completely out of your picture, do you think meeting somebody else might help?' Myles casually dropped in.

'As in a new partner, you mean?' Glanna screwed her face up. Myles nodded. 'And help what, exactly? I'm not lonely. I told you I'm all right. I met somebody at Kara's wedding, actually.'

'You did?' Myles Armstrong sat back in his black leather chair.

'Yeah. A woman. She was hot; hot and feisty. I liked her vibe. She has a boyfriend though.'

'Friendship isn't such a bad thing, is it?'

'It is when you haven't had a decent shag for so bloody long. I don't know what's happened to me. I had sex on tap – before I met Oliver, I mean.' She shrugged. 'But sex on its own without love is easy. Uncomplicated. No emotion to bare. Maybe the drink helped with my pulling prowess. And Hartmouth is not exactly leaping with hotties, is it?'

She checked her watch and jumped up. 'Time's up. I don't want to be encroaching into your evening. Thanks for this, Myles. As much as I'm a moany old cow, you do help me.'

'We still have a bit of time left, if you wanted to stay.'

'I don't have the patience.'

Myles stood up too. 'What are your plans for the coming weekend?'

'I'm going to get the wedding pic prints ready for Kara and Billy to view, then next Monday, as the gallery's closed that day, I'm heading to London for a couple of days, so I can visit Tate Modern and have a look round. I've booked to hear the artist Isaac Benson from Penrigan give a talk.'

'Wow, that's exciting. A little road trip.'

'Well, train trip as I no longer drive, but yes, it'll do me good to get a change of scene. Sadie Peach has offered to look after the shop for me. She knows what's what and can always phone me if there's a problem.'

'Are you taking Banksy?'

'No, you know how he likes to keep his anonymity, especially in the Big Smoke.'

They both laughed.

'He'll get spoiled rotten by my dad, so that's not a worry. I'm looking forward to it, a night and two days away from this place, and I love Isaac Benson's work. Just seeing him on TV the other night . . . well, I am deeply in lust with the man too.'

'What age is he?'

'Fifty-five, I think they said on the documentary – but what's that got to do with anything?'

'Just asking.'

'You're going to go all therapist on me and try to find out if I'm looking for a father figure.'

Myles shook his head. 'I wasn't at all. I'm just interested in the man, myself.'

Ignoring him, Glanna started to blurt out, 'I have a great relationship with Dad and true, I've always had a thing for older men. Even at school my first boyfriend was sixteen to my fourteen. There was complete controversy throughout the whole of Year 9, especially when we were found making out under the tuck-room counter in the sixth form block. There would have been even more of one if they'd known that I slept with Mr Dorkins from the woodwork department.'

She put both her hands to her face. 'He was so damn sexy. I was eighteen then and had left school, so it was all above board. Well, apart from the fact that he'd just got married. I met him in Storkers, the nightclub in Crowsbridge, now sadly closed. God, me and Carmel had some nights there before we went off travelling the world. It had a sticky carpet!' She grinned at the memories. 'Me and Dorkers. Ha! Dorkers and Storkers – I never thought of that before. Well, we were both steaming drunk and ended up having very noisy sex on *Ups & Downs* – my mum's boat, moored at the bottom of the hill at Riversway. It was so bloody hot! She's still got that boat, you know. Dad uses it sometimes, when the ferry's not running.'

'Was that just a one-off?'

'God, yeah. He sent me a huge apology the next day and hoped I would be able to forgive him and never mention it to a single soul. It was me who came on to him, so I found it all quite amusing at the time.'

'Did you sleep with other attached men?'

'When I was drunk, I would have slept with the Pope, if he'd asked me.' She let out a little laugh. 'Minus the one bout of chlamydia, I liked those days when I felt so free, and God only knows how I didn't get pregnant back then.'

'You don't feel free now, then?'

'It's different when you get older, isn't it?' Glanna said thoughtfully. 'It must be part and parcel of not having kids. Too much time to bloody think. My world isn't structured, which is every parent's dream, I expect. I know what I don't want though, if that counts.'

'What's that, then?'

'To grow old alone.' Glanna's phone alerted her to a text. 'Sorry, I'm expecting Dad to pop in tonight, and he didn't confirm a time.' She reached into her navy Longchamp tote bag for her mobile. 'Oh. He's there already.'

'Go, go, go. Enjoy the gallery.'

'I will. And Myles? Thank you for always listening to my nonsense.'

The therapist went to the door. 'We are booked in for the last Tuesday in July. You did want to keep our meetings monthly moving forward, didn't you?'

'Yes, please. And if I feel I need to see you before then, I can, can't I?'

The caring man looked directly at her, replying softly, 'I'm always here.'

Glanna headed to the apartment door and looked back.

'I'm glad you are.' She felt herself welling up. 'Bloody hay fever.' She sniffed loudly. 'I'll transfer what I owe you later.'

♡

Glanna whizzed in through the back gate of her gallery, got off her electric bike and parked it under the long porch outside the stable door. She could hear Banksy scratching to get out.

'Dad, what the hell are you doing down there?' Fred Gribble was crouched down as close to the stable door as he could get. He was wearing a flat cap and dark wrap-around sunglasses.

'I'm avoiding your mother.'

'She's not here. You know the only time she gets the ferry across to Hartmouth is if Jilly St John-Davis invites her over to the Dolphin for lunch and she's probably fallen out with her this year already, anyway.'

'It's not that. She told me she had got you one of those doorbells with a camera and that she could link into it from her phone.' Fred Gribble's Cornish accent seemed to grow more pronounced at this comment.

Glanna gave a bark of laughter. 'Yes, she did buy it, but do you really think I'd let her in on my comings and goings?'

Her dad's voice lowered. 'Maybe she was just worried about you being on your own for all this time and not drinking, you know. You are all right, aren't you, my love?'

'Yes, of course I'm all right. It's my choice to be alone. And come on, Dad, you know what she's like. She was checking up on you because underneath she realises that you should both be together still.'

Fred shook his head at her comment then, taking off his hat, revealed his newly cut, mousy-brown hair. Glanna leaned down to kiss him on the cheek, saying fondly, 'It's great to see you. Loving the hair – and look at you going all trendy and wearing a hoodie. You look twenty years younger.'

'I reckoned it was about time I bought meself some new clobber. I'm forever in old work clothes.'

Glanna had most certainly got her five-feet-ten stature and pale colouring from her mother, but her striking features came from her father. He was a fit man for his age, manual work keeping him agile, the Cornish sun giving his skin a year-round mahogany tone. At five feet seven, he reminded Glanna a bit of Tom Cruise.

But height wasn't the only interesting factor in the coupling of Fred Gribble and Penelope Pascoe. Glanna had always thought that her mum and dad's love story was very romantic and, in a macabre kind of way, still was. She had learned more a few years ago, when she had enquired where her middle name, Constance, had come from. Penelope, fuelled by a large Courvoisier, had then candidly revealed the whole history of her and Fred's non-marital affair.

Penny Pascoe told her daughter that she had grown up an only child (like Glanna herself) in a family of wealthy property owners in North Cornwall. Her beloved parents had died in a double drowning accident when their boat overturned on a lake during a holiday in Switzerland, shortly after Penelope had married her equally rich American fiancé Richard Adams, known as 'Dicky', whom she had randomly met in the grounds of Crowsbridge Hall when he had been visiting as a tourist. The grand and rambling Riversway House had been gifted to them by her grief-stricken grandparents. Life for a while seemed perfect, but then Dicky died in a tragic car accident on his way back from a surfing weekend with pals in Newquay only five years into their marriage. Heartbroken, Penny got very drunk at her husband's wake, which took place at Riversway, and when everyone had left, she slept with Fred Gribble, who was then just the handsome young employee on their estate who had made their impressive dining table.

Despite her grief, Penny gradually found herself falling in love with 'her Freddie', and he with her, despite her recent widowhood and the nine-year difference in their ages. Knowing the scandal it would cause for them to get together so soon after Dicky's passing, the pair kept their relationship quiet. When she fell pregnant a few months after Dicky's death, Penelope reverted to her maiden name, so that Glanna could take it too. Firstly, because 'Gribble' just wasn't a suitable name in Penny's eyes and secondly, because being the snob she was, she would never be able to bring herself to marry a penniless estate worker.

Penelope's insistence that they never publicly come out as a 'proper' couple had always upset Fred, but because he loved her dearly and didn't want to lose touch with his only daughter, their on-off relationship continued, with him carrying on working on the Riversway estate, the place that he also loved. Penelope, meanwhile, did not have to work. She lived the life of luxury provided by the sale of the properties in North Cornwall after her grandparents died, and by the life insurance after her beloved Dicky passed away.

The situation changed when Fred realised that he was far from the only man gracing Penelope Pascoe's opulent boudoir. For his own sanity and self-respect, he had to leave the main house. Well, kind of leave, as he agreed to remain working for Penny, for a salary, and live rent-free in the Lodge House, which stood at the end of the long, cedar tree-flanked drive. He had lived there now for the past ten years and, during all that time, he had never taken another lover, not one. Instead, at the local club in Crowsbridge, he had found companionship with his friends, with whom he played cricket and chess, and of course, he spent time with his beloved daughter, Glanna Constance Pascoe.

Glanna remembered that it had taken an age for Penelope to relay her dramatic story, and it wasn't until the end of it that she had asked her mother, 'So, what has any of that got to do with Constance being my middle name?'

Penny had given one of her 'looks' from under her

frameless spectacles and replied, 'Darling, surely you must be aware of Constance, Lady Chatterley and her gamekeeper lover Mellors, in *Lady Chatterley's Lover*? It is one of my all-time favourites.' She had then thrown her head back and given a tinkling laugh. 'And as Glanna means *pure* in Cornish, putting that in front made for an hilarious juxtaposition.'

Looking around him furtively, Fred Gribble unlocked the back stable door of the gallery with his own key and scurried into his daughter's kitchenette. After allowing Banksy time to patter outside to cock his leg against Glanna's bike and pee, he then quickly shut the stable door again.

'Dad, you're being really odd. What on earth's the matter?'

Fred began to talk at speed. 'I'm going on a date. I met someone on the Internet. Her name is Linda.'

'Dad, slow down.'

He took an accentuated breath. 'She works at Monique's – you know, the cafe that was Tasty Pasties at the end of Ferry Lane.'

'Mrs Harris, you mean!'

'You know her?'

'Dad, the market's like a family and she's very much part of it.'

'You're OK about it?'

'Yes, of course. Maybe this is what's needed to shake you and bloody Mother up.'

'She thinks I'm at the club in Crowsbridge.'

'You do realise that unless you are intending on only spending five minutes with . . . Linda,' Glanna found it weird saying her first name, 'you'll miss the last ferry back.'

'I booked a hotel.'

'Oh, have you now? You could have stayed here.'

'Not appropriate, Glanna. This is my third date with Linda, and ten years is a long time to be alone,' the man replied matter-of-factly.

'O*kaaay*. Enough information already. So does Mrs Harris – I mean Linda – not live alone, then?'

'Oh yes, she's been widowed for years, but I'm allergic to her ruddy cat. It's a right scraggy old fluffball, it is. Brings me out in hives and I can't breathe properly if I'm there too long.'

Glanna laughed out loud. 'Dad, just go and have a lovely time.'

'I intend to. I've left the light on in the Lodge and I'm going to turn my phone off when I leave you. I'll be back over on the first ferry. Your mother is rarely up before nine, so she won't have a clue.' He shrugged. 'Not that she'd care anyway. All I can say is, it's so refreshing being with someone where having the best watch or latest designer dress is not even on their list of things they want.'

'It's good to see you happy. Oh, and are you still OK to have Banksy on Monday morning through to Tuesday night while I head off to London? I've got Sadie looking after things at the gallery on Tuesday, but it's too much to expect her to take care of Banksy too, and I know he loves being with you.'

'Of course. I'll meet him Crowsbridge side as normal, yes?'

'Perfect. I'll speak to Billy and pop the hound on the first crossing.' She pushed her glasses up. 'And thanks so much, Dad. You're such an angel.'

'I do my best.' Fred Gribble gave a cheeky wink to his daughter. 'Right, I'm going to love you and leave you, missy.' He opened the door. 'It worries me if these stable doors are secure enough. Keep them properly locked, eh. You are insured, aren't you, kiddo?'

'Yes, of course I am. It's not just the stock in here I need to keep safe, you know.'

'The storage shed out here too?' He nodded towards the fixed structure in the back yard. 'Still no alarm, I see.'

'Dad! You are beginning to sound like Mum. It's all good. I can't be faffed with setting an alarm all the time, and anyway, it sounds like the only thing being stolen in Hartmouth at the moment is hearts, isn't it?' She put her hand on her father's arm and grinned at him. 'Now go and have some fun!'

She poked her head into the gallery to check all was in order and that the front shop door was securely locked, then she made her way upstairs to her comfy flat, accompanied by her trusty whippet. Throwing open the Juliet balcony doors, which looked out onto busy Ferry Lane and the market below, she lay flat out on her big cream sofa, making room for Banksy. Still exhausted from his morning run on the moor, making a harrumphing noise, the black whippet stretched out against Glanna's long culotte-covered legs and was soon asleep. Closing her eyes as she absorbed the street sounds that only a seaside market town brings, Glanna felt suddenly at peace.

Just as her art hut on the banks of the River Hart had been to her as a youngster, her flat was now her sanctuary. Penelope had insisted on kitting it out with an extortionately expensive bed and sofa, but it was Glanna herself, with her landlord's permission, who had hand-painted a beautiful mural of a rainbow over the estuary onto one of the white-painted walls. Above a medium-sized TV of her choosing was a framed limited edition print of one of Isaac Benson's seascapes, painted from the top of Penrigan Point. She had loved the dolphins in this one – three of them – their bodies just visible above the surface of the waves, and only if you looked closely. She also loved the names he gave to all of his paintings, this one being *Safety in Numbers*.

Glanna shifted comfortably, enjoying the warmth of Banksy at her side. She thought about her father and his antics, pleased that at long last he was moving on. Trying to find his own way and happiness. At sixty-nine years old, what was it that her mother was still chasing? Her dad really was a diamond of a man; he still looked good for his age and to her it was clear that her parents still loved each other. She wished that Penelope Pascoe could just see sense and stop wasting time. Everybody, even the Penhaligons, knew the score, surely – and did any of it really matter now after all this time? Love was love. Her mother was the problem. What Oliver had always said to her when she had relived any of her excruciating drunken moments, the ones she had remembered anyway, was that *other people didn't care.* That all most people worried about was themselves. Penelope's stuck-up neighbours wouldn't give her love life a second thought and if they did, sod them anyway.

Laughing to herself, she tickled the whippet's taut tummy, waking him up, and said into his twitching ear: 'Who'd have thought it, eh, Banksy boy? Your grandad, shagging *Mrs Harris*.'

Chapter 8

Eight o'clock Saturday morning, and the market was already in full swing.

'Spray carnations, two pounds a bunch, three for a fiver, every colour,' Skye Bligh's bright voice trilled from outside Passion Flowers.

'You say Barnarna, I say Bananna, hey Glarnar?' Charlie Dillon, purposely imitating her posh voice and pronouncing her name wrong, winked at the artist who was making her way to Monique's for her super-charged macchiato fix. Still holding the bunch of yellow fruit aloft, he then addressed Mrs Harris, who had nipped out of the cafe to get some fresh strawberries for smoothies and toppings.

'Just look at the size of these beauties, madam,' he said with a naughty glint in his eye. 'Perfect with a squirt of cream. Go on, grab a bunch and make sure to show me your knickerbocker glory.'

Pat Dillon slapped her irreverent husband, whilst Mrs Harris lowered her eyes and attempted a seductive pout at the rude greengrocer.

Glanna approached Skye. 'Hey, is Kara around today?'

'You're lucky.' The pretty blonde teenager gestured

towards the shop. 'She's here, but be quick, she'll be heading off again soon. Oh, and she said if I saw you to ask what colours you'd like for your first flower display.'

'OK, fab. Let me have a think about what would work, and I'll let you know Wednesday if that's all right with you.'

Skye put her thumb up as Glanna pushed open the glass door to be greeted by a knackered-looking Kara staring at a laptop. Her dad's fiancée Pearl was bending over a pram cooing at the tiny twins, like a loving grand-mother would.

'What are you doing back at work literally seconds after having those babies of yours?' Glanna asked, handing Kara a congratulations card.

'I'm so not working, well, here anyway. Having twins is like a conveyor belt of shits, tits and tears, and nobody tells you how much it hurts having a bloody Caesarean. I feel like a milking cow who's been zipped up with barbed wire.'

'Ow,' was all a shocked Glanna could manage.

'Thanks for this. I'll open it with Billy, if you don't mind.' Kara placed the yellow envelope into the back of the pram. 'The lovely Pearl is doing market days for the foreseeable future, but I wanted to just stop by and make sure that everybody is happy.'

'Yes, and you're going back to Bee Cottage for a rest before the next feed, aren't you, my love?' Pearl insisted. 'You've only been out of hospital a few days.'

'Yes, Mum,' Kara tutted, constantly delighted that her dad had found a woman who had already shown her more love than her biological mother had done throughout her whole life.

'I'm in love, so in love,' Pearl sang out at Glanna. 'Just look at the little darlings.'

'And yes, before you ask, my white witch friend next door was right with her boy and girl premonition,' Kara put in.

'One of each, that is sweet.' Glanna peered into the pram, relieved that the feeling she had experienced the other night must have just been connected to her thoughts of Oliver. It was that which had unsettled her, not the fact that somebody was about to give birth.

'Sweet? When they are biting at my sore nipples like piranhas at midnight, then start screaming again at 3 a.m., I have to confess that "sweet" isn't the first word that springs to mind.'

Pearl butted in, 'As soon as you go on to those bottles, me and your Billy will do some night stints for you, you know that, girl. No messin'.'

'I know. I know. And Pat has promised to help out as much as she can too. She and Charlie are coming round for dinner tonight – we're having fish and chips and they are bringing them, thank goodness.' Kara yawned loudly. 'I really must stop moaning or they'll start thinking I don't like them, when I love them more than life itself. And look, they are ginger nuts, just like me.' The proud mother then stood straight and said: 'Please allow me to introduce you to Red and Poppy Dillon.'

'Wow! Really beautiful names.' Glanna had always loved

the fact that, despite the Lady Chatterley connotation, her mother had given her a traditional Cornish moniker. She had yet to meet anyone else who shared it.

'We think so. They can embrace their glorious colouring then. They weighed in at five pounds each exactly, which is big, I'm told, for slightly prem twins. They are small but perfectly formed, and they didn't have to go in an incubator, which I was so worried about when I learned I was going to have an emergency Caesarean.'

'What a relief.' Glanna was impressing herself with her baby talk. 'Did you manage to enjoy the wedding though, up to that point of no return?'

'I had the best time, thanks – and what a story to relay to our grandchildren. I nearly gave birth in the kitchen of a cafe on our wedding day. Just in time to make them legitimate!'

Poppy started to stir, and Kara visibly cringed. All three of them stood stone still for a second. Pearl tiptoed her way to the back door to allow the pram easy passage.

Glanna reached into her bag, then whispered, 'Kara, I picked up your sister Jen's sunglasses the other night and put them in my bag by accident. Is she around this weekend? If so, I'll get them back to her.'

'No, she's back in London for the weekend. Is due down again next week, I think. She's probably got count-less pairs, so I shouldn't worry too much, but let me text you her number. Actually, I'll do it right now or I'll be sure to forget.' Kara fiddled with her phone. 'Done.'

'Brill, thanks. I will get on the case for selecting the

best wedding photos for you to choose from this week, and Skye just reminded me about my flower arrangement.'

'I'd forgotten about all that already too.' Kara laughed loudly, causing both babies to wake up and utter hungry cries. 'My cue to leave.' She raised one arm high into the air and headed for the door, pushing the pram in front of her. 'Motherhood, here I come!'

♡

Glanna ordered herself a Morning Macchiato coffee and, wanting to take a bit of time out before she opened the gallery, placed herself on a high stool at the window counter in Monique's and sipped at it slowly. On market days, most stallholders were present and correct from 6.30 a.m., setting up and preparing for the day, but experience had taught Glanna that a 10 a.m. opening time worked best for her clientele. The fact that she was far more a night owl than an early bird had been the deciding factor.

The hustle and bustle of stallholders and shoppers alike really did give the estuary town a buzz. The mixture of goods on offer, including antiques and antiquarian books, a clothes stall, jewellery and crystals, artisan foodstuffs, fresh fruit and vegetables, the gallery, plus the presence of a butcher, fishmonger and a baker attracted a varied array of shoppers of all ages. Sitting here gave her the best view down Ferry Lane towards the estuary, where on this clear summer's day she could see the *Happy Hart* setting off out towards Crowsbridge and the cars and passengers it had just dropped off now making their way up to the market and the car park at the top of the hill.

The screech of gulls streamed through the open door – a sound Glanna had long associated with sitting in her art room on the banks of Riversway, the place where she had found sanctuary after her split from Oliver. The wooden hut, lovingly built years ago by her father, with its unending view of the estuary, was where she would sit and think and paint and cry, quite often on Fred's shoulder, until the day Penelope Pascoe had seemingly grown an empathy gene and had surprised her with the purchase of the lease of the Hartmouth Gallery.

Glanna taking over the lease there wasn't the only change that took place in the market at the top of the hill. It had been a bit of a shock for the residents when Philip Gilmour, the eccentric and flamboyant owner of Tasty Pasties, had hung up his apron and headed to Cockleberry Bay in Devon with his new lover, Billy's twin brother Darren.

However the arrival of Big Frank's sister Breda Brady, a formidable southern Irish woman, and her long-term partner Enrico Donato, a fiery, loyal, and empathic Italian, soon allayed everyone's takeover concerns. The experienced cafe-owners, along with their ten-year-old son Rocco, were now a permanent and accepted fixture of the new Monique's Café.

Philip Gilmour had always insisted on cooking his prized pasties on the premises. The recipe, he declared, was so secret that even he had forgotten what was in it, but Mrs Harris knew and that was the main reason the new owners had kept her on. Now offering fewer varieties than before but still a traditional Cornish pasty and a cheese and onion option, this seemed to have gone down without complaint amongst the loyal clientele, and allowed the new owners scope to offer more varied ciabatta, cake and general cafe offerings with an Irish-Italian flavour.

'I'll give you a penny for them torts, so I will,' said Breda Brady, who was busily clearing the table next to Glanna.

'They're not that interesting, really.' Glanna drank the last of her coffee and stood up.

'And if it's about a man, he's probably not wort it.' The sturdy big-bosomed woman winked as she made her way back to the cafe counter.

Glanna shouted, 'Thank you!' as she headed for the door.

'You have a good day now, my love.'

Glanna wandered down to the Hartmouth Gallery. She had lied. Her thoughts *had* been interesting, to her anyway, and had very much to do with a man, namely the talented Isaac Benson and her bold plan to see if she could persuade him to exhibit one of his paintings in her gallery.

Chapter 9

Glanna handed a well-behaved Banksy with his lead on and his little overnight satchel containing poo bags, his favourite soft toy and blanket, and a packet of his treats to Billy for safekeeping on the first ferry of the day, then set off on the few miles to Truro station on her electric bike.

Even though it was early, she could tell it was going to be a hot day. The weather forecasters had predicted 28 degrees, 30 in London, so she was glad of the long cotton flowery sundress she had put on, currently hitched into her knickers so as not to catch it in the strong chain of her bike. Huge sunglasses covered most of her face and her own overnight bag hung precariously out of the basket on the front. As she pedalled, her phone rang and she fished it out of her bag to listen.

'Your father's having an affair!' Penelope Pascoe exclaimed dramatically, then ran on without a pause: 'Thursday morning, it was. The sun was up so I decided to go for a walk down the drive, knocked on his door and he didn't answer. I knew he wasn't there. I could sense it.'

'Maybe he was working or . . .'

'No, because I have a key and I let myself in, and I saw that his best blue shirt was missing, and the Versace aftershave I gave him was out on his dressing table.'

'Mum! You can't do things like that.'

'Well, I did. What's that dreadful noise?'

'I'm on my bike, on my way to the station. I've got my earbuds in.'

'Where are you going?'

'London. Tate Modern.'

'Oh! I could have come with you. Maybe lunched at Quaglino's, darling. I haven't been there for an age. It gets so bloody dull down here sometimes.'

'It's not a jolly, I'm researching – and when it comes to Dad, you made the decision you don't want him, so whatever he chooses to do is surely his business. You are hardly Mother Teresa yourself, now, are you?'

'That's different.' Penelope paused, then struck. 'You know something, don't you, Glanna? I'm well aware that he talks to you, tells you everything. And he's been in a suspiciously good mood recently.'

'I can't hear you that well, Mum,' Glanna lied, holding the phone a long way away from her face.

'Are you staying up there?'

'Yes, but back tomorrow.'

'So, who's opening the gallery up tomorrow, then?'

'Sadie – you know, the art student from Penrigan. She loves being involved and I'll be back by early evening anyway.'

'Do you trust her?'

'*Mum!*' Glanna's voice dragged in annoyance. 'Look, I'm about to park the bike up safely. I need to concentrate.'

'Not before you talk to me about your father, you're not.'

'Oh no, my battery is about to . . .' Glad of Penelope Pascoe's obvious concern at her father's antics, Glanna hung up. It was about time the woman realised what she would be missing if the kind and loving Fred Gribble were to leave her completely.

Glad to have parked her bike safely and caught her train to London in good time, Glanna settled down and relaxed. She had forgotten just how much she loved a long train journey. It was an opportunity to breathe and just be. The decision to close the gallery on Mondays had been for reasons just like this.

Glanna had been harping on to Myles about time passing, so from now on she decided she really should make more of an effort on her day off. As the train approached Paddington station, she couldn't believe how quickly the long journey had flown by. She had started off reading the newest novel from her favourite Cornwall-based author, Patrick Gale. Comfortably resting the hardback on the table of her pre-booked window seat, she had turned her phone off, free to escape in the pages of a well-written story without a single interruption or even an unwelcome thought. Having skipped breakfast, by eleven she had felt hungry so, opening her trendy black leather rucksack, she took out the cheese salad baguette that she'd grabbed from Monique's en route, a packet of Ready Salted crisps and a Coke Zero, and began to picnic at leisure, pleased to be alone at her table and slightly surprised that, on a Monday morning, the three pre-booked seats around her had been empty since Taunton.

After she'd finished eating, she turned her phone back on and began to read the messages that were now beeping in. Her dad had sent her a photo, of Banksy sitting upright next to him in his pick-up van, with the caption: *Six-mile forest run, B not me*, a smiley face, and a kiss. Her mother had messaged her, asking her to call her as soon as possible, and Jen had pinged the location of a bar in Clapham, coincidentally not far from where Glanna had lived with Oliver. It seemed such a long time ago now, but also a blink of an eye since the day she had left. The day she had walked away from somebody who had truly loved her, faults and all.

Pushing those feelings aside, she thought more cheerfully of the feisty Jen and their meeting at Kara's wedding. She sensed they were kindred spirits. There was a wildness about the woman that Glanna couldn't quite put her finger on, but whatever it was she liked it. And the petite blonde's reaction to her flirting had pleased her. After casually texting to say that she had Jen's sunglasses, the conversation had continued and had somehow led to Glanna meeting her for a drink this evening in Clapham. Their chat lifted Glanna: made her realise how much she had missed being around intelligent females of her own age.

Since leaving London, she had found herself living quite a solitary existence. Not quite fitting into the community of Hartmouth, apart from casual acquaintances made through the gallery, and relying on her dad and Myles, plus her beloved Banksy as well, of course, to keep her sane. Her mother didn't count, since Penelope was the one who usually undid all their good work. Getting back to Jen, Myles was right, as usual. Even if it would just be friendship with her and nothing more, it would still be refreshing for Glanna to have her company on a night out in London.

Glanna sent her mother a brief text to say that she would catch up with her as soon as she was back, then stood up and gathered her things together as the train slowed down to pull into Paddington. At the sight of the bustling concourse, Glanna experienced the usual feelings of mixed pleasure and pain. The surge of excitement that came from being back in her favourite city in the whole world also brought a painful reminder of her days of addiction and the failure of her longest and mainly stable relationship.

As she waited in the taxi queue, she scrolled down her phone and stared at the bearded hunk of a man with the seaweed-green eyes looking back at her. Here he was, the main reason for her visit: the one, the only, and the extremely talented and very mysterious, Mr Isaac Lowen Benson.

Chapter 10

As requested, the taxi driver had pulled in by St Paul's Cathedral, safely away from the stream of traffic. Getting out, Glanna crossed the road and walked over the Millennium Bridge towards Tate Modern, savouring the amazing sights to the left and right: downstream to Canary Wharf, and upstream past the London Eye and the Houses of Parliament and on, all the way back to the very source of the Thames.

It had always surprised Glanna that the Turbine Hall ramp entrance to Tate Modern resembled the way into an underground car park. As the gallery was housed in a former power station, it was never going to be a pretty building and one had to appreciate that, as with art and love, beauty was in the eye of the beholder. Thousands of people loved the iconic towers of Battersea Power Station too, although Glanna herself had never quite fathomed why.

Knowing that Isaac's talk was not until two, she had some decent time left to explore the other rooms.

First of all, Glanna swiftly found her way to the smallish lecture room where chairs were stacked against a wall beside a notice announcing the talk to be given by the artist. Two original paintings had been hung there, chosen by Isaac Benson especially to show the effect of light on a rugged Cornish scene.

After taking her fill of the paintings, Glanna felt desperate for a cup of tea. Sitting in the cafe, she made a mental note to visit the shop, which sold all sorts of art-related goodies. In fact, at home she often still wore the T-shirt that she had picked up here last time she had visited.

It was so good, coming back to London and being here at one of the sister galleries of Tate St Ives. As an artist herself, Glanna did appreciate different genres of work, but that didn't mean she liked everything. Abstract art had its place, but she would never hang it in her home – or in her gallery, for that matter. Painting in watercolours, she had discovered long ago, was her own preferred medium, although she did occasionally work in oils. Glanna was so grateful for her God-given talent. Through art she could express herself, release her pain and give shape and colour to her memories, hopes and regrets, with that ever-present symbol of hope, the rainbow.

Sculpture was another of her passions, be it made out of clay, stone, wood or any of the other materials used today. Life-sized classical nudes were a favourite, and in the old days she would spend hours in the British Museum and the Victoria & Albert, studying the figures there. How was it, she would ask herself, that sculptors from all centuries and from all over the world could take a cold block of stone and out of it bring a figure to life, a figure that was alive with warmth and personality? Their genius filled her with awe.

During her university course at the Slade, Glanna had not particularly enjoyed drawing people, although portrait studies and life drawing sessions were a part of the curriculum. For Glanna, like Isaac, the natural beauty of the world was the subject she loved most to explore.

She looked at her watch: half an hour before the talk began.

She was weaving her way through the crowds of visitors when she heard weird noises and couldn't resist investigating. Entering a darkened room, she looked up at a towering Dalek-like structure, built from what appeared to be old-fashioned radios; some of which not only emitted noise but sporadically shone bright lights in varying colours. It was a lot to take in. How on earth had she missed this when she had visited before?

Intrigued by what the huge exhibit represented, she tagged on to an animated French tour guide chatting away in accented English to a group who hung on his every word.

'So here we are at the famous *Babel* 2001, acquired by the Tate in 2008. Described by its creator, the Brazilian conceptual artist Cildo Meireles, as a "tower of incomprehension", it is based, of course, on the Old Testament story of a tower that was built tall enough to reach heaven. This offended God, and as a punishment He caused the builders to speak in different tongues. After that, of course no one understood each other, and this mutual incomprehension led tragically to the beginning of mankind's conflicts.' The Frenchman gestured at the tower. 'Note how the indigo-blue lighting, combined with the background mutterings of all those radios tuned to different stations, increases our sense of confusion. This Tower of Babel truly is, one might say, an actual *tour de force*.'

The group left, following their guide and, feeling a troupe of noisy schoolchildren crowding in around her, Glanna too was about to head off when she felt a strong hand rest on her shoulder. For a moment, time stood still and the clamour receded as she absorbed the familiarity of the touch, which spoke of comfort and love, and kindness and passion. Her eyes closed, she wanted the hand to stay exactly where it was so that, just for a little while, she could pretend everything was the way it used to be.

'It's about bad communication this one, isn't it?' a deep voice said, the hand still firmly on her shoulder. Glanna felt a pang of profound emotion as she turned to look up and into the eyes of the one man she had truly loved. *Oliver.*

'My speciality, that,' Glanna replied lightly, and felt a sudden leap in her gut.

'We can't always be on the same wavelength, not all the time, anyway,' Oliver Trueman said gently, and for a split second their eyes rested on each other's souls.

Glanna tried to pull herself together. 'Anyway, this is a surprise, and a very nice one at that,' she managed, and found that her breathing had become irregular.

'I'm teaching art now, three days a week at a secondary school,' Oliver explained, nodding towards his small gang of young pupils. 'Hence I occasionally bring this lot, who are studying Art GCSE, to visit galleries.'

'Well done, you. I know how much you wanted to do that.' Her face lit up, then she grinned. 'Beats dealing with those blinking addicts, I bet. Or are you still at Brightside too?'

'Oh yes, I'm still there. To be honest, it's sometimes easier to manage those reprobates than this lot,' he joked, as the kids' incessant chatter and some play fighting were now almost drowning out the collective sounds emanating from the Tower of Babel itself, which was quite a feat.

How much more small talk could they manage? Glanna thought. And then he said it.

'How are you?' Those three little words that, during her worst bouts of bad mental health, had been known to make her cry for no reason.

'I'm . . . well, I . . . I take Mondays off so I came . . .' Glanna felt suddenly sick. She wanted to keep talking, but at the same time she wanted to run out of the building and jump right into the Thames which flowed outside.

'Mr Trueman,' moaned a voice, 'tell Leon to stop bashing me.' The small group of young teens were standing around the structure, some trying to listen to the radios and others making *Dr Who* Dalek sounds. Thank goodness they were taking no notice of their art teacher.

Relieved at this timely interruption, Glanna gulped and regained some of her composure.

Oliver's face looked slightly pained. 'Look, I'd love to chat, but I need to get this lot back to school, now that the Isaac Benson talk has been cancelled. I imagine that's why you are here – for the talk, seeing as he's a Cornish artist? Such a shame.'

'Cancelled? Oh no, what's happened?' Glanna said, dismayed. 'I was at the little lecture room a while back, wanting to look at the paintings before the talk. It was open, and other people were milling around in there. Why cancel at such short notice?'

'I don't know. I nipped up there a few minutes ago to check out the seating so I could get this lot sitting together in one area, but the room has been closed off and a new notice has been put up.'

Glanna's face fell. 'Oh – and I've come all this way. Unbelievable . . . but at least I got to see you.' The words escaped before she could stop them.

She looked at Oliver and took in his whole being. Dressed casually in dark jeans and a school-branded dark purple polo shirt, he was sporting his trademark white Nike trainers, and his once-cropped hair was now a short trendy afro. She had the urge to reach up on tiptoe and run her hands through his hair, to tell him all the things she wanted to say. That she missed him. That she was sorry. That she had never meant to sleep with that barman. And that she hadn't really wanted to leave him. But Oliver wasn't stupid. He already knew that. Well, he knew the unfaithful bit, at least.

'I tried to message you, to check you were doing OK, you know,' he told her.

Glanna remembered the anguish of changing her phone number to avoid all contact with Oliver and her old life. At the time she had felt it was the only way she could heal herself and move on.

Breaking the silence, his tone lightened. 'You look great, by the way.' He then looked round to check what his charges were up to. They were still examining the weird and wonderful Tower of Babel, and some were taking photos of it and of each other standing by the structure and adopting strange poses. In other circumstances, Glanna would have been amused. The attendant was keeping a close eye on them.

'Thank you,' Glanna said. 'Must be the sobriety – or the sea air, maybe.'

She could sense his relief at hearing those words. 'You still living with your mum then at Riversway?' he asked.

'God, no! I settled in Hartmouth. There's a whole body of water between Mother and me, and that suits me just fine.' She went on, 'Actually, thanks to her I have opened a little gallery.'

'Wow, that makes me so happy.'

'Sir! What time are we going?' one of the girls nagged. 'I'm bored, sir,' another added.

'Look, I'm so sorry, Glanna, this isn't a good time. How long are you up for?'

'Just tonight.'

'What a pity. I have plans later that I can't change, but I'd love to chat more. I know – breakfast, how about breakfast? I have so much to tell you.'

'It'll have to be early; I'm getting the 09.04 from Paddington.'

'OK, not very glam but how about 8 a.m. at the Costa in the station? You won't miss your train and I know how much you love their toast.' His voice lilted at the memory of the morning after they'd first slept together, walking hand-in-hand to the local Costa to get strong coffee and her favourite granary toast, butter and marmalade combo.

'OK.' Glanna nodded wildly. 'Good idea.'

Two of the boys started tussling again. The group was getting restless.

'I have to go. I'm on the same number. Until tomorrow.' He squeezed her shoulder with his huge manly hand again and, before she could tell him that she had long since deleted his number, he was gone, shepherding the kids out of the room.

Glanna looked up at the giant Babel exhibit and a flood of questions filled her mind. Why, when in relationships, did most people speak in different tongues? Why had she been such a fool as to let a man like Oliver Trueman slip through her fingers? And why, most importantly of all, had she not wanted to have his children?

She started to walk slowly back towards the exit of the building and out to the path beside the Thames. Something Star Murray had once said in a passing comment – that nothing in life is a coincidence – rang in her mind. After all, it was a random encounter in Ferry Lane Market that had brought Star and Jack Murray together.

Maybe, Glanna thought, this was the chance she had been given to lay herself open, to drop her guard and see what happened. She'd found it hard when Myles had told her it was OK to be vulnerable where love was concerned. But tomorrow at 8 a.m. in Costa Coffee on the concourse of Paddington Station, vulnerable is exactly what she planned to be.

Chapter 11

'I didn't expect you to be here before me.' Jen Moon threw her handbag down on the outside table of the busy Clapham bar. 'Shit, it's still bloody hot.' She pulled a tiny can of deodorant from her bag and discreetly sprayed her armpits. 'Want some?' Glanna shook her head. 'I was going to get a bottle of white, OK with you?'

'I'm good with this, thanks.' Glanna held up her bottle of Peroni Libera.

'Oh yeah. I forgot. You don't ever drink alcohol, then?'

'No, not now. Here are your sunnies before I forget.'

Jen carelessly threw the glasses she was currently wearing into her handbag and replaced them immediately with the huge Guccis. 'I missed these bad boys, thanks.'

Glanna raised her voice above the traffic noise. 'Go on, get yourself that drink. I'll keep our space here in the shade.'

Jen returned with an ice bucket containing a bottle of what Glanna noticed was her own once-favourite New Zealand Sauvignon blanc. The other woman poured herself a large glass and took a big swig.

'God, that's better,' she sighed, and had another quick swig. 'Markus – you know, my fella – he's wanting to rent out our Putney penthouse and buy a house with a garden in Wimbledon. I say he's got more money than sense, but being an accountant and the way property prices are in London, it would be a great investment. But oh, my God, spending an afternoon being dragged around to view houses in this heat is no fun. How was the exhibition?'

Glanna took a sip of her beer. 'It was going to be a short talk based on the theme of Light in Cornwall, showing just a couple of Isaac Benson's paintings to illustrate his ideas. I found out today that his main exhibition is going to open back at the Tate in St Ives in a couple of months' time.'

'So, what's he like and how was his talk?'

'That's the thing. It was cancelled at the last minute, with just a note saying that due to unforeseen circumstances, Isaac Benson would not be available today – and then it directed everyone to the Cornwall event.'

'So, you've come all the way to London and he's exhibiting down the road from you. Unbelievable.' Jen took another big slurp of wine.

'Tell me about it!' Glanna agreed. 'It would have been amazing to see him in the flesh though. I was secretly hoping to persuade him to display one of his canvases at the *Hart*mouth Gallery. What a coup that would have been.'

'You've got some balls.'

'Well, faint heart and all that.'

'I told Markus you were going to that talk, and he

informed me that Isaac Benson lives not far from Hartmouth, is that right?'

'A forty-minute drive away, maybe. He lives at Penrigan Point, off the moor, miles from anyone. He's so elusive, that's what made it even more exciting that he was coming to London to give a talk in person. I was surprised to even see him on the TV the other night, but no doubt that pays well without him having to meet the great unwashed, otherwise known as his audience.'

'You creative types,' Jen teased. 'Us number-crunchers are far more predictable and straightforward.'

'That's for me to find out, isn't it?' Glanna smiled, then swallowed some more of her cold drink. 'Anyway, it wasn't time wasted as it was great to spend time there, and also—' Glanna stopped short. She hardly knew Jen, and how could the other woman begin to understand even a smidge of what she and Oliver had been through together, and the way Glanna felt right now? Because she had definitely felt a surge of something. Was it love? Was it simply old habits reasserting themselves? She didn't know. But one thing she was sure of, and that was how excited she was to be seeing him tomorrow, if only for an hour. A chance to tell him exactly how she was feeling.

'And also?' Jen prompted. 'You were going to say something else?'

'Um, just that it's a treat to be back in London for the night.'

'In that case, we'd better make the most of it, then.' Jen reached for a handful of ice from the bucket and put it in her wine. Then, placing her cold hand on the back of Glanna's, she added, 'Hadn't we?'

Glanna checked her watch, a Cartier Tank Américaine with a black leather strap that Penny Pascoe had given her for her birthday last year. It annoyed Glanna that her mother was so reckless with her money sometimes, but not enough for Glanna to have given the timeless timepiece back.

'It's only just gone six,' she told Jen.

'Good! The night is yet young.'

Glanna liked and related to the cheeky glint in her pretty companion's eyes. 'So, do you think you will move back down to Hartmouth, then?' she asked, thinking it might be quite nice to have Jen around.

'I may, but with Markus wanting to buy this new property, it doesn't look like he will. We just had the biggest row actually.' Jen bit her lip. 'He says he's not ready to give up and settle in a sleepy Cornish town.'

'Hartmouth's not that quiet, but compared to here it is a bit morgue-like, I suppose.'

'Don't you be sticking up for him.'

'I'm not. Thing is, I thought like him at first but now I'm enjoying the peace and the beauty of living by the sea. How old is he?'

'He's fifty, so he's not exactly a youngster. His daughters are here in London too – teenagers now, thank goodness. The times I gritted my teeth through visits to the zoo and so-called "family",' she used her index fingers to make inverted commas, 'holidays.'

'That you went on with his girls, you mean?'

'God, no. They all went without me. Mummy in tow too. Quite bizarre, but that's all stopped now that they are older.'

'I think that's quite sweet really. Doing it for the kids and all that.'

Jen rolled her eyes. 'He said he wants to wait until they are both ensconced safely in university before he moves to what he called "the arse end of nowhere". Charming! I can't see the sense in it, frankly. Have car, will travel and all that. Don't get me wrong – I have to value his qualities as a father, but it also pisses me off. I have never been number one with Markus, but that's what happens when you fall for a man with kids.'

'Sorry to play devil's advocate here, but I can see both sides.' Glanna wafted her sundress around her knees to cool herself. 'You want to be near your sister and your new nephew and niece in Hartmouth, and set up your own business with Jack, and that seems perfectly fair and reasonable. But Markus sees the majority of his life as still being up here.'

'Yes,' Jen said gloomily. 'While I am so over London and so over being second best.' She refilled her glass to the brim. 'All partied out, that's me.'

'Yeah, right.' Glanna felt the wonderful sensation of lady lust rearing its naughty head. 'What age are you, if you don't mind me asking?'

'I'm early forties and holding right there.' Jen ran her right hand through her perfectly cut smooth blonde bob. 'You?'

'Thirty-nine and holding right there myself, or I would be if my mother wasn't insistent on me having a grandiose, fuck-off fortieth birthday party at Riversway, my family home in Crowsbridge.'

'Oh.'

'Yes, oh indeed.'

'And before you ask,' Jen drank, 'no, I don't want children of my own.'

'Can I just say snap, hallelujah and cheers all at the same time?' Glanna chinked her bottle of beer with Jen's wine glass.

'How refreshing. You get sick of the question too, I bet?'

'It's not so bad in Cornwall as I keep myself to myself down there.' Glanna leaned her head back and relaxed, making a sighing noise. 'I'm glad I've met you.'

'Yes, we can be kindred "no kids" spirits together.' They chinked again. 'I will amend my story slightly,' Jen went on, 'as I do love Markus very much and he didn't make the baby decision for me, just cemented it. I've always been a career girl, Glanna. I left Hartmouth as soon as I could. And, well, when I met him, he not only had two kids already, but he had also had the snip. He was straight up with me and said that he intended to retire at fifty-five and had done his time as a father to young children. And that was the deal with him. I could run then or stick it out and enjoy the good times. I stuck it out.'

'Do you regret your decision?'

'Not at all. Like I say, I never had the maternal urge. I lead a very blessed life with him, and what's more he's got the biggest cock.'

They both fell about laughing.

'And now it's your turn,' Jen said. 'How's your love life?'

Glanna was just about to come clean with her own story, when her jaw dropped to her knees and her heart to her ankles. Letting out a little gasp, she grabbed the food menu that was on the table in front of her and put it up to her face.

For there across the street, guiding a pushchair through the summer evening revellers, was Oliver Trueman. Inside the pram, with just a nappy on, smiling and shaking a noisy teething toy, was a beautiful curly-haired mini-him. And by Oliver's side strolled a naturally pretty and friendly-looking woman with short brown hair, wearing shorts and a T-shirt, to whom he was chatting animatedly.

Sensing that something serious was afoot, Jen gently put her hand on top of Glanna's. After checking to see if the coast was clear, Glanna removed the menu to reveal tear-filled eyes.

'Any left in there?' she said, and pointed to the bottle of wine sitting in the chrome ice bucket.

Jen nodded. 'Yes, but don't you—'

Glanna dismissed Jen with a wave of her hand, before heading straight for the Ladies' toilets, entering a cubicle and sitting on the closed seat with her head in her hands.

This hurt. Hurt more than she had ever thought it would. Oliver with another woman she could almost stand, but Oliver with another woman *and* a baby – that really was too much to bear.

Chapter 12

It was already getting light when Glanna was awoken by the non-stop ringing of a mobile phone coming from under the bed. Jen groaned as she stirred and fumbled firstly on the side table and then around the crumpled bedsheet to try and find the offending article and turn it off.

Switching on the bedside lamp, she shot up with a start. 'What the fuck? There's me expecting to see a silver-haired man lying next to me and it's a nigh-on naked bloody woman!'

Glanna ignored her new friend's dramatics, remaining motionless.

The phone stopped then started ringing again. Jen jumped out of bed and went down on all fours, blindly swinging her arm backwards and forwards under the bed to locate the phone, which stubbornly refused to cease ringing. Finally she found it.

'It's only 5 bloody a.m.,' Glanna mumbled, looking at her watch.

'Yes – and my boyfriend is obviously wondering where the hell I am.'

Jen climbed back into bed and phoned him back

immediately. 'Markus, hi, I – I mean *we*, me and Glanna, that is – we're at,' she snatched up the branded notepad on the side, 'a Premier Inn near Paddington.' She made a face.

'I must have crashed out. Sorry . . . Yes, I know I always usually text you . . . I'm fine . . . yes, yes . . . Let's breakfast at the Yard in Putney. I need to come and get my car anyway, but I must have at least an hour's more kip as I'm driving back down to Dad and Pearl's later. Love you.'

Jen hung up as Glanna, in her skimpy lace underwear, went into the bathroom to pee, leaving the door open while she did so, then coming back to fill the plastic hotel kettle, before climbing into the comfy king-size bed.

'Shit, it's warm in here.' She threw the crisp white sheet down to her waist 'Look, I wanted to say thank you, Jen.'

'Thank you for what? We didn't – you know . . . do stuff, did we?' Jen's hair was all over the place. Her mascara smudged under both eyes. Red lipstick marks smeared over her pillow.

'No, we didn't. Your face!' Glanna laughed. 'And it wouldn't have been so bad if we had, would it?'

Jen groaned. 'Leave me alone. I feel so rotten. I played around at university with girls a bit, but I really do like cock too much to veer down that road again.'

Glanna shook her head in amusement. 'Don't worry, it's all good.'

Jen stood up, located her short summer dress on the

floor next to the bed and pulled it over her own under-
wear. 'So what *are* you thanking me for then, Glanna
Pascoe?'

'For telling me I didn't need that drink. I really appreciate that. It was the first time in a very long time that
the temptation had even crossed my mind. Jen, I'm so
bloody glad I had the strength to resist, supported by
you. And thanks so much for listening to my woes.'

Blinking, Jen reached into the depths of her memory.
'It was me going on about Markus and our row, more
like. Poor you, your ears must have been bleeding.'

'You were fine. You were funny, in fact.'

'Ah, but Oliver, right? Your ex? I remember most of
what you told me.' She put her hand to her forehead.
'Ugh, I feel terrible. White wine on an empty stomach
on the hottest day of the year, so wise . . . NOT!'

'Now, that is something I don't miss – the hangovers.
I've got some paracetamol in my bag, if you want some.'

'No, it's OK,' Jen groaned. 'I just need a long shower
and to be nil by mouth except for lots of toothpaste. And
please don't go all drink police on me, Miss Sobriety.'

'Course I won't, and talking of Oliver, I was actually
glad I saw him and even more glad that you were there
to talk to.'

'It must have been such a shock,' Jen said kindly.

'Yes and no. He's a good-looking man, he wanted a
family. What's the crime in him getting what he wanted?
The woman he was with looked like what my mother
would call "a nice girl",' Glanna mimicked Penelope's

99

affected voice. 'But that's probably what Oliver needed and deserved. I was lucky he put up with my opinions and tantrums for so long.'

'You don't get to choose who you fall in love with; love chooses us,' Jen croaked, going over to the kettle and switching it on.

'Bloody hell, look at you getting all profound when you're feeling half-dead.'

'I truly believe it. I mean, look at me. I'm with an aging sensible accountant with two moody teenagers, a grabbing ex-wife but . . .'

'A huge cock,' they said in unison and burst out laughing.

'Are you going to meet him for breakfast?' Jen asked now. 'Oliver, that is?'

'What's the point? I sound such a bitter old cow, but I really can't face him now. And I know that's so weak. He's happy, he's got what he wanted, and a conversation will only make me sad. It's no one's fault but my own that I've been treading water since we split.'

'You could be friends, maybe?'

'Come on, Jen, when has anyone ever stayed friends with someone they've truly loved? It's not possible.'

'Yeah, you're right.' Jen was now lying back on her lipstick-stained pillow, eyes flickering with tiredness, the hangover now taking over her senses. Her speech was slow and sleepy. 'So do you date men *and* women, then?'

'Probably a bit like you. I've never dated a woman,

but I had a few sexual encounters in my previous life, and I do appreciate the female form. So much more aesthetically pleasing than a man's, don't you think?'

'Oh,' was all Jen's addled brain could muster.

Glanna made a little moaning sound. 'About Oliver, the only shit thing is, I haven't got his number to let him know I won't be coming.' She ran a hand through her hair. 'He wasn't to know I'd deleted it like a teenager. I still can't go through with it though. You are still OK for me to come back in the car with you to Cornwall, aren't you? I'd much rather be with you than go alone from here. And I'm scared of bumping into him at the station.'

'Yes, of course. You might be driving at this rate though, mate. I'm probably well over the limit still.'

Glanna ignored both this comment and the now boiling kettle, and snuggled in next to her hungover bed mate. This unexpected closeness to another human being caused her voice to wobble with emotion. 'Would you mind if I hug you, Jen?'

Jen shuffled to get comfortable then, feeling hot tears of sadness begin to drop onto her neck, she pushed her slight frame into the little spoon position against the tall willowy body of Glanna Pascoe, saying, 'It will all work out fine, you know.'

Glanna sniffed loudly as the petite blonde continued, 'And whatever happens, you may have lost a lover, but you've gained a friend in me, and I'm not going anywhere.'

And as a slight smile graced Glanna Pascoe's quivering

top lip, Jenifer Moon let out a little snort then began to snore softly next to her.

Oliver Trueman drained his coffee and looked down at his phone for the umpteenth time. He'd got here early, at ten to eight, and it was now twenty minutes to nine. Her train would be ready for boarding shortly and leaving in twenty-four minutes exactly. That would barely leave enough time for a hello and goodbye. For all of Glanna's faults, being late had never been one of them.

How presumptuous he had been, Oliver thought now, annoyed with himself, to assume she would have kept his number in her phone. Best scenario was that she had deleted it then, with a valid reason for not making the meeting, had no way to reach him. It was so frustrating.

Meeting Glanna again, so unexpectedly, had thrown him. He had felt the very same jolt that he had experienced when he had first bumped into her in the corridor at Brightside House. Glanna Pascoe . . . even her name had sounded exotic, and with her tall stature, white-blonde crop, high cheekbones and huge eyes behind her expensive glasses, she really was a stunning-looking woman. Her wit and wisdom, with intelligence beyond her years, made her seem such an old and interesting soul. At first he had found it hard to believe that such a talented artist was amidst his class of addicts. But as he spent more time at Brightside he learned that, like other illnesses, addiction didn't care who it affected. Age, creed, colour, wealth, background . . . addiction made no distinction as it seized victims in its grasp, and only the strong-minded or the very lucky escaped its destruction.

Meeting Glanna was as if a light bulb had been switched on, not only in that house of hope, but also in his heart. There was not one person there who didn't like her, staff and fellow housemates alike. Even on her darkest days of thinking she couldn't get through it, Glanna somehow managed a joke. Then she would grit her teeth and say, 'I will do this.' And he had truly believed that she would.

His thoughts were broken by a 'Mind if I sit 'ere, mate?' from a scruffy-looking man. Oliver nodded then stood up and walked towards Platform 1 where the 09.04 Truro train was now boarding.

Blagging his way through the gate, he walked the length of the train and back again, searching for Glanna. He had so much to tell her. About his new job and changes at Brightside, about his new flat and life which included Clarence, his beloved son. She had looked well too and apparently had stayed sober – and for that, he really was happy and relieved.

But Glanna not showing up, whether she had his number or not, had proved that she wasn't that bothered about catching up or re-establishing their friendship – something which, in the days and months after they had split, he had longed for so badly. He wasn't one to push that. From his training in dealing with addicts at the centre, he'd soon learned that, addicted or not, people do what they do – and when they are ready, if they want to come to you, they will. Glanna, although seemingly keen to meet, obviously wasn't ready.

Passing back through the ticket barrier, thanking the guard who had let him through, he walked out of the busy station and up the side road onto Praed Street, crammed with traffic in the rush hour. The humidity of the day and night before was about to be broken with a storm, by the feel of it and by the black clouds gathering. A couple of minutes later, as big drops of rain started to fall on his lifted face, getting heavier and heavier, a rainbow began to form on the horizon, causing Oliver to instinctively reach for his phone camera. It was then it hit him: that whatever he had had with Glanna, it was now well and truly over.

Chapter 13

'No, of course you can't join us,' Glanna told her dad. 'I'm not sitting for two hours staring at my own father naked.' She moved the exquisite display of flowers that Skye Bligh had just delivered from Passion Flowers to the end of the counter.

'Well, for goodness' sake don't let your mother get wind of what you're planning as she'll be in like Flynn, offering herself as a model,' Fred Gribble advised. 'That woman can never wait to get her kit off. A glint of sun lands on the parquet flooring and your mum's stripped to her birthday suit on the croquet lawn before you can say David Dickinson.'

Glanna laughed at both the image of the mahogany-hued TV antiques expert and her mother outrageously flaunting her aging body. 'I love you, Dad, and all your craziness.'

Banksy, tired from a long walk over at Crowsbridge Forest with his grandad, gave Fred Gribble's hand a cheeky lick, then loped back upstairs from his gallery bed to the basket in front of the Juliet balcony overlooking the market so he, just as his grandmother Penelope Pascoe liked to do, could catch some rays whilst sleeping.

'And I love you too, my girl.' Fred cleared his throat. 'But why have you suddenly decided to run a life drawing class?'

'Why not? Basically, me and Jen – you know, Kara Dillon née Moon's sister – well, we discussed it on the drive back from London yesterday. It's not even as though I myself like life drawing, although I admire the work of others. The thing is, Dad, I do feel something lacking in my life. I'm not even sure if it's a partner. I am sure though that I need to fill my time with more than painting and sitting in the flat upstairs.' Glanna looked sad as she added, 'I've wasted so much of my life, Dad.'

'You've travelled the world, my girl! How many people can say they've done that? I for one sure can't.'

'I drank, partied and slept my way around it, you mean.' Glanna knew she could be brutally honest with her father. 'There wasn't exactly a lot of sightseeing involved. I was so young then and took it all for granted. In fact, when I look back, it's all rather a blur. What I need now is to find some peace.'

'Jesus, don't start on this mindfulness and finding yourself business now, will you?' Fred said, looking startled.

'I'm not, I'm just looking after myself. Glanna Pascoe Inc. from now on is giving herself a lot of TLC.'

'So, London was good, then? How was the great artist's talk?'

'He didn't show, but someone else did.'

'Go on.'

'Oliver.'

'Oh princess, how did you feel?'

'I realise I miss him, but he has a baby now and looks so happy. And like I say, I don't know if a partner is the answer.'

Fred sighed. 'Oh Glanna, has he really? It's only been two years, so that was quick, pet. Well, I never.'

'I don't want to talk about it any more.' Glanna opened the till to check whether she had the correct float in there and to distract her feelings from spilling over.

Fred Gribble's voice lifted. 'So, how many are in this group, then? And how are you advertising it? You might get a load of weirdos. I don't know how all this naked stuff works.'

'It's art, Dad. And it's serious work requiring utmost concentration – no time to perve. I'll soon be able to tell who is there for the wrong reasons and they'll be out on their ear sharpish. So far, there's me, Jen and Sadie. I'll be running it and Sadie and I will be doing a bit of teaching during the two-hour classes, with a break in between. Everyone who joins up will have to be willing to participate as models as well as artists. That's how I've planned it so far. I reckon that until I can afford to hire models, posing for the class may actually teach us all, including me, more about the body.' Glanna frowned. 'Attracting a few more people who won't mind taking their clothes off for one of the sessions may be difficult, but the rule will be that they can cover certain areas up if that makes them feel more comfortable. I certainly fit into that category.'

While Fred took all this in, his daughter went on: 'I've put a notice in the window, hoping to interest local people, and I'll also put something on my website. It's just a six-week course, so we need three more participants, ideally men so we get the chance to have a go at both sexes, so to speak.'

'How will it work, then?'

Glanna explained. 'My studio upstairs is big enough for six of us. I will create a comfortable setting, with no draughts, and each week one of us will choose a naked pose, or near-naked. The others will draw or paint that person, then at the close of each evening session, we will vote for the best picture. At the end of the course, the artist with the most votes will win a one-year membership with the chance to take a friend free to all the exhibitions in the four Tate galleries – Tate Britain, Tate Modern, Tate Liverpool and our very own Tate St Ives. It's a great prize – wouldn't mind winning it myself,' she joked.

'How much are you charging the punters?' Fred asked.

'I'm charging ten pounds per person per session – sixty pounds each in total for the whole course – which will go towards the prize and also materials et cetera for the session. Not a huge reward financially for the business, but it's another little income stream, plus I've always been a bit rubbish at drawing people, so it's a good learning curve for me too.'

Glanna's eyes sparkled as, for a few moments, she forgot all about Oliver and pictured her new idea working out.

'I'm excited to be mixing up my skills again, and most of all I'm hoping it will be fun.'

'You can't win the prize, no?'

'If I do get the most votes, which I very much doubt, I will donate the value of the prize to the whippet trust where I found Banksy.'

'You are kind. Actually, Linda said she was looking for a new hobby the other day, so maybe I should mention it to her?'

'If you want to. I don't suppose it really matters if there are more women than men. And yes, talking of the lovely Linda, how was your night?'

'Very nice, thank you.'

'Only "nice"?'

'When you get to my age, you take a *nice* and you're grateful for it.'

'You're only sixty, Dad, that's not exactly ancient. Personally, I'm never going to compromise.' Glanna started lightly dusting off some of her own rainbow paintings which she had put in the front window in light of losing Sally Jefferson and not having had time to move around any of the *Seascapes in All Seasons* pieces yet.

'If I'm honest, it was a bit tricky,' Fred admitted. 'Glanna, I know you're my daughter, but . . .' His voice lowered to a whisper. 'I thought your mother was bad enough, but this woman is sex mad. Kinky is what they call it, I think. She opened her overnight bag and inside – well, I couldn't believe it. There were things in there I've never seen in my life before. Paddles, whips, handcuffs, flavoured massage oil. A nurse's outfit! And those curves!' He grinned despite himself. 'I've heard the term "big-bottomed girls" before, but after your mother's stick-like frame, I wasn't quite sure what to do with all that pulsating flesh.'

'Dad!' Glanna burst out laughing. 'That is so funny, who'd have thought it? They do say the quiet ones are the worst.'

'Yes, it's not just pastry she knows how to handle, I'll tell you that.'

'Stop!' Glanna put up her palm, flat out. 'That *is* enough information now. Ask her to pop in about joining the class, then, as we welcome figures of all kinds, but I doubt if seeing naked men in front of her will dampen her ardour. Probably do the opposite.'

Fred laughed. 'She'll be chasing them around the studio with her wet paintbrush.'

'Ew.' Glanna screwed her face up. 'Let me just wipe that euphemism from my mind, shall I?'

The shop bell went, signalling the arrival of a customer who, after pleasantly acknowledging Glanna and her father, went to the back of the shop and started browsing.

Fred Gribble leaned up to kiss his daughter on the cheek. 'You have a lovely day, now, won't you?'

'I will – and thanks so much for looking after Banksy. You've properly tired him out with that walk.'

Fred reached the door then, turning around, said quietly, 'For all her faults, I still love your mother, you know.'

Glanna put her hand on his shoulder. 'I know you do, Dad. But don't lose yourself trying to hold on to someone who refuses to show they care.'

'That's all over now. I'm sick of trying to make her see me when I am clearly invisible to her.'

'Good.' Glanna felt heartened. It was exactly what she needed to hear. 'I just want you to be happy, and if that takes the shape of playing doctors and nurses with Mrs Harris, then go for it, I say.'

'Shhh.' Fred Gribble giggled naughtily and put a finger to his lips. 'Right, I have to get back to Riversway. The awful posh neighbours are over for the afternoon, and I was in the middle of cleaning the pool.'

Glanna opened the door for her father, making the bell ring again, and kissed him on the cheek. As she watched him drive down the hill towards the ferry, she sighed a little. The role of go-between from her mother to her father and back again had been forced upon her for too many years now, and she wanted out. If she played this right, Glanna thought to herself, with any luck it would soon be the last time that she would ever have to do this.

There was no point in telling her father that her mother still loved him and was jealous of his antics. It was too soon. First, Penelope Pascoe must be made to experience the genuine fear that she was on the verge of forever losing faithful, loving Fred Gribble – the only man she had ever properly loved. Only then might the deluded woman be compelled to stop play-acting and show Fred just how much she *did* care, in order to win him back.

Chapter 14

The following Monday, Glanna awoke early to the sound of heavy rain splashing against her bedroom skylight. Her day off plan had been to go for a long walk around Penrigan Point then, weather permitting, she would paint the view from the top. After that, she would treat herself to a meal at the car park cafe there, then come home and ring around some local artists to see if they'd be interested in taking her coveted window slot to replace Sally's ceramics.

Jen had hinted that she might join Glanna on the walk, but on hearing a text bleep in, Glanna knew immediately that it would be her fair-weather friend with an excuse. Jen wrote that she now had a client meeting in Penrigan at ten, so would happily drive Glanna to the car park and meet her later, but would have to drop out of going for a walk. Checking her weather app, Glanna was pleased to see that the sun would be coming through shortly, but with the possibility of a thunderstorm at lunchtime. Springing out of bed, she showered and went to wake up Banksy, who was still sound asleep in his dog basket in the lounge.

'Are you pretending to be asleep because it's raining,

you soft dog?' The smooth-haired whippet detested being out in the wet, and was also inclined to be a bit lazy. Giving a doggie sigh, her beloved pet slowly got out of his basket, shook his body, then nuzzled into her knees. She bent down to kiss his pointy snout, saying, 'I've got some snippets of cold chicken to go on your chicken and brown rice biscuits.' Banksy gave a quick bark and ran into the kitchen, with Glanna following. 'The rain's nearly stopped – look,' she told him, getting down his clean bowls and running the cold tap for his water. She opened the fridge for the slice of cold chicken and, while chopping it up to sprinkle on his biscuits, she turned to add, 'And by the time we get up to the top, you will be able to run around in the sunshine.'

It was at times like these she really did wish she had a car. Penrigan was too far to get to on the electric bike with Banksy running alongside and, due to the lack of a train station in Hartmouth itself, it usually meant her getting a taxi. Sometimes Kara would invite her to hop into the Passion Flowers van when she was out on deliveries, but with her on maternity leave now, even that was not an option.

Ever since the day of the accident when she had drunkenly driven into the back of the parked Range Rover, she had chosen not to drive again. Despite not suffering any lasting injuries herself, the scenarios of what 'might have been' – such as killing someone through her drunk-driving – had severely knocked her confidence. She found it strange how nobody had ever commented on the scar above her eyelid. Maybe it had faded enough that she was the only one who was aware of it – or maybe nobody looked that closely at her. But for this, she was glad, as it had certainly been far from her finest moment and the injury was not one she wished to explain.

Fed and watered, she and Banksy made their way out of the back stable door of the gallery. As she shut the gate behind her, Star was just coming down her back stairs, waving to a flustered-looking Jack who was holding a screaming baby Matthew.

'You OK?' Glanna shouted over.

'Not really. Mum's not well and she was supposed to be having Master Murray today. I've got a huge online order to fulfil, so me and Daddy Bear are having to share the load.'

'Bless you. Is there anything I can do to help? Never fancied having one myself but I seem to be pretty good with the ones I can hand back.' Glanna thought back to when she and Oliver had babysat for the two kids of a work colleague a few times. Children did seem weirdly drawn to her, 'a bit like when a dog knows you are scared of it,' she used to quip.

'No, you're fine, we will manage somehow. By the way, you don't know anyone who wants to buy a car, do you?' Star waved the handwritten *For Sale* board she was holding at Glanna.

'This is so weird; I was only just thinking earlier how much easier it would be if I had transport other than my bike.'

'See? I knew that already.' Star winked. 'It's my little convertible Smart car. I can already see Banksy sitting head held high in the passenger seat with his little black nose twitching in the wind. It's not exactly a family car, is it? So as much as it saddens me to say goodbye to my little beauty, she's got to go, I'm afraid.'

'How much are you selling it for?'

'Well, I'm the most rubbish driver so the dents are free, and because I haven't got the time or inclination to get her fixed up, she's just three thousand for cash.'

'Umm. I do love your little car. Can I just think about it today, and if you do sell it before I decide, then it's not meant to be?' Glanna's voice shook a little with the fear of driving again.

Star was opposite her now. Feeling the woman's anguish, she put her hand on Glanna's thin arm and shut her eyes for a second. 'I'm being given that it's time, the right time. For a lot of things for you actually.' There was a short pause then she made an oohing sound as if she was coming to from some sort of trance. 'I'll do you a free tarot reading if you'd like one, when I get a second.'

'Er, that kind of thing is not really for me but thanks anyway,' Glanna said hurriedly. 'OK, we'd better go, hadn't we, boy?' She looked down to Banksy, who was waiting patiently. 'I'm meeting Jen at Bee Cottage.'

'No sparkly collar today, then?'

'No, it's harness day as we are going on a long walk.' The whippet was wearing his special Aztec-patterned coat and harness that had a handle so that Glanna could lift him if he was getting tired.

'Lucky old Banksy,' beamed Star. 'Well, have a lovely day and let me know about the car when you've had time to think about it.'

The car park was surprisingly only half full when Jen dropped Glanna at the base of Penrigan Point. Probably because the rain had only just stopped and, with the kids' summer school holidays not yet upon them, it wasn't quite full on tourist season yet. Glanna waved Jen off then, tying the docile Banksy up outside, she went inside the cafe and got herself a takeaway coffee. She was feeling cheerful. It was so nice to have somebody of her own age to confide in for a change, and to feel the excitement about the life drawing class, which would also be a shared experience that she would be able to discuss with her new friend Jen. Being single, she had struggled with that. Moments were always better shared, and opportunities to share had been few and far between lately. So used was she to her solitary existence that even the sound of her own sudden laughter had almost made her jump the other day. How sad was that!

Inside the cafe, a spotty student was working behind the counter. Glanna saw him check out her nipples, which were slightly protruding through her close-fitting white

T-shirt. She rarely wore bras in the summer; they just added an extra layer of heat in her opinion and she was lucky enough with her small, pert breasts to get away with it. Her cropped jeans, white Kurt Geiger trainers and Versace prescription sunglasses (yet another gift from her mother) completed her outfit which, with the sun now coming through and the ground drying out quickly, was perfect for a walk up the cliff path.

'Come on then, Banksy boy, we are going on a long and lovely walk and Mummy might even paint something today.' She released him from his harness and he ducked under the stile which signified the start of their walk. Climbing over, she made her way up the gorse-lined cliff path; the bright yellow flowers were still hanging in there from their spring arrival. Glanna stopped to unclip the lead and put it in her black rucksack, which also contained her drawing pad, micro-palette, bottle of water, doggy-doo bags and Banksy's collapsible bowl for when he got thirsty. The air, fresh from the recent showers, caused her to inhale deeply.

Thinking and walking had helped her so much over the past couple of years. Had relieved her tension when she felt like she was going to blow. It wasn't a drink she needed, Glanna had come to realise, so much as this pure air and water – as well as the endorphins that exploded through her when she challenged herself physically. Hills were a bit like life, she thought. Obstacles. The climb was often hard, and you doubted your ability to get there, but when you reached the top and took in the view, boy was it worth it. And then, looking down, you came to see that you had made a fuss about nothing, that getting up there hadn't been as difficult as you had thought. Myles had taught her so much, including the truth that a lot of life was about facing a challenge head on without fear. How often since then had she discovered that the worry of something was far harder than the actual execution.

The life drawing class was due to start next week. She had picked Tuesdays, as Jen's compromise with Markus was that she would work in Hartmouth Tuesday to Thursday and go home to him for the weekends. When he had his kids for the whole weekend, Jen would stay down here. So, it was a win-win really. Markus could have valuable time with his girls without Jen moaning and Jen didn't have to join in.

Mrs Harris was now also booked on the course and had paid up, and Glanna was already intrigued to get to know Hayden, who worked on the ferry with Billy and had signed up just recently. The brooding young ferryman, who on the surface gave no impression of being the arty type, would be interesting. And now she knew what went on under Mrs Harris's apron, Glanna wondered what that woman would bring to the easel. She liked the idea of getting to know everyone. In fact, that was another thing she had found since she had been sober: she had time for people. She found herself having a lot more to say and made time to listen. Before, it had all been about being with 'her tribe', those who would help send her into drunk and drugged oblivion, where she would be lucky to remember her own name, let alone those of others, or care what was going on in their lives.

Banksy came back by her side for a second, licked her hand then, on seeing something move in the bushes, the eager hound tore ahead up the cliff path. Glanna took another lungful of clean sea air and lifted her face to the sunshine. Yes, getting out of London had helped in her quest for sobriety, but as time went by she realised that perfect moments like this were the reason she had relocated to the Hartmouth area. To feel small in a huge world of natural beauty. To realise what was really important. Oliver had moved on, it seemed, but he had definitely helped her to move on too – and for that she would always be grateful.

Glanna's expression grew sad. All of this was good positive stuff, but who was she kidding? The pain was still there, the pain of seeing him with his own child and another woman, who had looked genuinely nice. Glanna had ribbed her father for using the 'nice' word but after all, 'kind' and 'nice' were the two things (if we were all honest with ourselves) that most of us wanted out of a relationship. True, a bad boy or girl might make the blood run faster, but that didn't make for a happy life. She had had all that. Dancing on tables after a vat of tequila in Antigua, then shagging the maître d' of her hotel on a deserted Caribbean beach. Meeting a millionaire in Monaco and snorting cocaine off his stomach inside his humongous yacht. Flying to Paris in a private plane for lunch on the Champs-Elysées and back on the same day. The experiences had been amazing, but she was just one of many who had done similar things with these playboys. Glanna knew she was a fantastic 'plus one'. Tall, attractive, worldly. But that was it: she had always been just a plus one and never *the* one. Until Oliver, that was.

Seeing Oliver as a father was something she had always dreaded. And the feeling when she had spotted him and the child had rocked her with its intensity. Made her understand what she had given up. Myles had asked her why she didn't want children. She had found it easy to spout off the practical reasons, to moan about the noise and lack of freedom, but was it that – or was her own noise hiding the actual reason? The reason she had hidden her real self behind alcohol for so long too?

She had got so used to the feeling of missing Oliver that it had become a normality. The pain just sat within her, like a hole in her heart that needed to be filled, and although she was making all these new plans, she wasn't quite sure yet if they were the answer. Maybe they were just sticking plaster over the wound for now, but at least with her trip to Tate Modern and setting up the life drawing class – even coming up here to paint on her day off – she was taking positive action to keep herself going. Although none of it made sense. A man had loved her, she had loved him and when, on wanting to seal their relationship with not only marriage but the ultimate gift of love in having a child together, she had betrayed him, then run as fast as Usain Bolt to get away from the situation.

With all these turbulent thoughts zooming around her mind, and whilst these feelings were so close to the surface, Glanna wondered whether she should see Myles again before the month was out. It had taken years for her to get her head straight after she had first started having therapy, and by now she was beginning to enjoy learning why she unconsciously behaved the way she did in various emotional situations. She sometimes dared to challenge her own psyche, but she was now noticing that it quite often whispered the right way to act or turn, most of the time, anyway.

Just then, the top of the cliff path flattened out to reveal a vista of sea and sky, stretching to infinity. A lone cormorant bobbed up and down on the white-tipped waves and the seagulls suddenly came alive, flying out from their rocky hideaways and shrieking in greedy delight as they headed for what must be a shoal of fish, far below.

At the sight of his mistress, Banksy, his sheer black coat gleaming in the sunshine, came tearing back alongside Glanna, sniffed up at her rucksack asking for a treat, then tore off again. She had no fear of him falling for he was so used to the cliff top, and the moorland which stretched behind it, that he could be here in the dark and not lose his way. Even with the beach so far below, she could hear young children's excited cries carrying on the brisk breeze. Both the pier and beach at Penrigan now looked so small, with tiny figures enjoying the sights, sounds and rides that the sea, sand and old Victorian boardwalk had to offer. After not being around children for so long, suddenly they were everywhere.

Oliver would have a toddler in no time and Matthew Murray crying this morning had made her offer to help – what was all that about? And then there were Kara's twins, Red and Poppy, who she did find very cute. Was her mindset changing?

She had seen how being a mother was a hard and often thankless task. Being a daughter to a mother like hers, even harder. And the thought of what pregnancy did to your body! Glanna made a grimace. Penelope had never let her forget the one lone silver stretch mark on her belly, nor the fact that she was so sick during her pregnancy that, in the first three months, she had asked Fred to wake up Harry Moon in the middle of the night to run the *Happy Hart* over to Penrigan General as it would be quicker to go by water than by road, for fear of her dramatically dying of dehydration.

Kara already looked like she was asleep on her feet and had no spare time at all. That was no way to live. Glanna shuddered. No, motherhood definitely wasn't for her. Oliver had made the right decision in finally allowing her to walk away, Glanna decided, and as much as she still had strong feelings for him, it was all for the best. 'Yes,' she said aloud to the sea-fresh air. 'The best for both of us.' Especially now he had obviously found love and had become the father he had so longed to be.

Glanna walked as close to the cliff edge as she dared, a lot further back than in her drinking days, when she had no regard for herself or her body. She put both her arms out and slowly moved them up and down as if they were angel wings. Tipping her head back, the stiff breeze whisked around her, causing a stray hair to catch her eye and her to rub it. Ignoring a couple who were walking behind her and absorbed in each other, she whistled for Banksy and then looked down and gasped. For there, clearly visible swimming along beside a fishing boat, was a little pod of three beautiful dolphins, their playful curiosity shining through as the fishermen lobbed fish up in the air, causing them to leap out of the water and catch the fish in their smiling mouths. Glanna could hear the faint sound of children and adults alike applauding at the unexpected free show from such beloved creatures.

Dolphins always reminded her of the framed Isaac Benson print on the wall of her flat. But those dolphins were silent, in hiding – unlike the ones playing down in the sea – showing off their true joyful nature. She looked across in the direction of where the great painter's house was situated. It lay a good distance along the cliff path ahead. Surrounded by a stone wall, it was only accessible by one dirt track along which Isaac would drive his old Land Rover to go shopping for groceries or to meet the few guests and any deliveries he received.

As greatly as she'd longed for a peek into the private view of his world, she had never dared to walk that far. The cliff path at that point was downright dangerous in parts. And as for daring to risk the drive up to his house, rumour had it there was a huge gate halfway up with sensors on it that alerted the main house should any unauthorised person come within two metres of it. This was why it had amazed Glanna that one allegedly so protective of his privacy should have allowed television cameras into his house. Saying that, the programme had only showed the outside of the old granite farmhouse, plus the interior of his amazing studio, which was linked to the main farmhouse with its own entrance. Viewers were shown just one still shot of the sister he lived with. She was riding a horse – in a photograph so grainy it looked like it could have been taken in the nineteenth century. Most peculiar, and merely whetting one's curiosity more about the whole strange set-up.

Dismissing the forecast of a storm on her weather app, Glanna checked the sky and shrugged when she saw no black or purple clouds in sight. Remembering her vow to make the most of her days off, she summoned Banksy, gave him another treat and attached his lead back on the harness. Texting Jen to say that she was happy to get a taxi home, she began to walk further along the spectacular cliff path, deciding that they would go as far as it was safe to do so. Even catching a small glimpse of Isaac's house from a distance would be something, and it was too lovely a day not to make the most of it. As soon as it got a bit dicey underfoot, they could turn back.

The further they rounded the bends of the cliff, the fewer walkers there were until they all petered out. At the same time, the views became wider and more stunning. On an ocean that seemingly stretched for miles, Glanna saw the black silhouettes of trawlers and a gigantic cruise-liner on the horizon. A small lone plane cut through the sky like a giant seagull, leaving a plume of white smoke in its wake. Various seabirds soared on the wing near Glanna and Banksy, catching the breeze. Glanna was thrilled to see some colourful-beaked Atlantic puffins snuggling against the clifftop ledges, and laughed as the whippet give a small bark of approval for their perfect walking spot.

It was only when sporadic spots of rain started falling through a quickly darkening sky that Glanna realised she had pushed her luck too far. She could recall her dad, who had listened religiously to the shipping forecast for as long as she could remember, giving her a good telling-off in his Cornish accent for going against a weather warning and ignoring her own knowledge of how quickly a coastal storm could blow in and cause havoc.

With no time for even a glimpse of a rainbow, the sky had turned a charcoal grey, and the temperature was beginning to drop. Birds were now crying their annoyance at the sudden atmospheric change which even they hadn't seemed to expect. Pulling Banksy's lead in tighter, Glanna tried to comfort her companion who, not liking cold and rain one bit, had begun to shiver.

'I'm sorry, boy. It's all my fault. We need to get back to the car park cafe as the storm is coming after all.'

Just as they turned around to retrace their steps, a

massive fork of lightning sped from sky to sea, quickly followed by the largest clap of thunder Glanna had ever heard. Reverberating around the clifftops, it caused a terrified Banksy to do the unthinkable and run. Glanna, unable to keep up with the speedy whippet, lost her hold on the lead and he was off! Up the banks and down again, the lead flailing behind him, at times racing so near to the edge of the cliff that Glanna really did think this time he might tumble. Then, as another massive crash sounded above them, the terrified whippet shot right up over the cliff bank and towards open fields. Within seconds, she lost sight of him.

'Banksy, *Banksy!*' Her frantic calls were lost on the rising wind, and the rain had soaked through her thin clothing, making her tremble with chill, and pouring down her glasses so that she was nearly blinded. In terror of losing her beloved pet, all through her own folly, Glanna began to scream as loudly as she could: '*Banksy!* Come back to me. Come back to me . . .' Her tears were now indistinguishable from the rain that was dripping off her sodden fringe. Glanna's panic was immense. She knew there was no way she could climb up the bank of the path and get up to reach him, especially now everything was so slippery. She tried to think calm thoughts, then decided that if she just walked back the same way she had come up, she would be fine. She just had to stay away from the cliff edge for fear of getting blown over, and then pray that Banksy heard her calling and came back to her. Sobbing in anguish, she roared,

'*BANKSY!*' again at the top of her voice, louder than she'd ever shouted before in her entire life.

Clinging on to the rocks for safety, she began to edge her way slowly back. She was just beginning to feel slightly safer, when a huge lone figure wearing an ankle-length raincoat, the hood pulled right over their head and covering half of their face, loomed up right in front of her.

Knowing she couldn't run either way, Glanna froze on the spot like a frightened rabbit. The figure, who was holding some kind of old-fashioned lantern in one hand, held out his arm to her and, in a deep and reassuring voice, called over the elements, 'It's all right, young lady, you're safe with me. Quick – get yourself in here and in the dry.'

Chapter 15

At Riversway, a naked Penelope Pascoe put her mobile back down on to the bedside table and then walked over to the huge mirror on the end wall of her boudoir. The bedroom was light and airy with floor-to-ceiling windows giving magnificent views down to the estuary. It really was an incredible room.

She loved extreme weather and delighted at seeing the heavy branches of the oak trees, thick with leaves, bowing and dancing in the strong wind and the rain now slashing down in diagonals and smashing against the windows. Thank goodness Fred had had the sense to put the cover back on the swimming pool though, or that would be full of all sorts of debris and even creatures by now. He'd always told her that he could smell when the weather was about to change, and as ridiculous as it sounded, he was usually right. That was the thing about Fred, he was so bloody practical and dependable.

Saying, '*Ouch!*' at the sudden stabbing pain in her hip which had niggled her for a couple of months now, the woman looked back in the mirror then put her hands under her slightly drooping breasts, pushing them back into the position at which they had always sat, right up to her early sixties. Turning to the side, she sucked in her slightly rounded stomach and frowned at the crepey skin around her knees and upper arms. Running her finger along the silver stretch mark on her belly made her think fleetingly of Glanna. Penelope had complained so much and so often about that single tiny blemish, caused by such an important event in her life. Wasted breath now. She'd rather have ten of those under her belt than everything else that was either sagging down or growing on her.

God, aging was difficult, especially when you still had the mind and sex drive of a woman of less than half her age. Also, it was difficult to swallow the recognition that, during all the years she had wasted wanting the perfect figure and face, when she now looked back at photographs, she really had it all going on. Sadly, now, she realised that the only person who was bothered by her imagined imperfections was her! Yet still she had regular massages, facials and skin peels, and rubbed various potions on to her face, but age tended to laugh in the face of these expensive treatments. She had vowed never to go under the knife, but with Karl Muller showing a lack of interest for the first time in six years and no other young men to mention at present, maybe it was time.

Penelope knew she was lucky to have good genes. Her forthright and forbidding mother, Demelza, had always been an attractive woman right up until her untimely death in the freak boating accident. Penny found tears pricking her eyes at the thought of her loving father who, in his bid to save his wife, drowned too. She had never got in a boat again. Her grief had been immense. She had just married Dicky Adams. It had been such a difficult time and then, when Dicky died too, she had worn black for six months and told all her friends that she thought her family were cursed, like the Kennedys. Now she sighed, remembering how the only constant throughout this dreadful time had been dear Fred. As young as he was, he had a mature head on his shoulders. Calm, sensible and kind, it was Fred Gribble who had kept her sane back then. She looked out again at the violence of the storm, fearing that even the oaks might fall, and remembering . . .

Poor Fred. Oh, how he had loved her. But even he could only cope with so much, and when he finally turned his back on her due to her constant infidelities, rather than stop, she had continued to invite a string of younger lovers to her home and into her bed. The grieving widow was surprised, in fact, by how many younger men were attracted to the more mature woman. And when Karl's visits had begun to dwindle due to his family commitments, she had turned to dating apps to find partners, and on occasion had lured holidaymakers, usually married men bored with their wives and the kids, for a quickie in Glanna's old art room on the riverbank.

Penelope was lucky that her alabaster skin had always remained soft and clear and that her hair, still long and now a beautiful, dyed chestnut brown, was still thick and luscious. She was tall and had always managed to stay slim without too much effort. She had an enviable figure, but now that wrinkles were beginning to appear every-where, some part of her wished that she had had a fuller figure and face. 'You never see a wrinkle on a balloon, do you now, madam?' Mrs Maynard, the rotund house-keeper, informed her when Penny Pascoe gave voice to her woes about growing old ungracefully. Then the plump woman would add, smugly, 'It's either your figure or your face. You can't keep both, and that's a fact.'

Penelope sighed and pulled on the luxurious patterned silk dressing gown, bought whilst on a stopover in Singapore when she had flown out to meet Glanna and Carmel, who were at that time staying on Magnetic Island in Australia. Lying back on her bed, she reached for the *Country Lives* magazine she had been reading earlier. Unable to concentrate for the thoughts whirling around her head, she threw the magazine on the floor then, propping herself up on three pillows, looked out again at the angry elements.

Sex with the 45 year-old Crowsbridge dentist, Karl Muller, had always been OK but very organised. Without fail, on a Monday morning, every fortnight and holidays permitting, he would come to the back conservatory door and knock three times. Until recently, that was. Penelope would meet him in one of her many sexy robes, then lead him straight to her boudoir, where underneath he would discover that all she was wearing was a lacy under-wear set, Chanel No 5 and a pair of her Manolo Blahnik 'bedroom' heels.

She found his slight German accent a turn-on and loved the way that he always showered before sex, as well as after, so was as clean as can be in order to carry out their routine. Oral sex followed by the missionary, changing to the doggy – and then, for what he always announced as 'the money shot', he would insist on finishing himself off on her breasts. However, the arrival of his fourth son had disrupted their morning trysts. He had never stated the ending of the affair, if that's what you could call it. Even after all this time, they rarely conversed about anything of a day-to-day or caring nature. In fact, she had no idea of any of the names of his children, nor even of his wife for that matter. In reality, their coupling was more like some kind of non-paying sexual transaction, where both parties were benefiting, physically at least.

Despite all this, rejection wasn't something she was used to, and it had annoyed her that he had turned her down this morning with such little notice. Rude! She wouldn't have bothered putting her face on, let alone her black suspender belt with a new pair of nude silk stockings and black silk panties. He had made her feel cheap.

She sat down in her window seat and stared out blankly at the storm raging outside. A lot of her friends were away on holiday. The Penhaligons were now at their place in Puerto Banús in southern Spain. She had declined their offer to join them, as they had also invited Jilly and Jonty St John-Davis, whom she could only stand in small bursts, plus she was sure that Rachel, the Penhaligons' tart of a daughter, was shagging Jonty behind all of their backs.

Penelope regretted none of the wonderful sexual experiences that she had enjoyed during her life. She thought of the young men with their smooth bodies, boundless energy and devil-may-care attitudes, loving the fact that they not only had access to a beautiful older woman but also a swimming pool, stables and a tennis court if they so wished. They fawned over her in exchange, attending to her needs. But lately she had begun to find it all so bloody soulless. None of those she picked wanted more than a dalliance with a sexy mature woman. And those who did want more, she found she didn't fancy. In fact, they made her want to run a mile. Nothing seemed to have any meaning. She was bored. All the money, which she once had enjoyed spending so readily, was no use if she had no one to spend it on or with. She didn't count her daughter in this as, despite her objections, Glanna did seem to enjoy it when Penelope spoiled her.

Her bedroom and dressing room at Riversway contained enough jewellery to set up a shop, and clothes and shoes galore. She also had so much expensive make-up, sufficient to keep ten more series of *Strictly Come Dancing* going. But even the sheer size, space and grandeur of Riversway, which she had always adored swanning around in, had lost its appeal. After all, she was only ever in one room at a time and unlike before, when she would have guests visiting and staying every fortnight, she now only occasionally had her neighbours over for lunch, a swim or a ride. Lately even Glanna, her only child, appeared to do everything in her power to avoid seeing her.

Penelope's bedroom had become her sanctuary, the only place where she felt safe. By now she had at long last realised that money created freedom, but what really made for a great life was the people you spent that freedom with, the people who knew you and cared about you and your future.

She looked down to see her Freddie, full waterproofs on, making sure that Blake and Krystle, her two horses named after characters from her favourite old TV series *Dynasty*, were locked in securely. No doubt he was comforting them in case they were skittish and scared of the dreadful weather, because that was the kind of man he was. So loving, so thoughtful and actually bloody good in bed too! He had been just twenty to her twenty-nine when they had met. So hot, so willing. In fact, she had never had better sex with anyone else in her life – and with her sexual history, that was some kind of accolade. But Freddie was just a humble estate worker – so how could she have possibly set up home with him? He even spoke in a common way, and she was constantly correcting his use of haitch over aitch. But how they had laughed and laughed, lying in this big bedroom and watching their favourite *Carry On* films together, and how delighted he had been, despite the circumstances and Penelope still grieving for her late husband and her parents, when she announced that she was pregnant with his child. She would never forget the expression on his face when he heard that he was to be a father.

Fred was a gifted natural cook too, but it was their after-sex cheese and ham toasties and a pot of Lady Grey that had become his speciality. Knowing how much his lover adored tea, Fred had also bought her the Swan vintage Teasmade which still sat on her bedside table and which she still used to this day, religiously. She would never admit this, but it was the best and most thoughtful present that anyone had ever bought for her. And yes, some of the nicest times she could recall in her life had been spent with her dear Freddie Gribble.

Forty years and more she had known him properly. And all those years he had lived with her or in the lodge house. And during all that time, she had had the security of him loving and protecting her, even if it was from afar. After he had moved out of the main house into the lodge, once a week he would drop by to bring her up to date with what was happening with the estate grounds and the outside staff over a cup of tea – English Breakfast for him, Lady Grey for her. That arrangement had stopped recently, and that was when her suspicions were aroused that he was seeing another woman.

As another huge clap of thunder reverberated about Riversway, Penelope Pascoe sighed and felt ashamed. Fred Gribble was the only man who had ever taken her face in both of his hands and said, 'I love YOU!' He had to spell out what YOU meant. He didn't care for her fancy clothes or perfect figure, her rich trappings or lifestyle. He loved what was inside. He loved *her*.

Penelope's breath hitched for a second. All of a sudden she realised she wasn't just bored or lonesome, it was the alien feeling of jealousy and the constant gnawing of potential loss that were causing her uneasy state of mind. She had already lost so many of those who had loved her. Unknowingly, by living with the fear of losing others, she had pushed away those she had loved. And suddenly overcome by a feeling of intense grief and pain, Penelope Pascoe started to weep.

Chapter 16

Glanna took the big man's hand as she shuddered from the cold and shock. She knew that, realistically, trying to negotiate a slippery cliff path in a raging storm wasn't an option – she would have to wait until it had passed by before she could look for Banksy again.

Entering through a concealed opening in the cliffside and free from the pouring rain at last, she took off her prescription sunglasses and tried to wipe them somehow. Blindly, she felt a piece of cloth being put in her hand; her teeth chattering, she managed to dry her glasses and put them on.

She gasped as she looked around her. For the opening in the cliff had revealed a small, cave-like area with a roof that must have been at least eight feet high. In one corner she saw a worn milking stool and a low-set easel. In the other, a battered old rucksack. A used disposable barbecue sat in a natural hole in the granite, with a battery-operated candle lantern on top. Despite the commotion of the storm outside, a sheepdog slept soundly on a hessian sack next to the stool. Without a word, the big man dragged a thin fence panel over the gap, and pulled back the hood that had covered his face. He held out his hand in greeting.

'Isaac Benson,' the stranger said. The sudden peace from the elements inside this man-made room was a relief to both of them.

'Oh my God. Shit. I . . . err . . . I know who you are.' Glanna tried to think straight, but with her hair dripping down her face, and her T-shirt and jeans soaked through, it was hard. In the end she managed to say, her voice wobbling slightly, 'I'm Glanna Pascoe. Thank you for rescuing me.' She placed her ruined art bag on the floor.

'Ah. You're the lass who's got the *Hart*mouth Gallery now, aren't you? A flyer was in the local paper about some seascape exhibition you're running there. I like the look of your work. Rainbows. Personally, I leave them alone. They are hard to get right.'

'Thank you.' Glanna blushed.

'I might have known it would be another mad artist getting caught out on the cliff path in this inclement weather. Your place not open today, then?' Isaac's voice was soft, almost hypnotic.

'Er . . . no. I take Mondays off, so I can do other things, which include my own work, painting for myself.'

'I see.'

There was another huge roar of wind that reverberated around the clifftop.

'Oh God! I need to find him.' Glanna made a loud whining sound, not unlike one of Banksy's noises.

'Worry, like guilt, is a wasted emotion. Animals, like humans, can and will survive most things that are thrown at them.'

'But . . .'

'I have lived long enough up here to know he will be OK.' Isaac softened. 'I promise you.'

Close up, in real life, the man was even more striking than he had appeared on the TV screen. His face was ruddy, his beard long and wild, with a weird, blackbird-feather shine to it, and his thick hair was tied up in a neat man bun. His deep-set green eyes were all-knowing, his hands huge. Glanna thought he was not unlike the actor Jason Momoa. Neolithically strong and handsome. As if he could wrestle a bear and the bear would lose.

'Here, you must be freezing, take your top off and put this on.' He threw a green jumper at her. 'That should cover most of you. I will turn my back.'

Glanna did as she was told, her hands fumbling with her T-shirt, which was hard to remove as it was stuck to her skin. After she'd put on the long jumper, she also pulled off her jeans and hung her wet things on a projecting piece of rock. The soft jumper, falling to just above her knees, resembled an ill-fitting mini-dress from the 1960s, but it instantly warmed her.

Isaac noticed her pulling it around herself to ensure she was keeping her dignity.

'A body is art itself, Glanna,' he commented. 'Like the landscape, changing with time and age. Whatever the season, it is a thing of beauty. And men don't worry about those changes, like you women do. I can assure you of that.'

Not quite sure how to take this hulk of a man before her, she smiled nervously.

Seeing this, Isaac changed the conversation to more conventional things, asking, 'How's it all going with the gallery, then? I hear Ferry Lane Market is a busy one, so I dare say you turn over a few pieces a week there.'

'Business isn't too bad. I'm learning every day. I was supposed to have Sally Jefferson exhibiting this month, but she had to let me down.' Glanna was surprised at how soft and fragrant-smelling her new garment was.

'Oh, did she indeed!' He scratched his beard. 'I hear she's quite the prima donna, that one. And that it's actually her husband who is the potter, while she just does the painting of the lovely things he makes.'

'How do you know all this stuff?'

'Oh, I know everything about the art – and the artists, as it happens – around these parts.' Isaac sounded far older and wiser than he looked. He reached for an orange flask from his rucksack. 'Coffee?'

'That would be lovely, thank you.'

He handed her a small plastic mug full of hot dark liquid. 'No milk or sugar, so like it or lump it.'

'Perfect.' Glanna took a sip and felt life flooding back into her veins. She couldn't help herself; the words came tumbling out, making her sound like an adolescent adoring fan girl. 'I can't believe you know who *I* am,' she gushed. 'I mean – you're Isaac Benson. *The* Isaac Benson.'

'Just a man who has been given a gift with his hands

and creates from the heart, that's all. I'm no kind of deity, I can promise you that.'

'I have to disagree. You are a genius,' Glanna said, sincerity in her voice, the gushing gone. 'Art is made to inspire, to make us question everything. It can bring awe, excitement, and outrage. And you do all of that.'

'I see. Well, I reckon if you painted just using your passion on the subject, you too could be an artist like that.' Isaac's expression didn't change.

Glanna's face reddened at the big man's tongue-in-cheek comment. 'I went all the way to Tate Modern to hear your talk. But it was cancelled.' She took another sip of her steaming drink. Now faced with the reality of him, she was far too nervous to broach the subject of him exhibiting a canvas in her gallery.

'You did? That was kind of you. It's in St Ives now. The date will be announced soon, I believe.'

'So, what happened?' she dared. 'Why did you cancel at the last minute?'

'Ah. The job of the artist is always to deepen the mystery.'

'Francis Bacon, wasn't that?' Glanna immediately noted.

Isaac, impressed at her artist knowledge, casually poured himself a cup of the strong black coffee. A distant rumble of thunder could be heard outside. The storm must be moving away; the rain now not at such a catastrophic level. Glanna hoped and prayed that her boy Banksy had found shelter somewhere. If he had been hurt, she would never forgive herself. Once the rain stopped, she would leave here and search for him. He wasn't a great big strong dog like the sheepdog still asleep on the floor here, and she willed for her beloved black whippet to come to her.

Isaac rested his cup on the floor then, taking off his anorak, revealed long beige shorts and a faded light-grey T-shirt. He looked European, Glanna thought. There were few Englishmen who could wear shorts that well. His legs were hairy. His calf-length black and tan sailing boots somehow went with his attire. Scrabbling in his rucksack, he held out a small hand towel.

'Here. It's the dog's but it'll dry your hair off.' He clocked the look on Glanna's face. 'It's clean.'

Glanna put her coffee cup down on the floor, took the towel, then gestured down to the peaceful bundle of brown and white fur. 'I can't believe he or she has slept through all of this commotion.'

'Dear old Beethoven. The fact is, he's stone deaf. Was born like it. I mean, what use is a deaf sheepdog to anyone?' His face remained straight, and Glanna was too frightened to react. 'You are allowed to laugh, you know. Yeah, this fella has been a constant companion for me and my sister, he has. And I haven't had sheep for years anyway.' He laughed, causing his eyes to shine.

And as if reading her mind, he then said gently, 'You've no need to fret, Glanna. Your Banksy will find you.'

'You know my dog's name?' Could today get any stranger?

'I think the whole of the cliffside heard you bawling it.' The big man then went to the opening in the rock, put two fingers to his lips and let out a shrill whistle. He cocked his ear to the right, stood for a moment then did it again. All the time, Beethoven's ribcage rose and fell slowly, signifying the dog's deep slumber.

Suddenly there was a whining and shuffling outside the makeshift entrance to the cave. Isaac pushed the fence panel aside, making room for the soaking wet whippet to slip through. Then, taking the towel back from Glanna, he unclipped Banksy's now filthy harness and proceeded to rub the frightened hound down. Taking a couple of treats from the pocket of his shorts, he gave them to the whippet, then lifted him gently to lie by the side of his own dog. Without any kind of reticence, Banksy snuggled into the big warm body of the sheepdog as though they had been lifelong friends.

Hugely relieved, Glanna went over to stroke his soft ears. Banksy sleepily opened his eyes and looked at her as if to say, 'Maybe you should take a leaf out of this bloke's book: he really knows how to look after a dog.'

'So, you paint here often, do you?' Glanna said shyly, turning back to her host.

Behind his beard, Isaac's lips twitched. 'I bet you say that to all the artists.'

Glanna planted her palm on her forehead. 'Mortified. I've been wanting to meet you for years and I come out with that.' She said, suddenly emotional again, 'I'm all over the place.'

Isaac took over. 'I saw you, and I thought to myself: What's that stupid woman doing, walking the Penrigan cliff path so far along with a storm upon us?'

As he spoke, Glanna noted his Cornish accent was even stronger than her dad's. Loving the irreverence of this man, she teased: 'So do you have cameras in here too, then?'

Isaac raised his eyebrows. 'You came so close to us that I had no choice but to step in and help you before you had a terrible accident.'

Seeing that Glanna was edging nearer to the easel in order to look at the painting in progress there, he held up a hand to stop her and said: 'I would appreciate your respect of my privacy. Nobody knows about this little gem of a secret studio. And I mean *nobody*. Well, apart from Beethoven. I like to keep myself to myself in all areas of my life. Trust is big in my world. Somebody dared to break it once. The outcome was very poor on my part.'

Glanna nodded furiously at this serious outpouring. 'Of course. I am a private person myself. So, I get it. I will tell no one, and that is a promise.' She sighed. 'It's so peaceful here – and what an incredible view when the weather is good.'

'Yes, it stays cool in here in the summer although it's freezing in winter, but it's from that view from this clifftop where I get so much inspiration, with the dolphins especially. They should be back when the weather clears. They really are such beautiful – and such intelligent – creatures.'

'I saw them earlier. I love them too. Although I prefer it when they are not showing off and performing for an audience,' Glanna said.

Isaac carefully covered up his work in progress, then gestured to the little milking stool. 'Take a seat, Glanna. It is Glanna, like Hannah, isn't it? Not Glarnar, which would make you sound *very* posh.'

'Glarnar,' Glanna repeated. 'I get that a lot, yes, but Glanna like banner, I usually say.'

'I like it.'

Glanna liked him. She sat down on the stool, keeping her knees covered with the jumper for decency's sake. It was uncomfortable with her long limbs. How all six foot six of Isaac Benson managed it, she had no idea.

'I bet you're wondering why on earth a man with legs as long as Penrigan Pier should choose to sit on a stool fit for a Lilliputian. I'll tell you why: because it takes you right out of your comfort zone, that's what it does. Gives you a new viewpoint. An old art teacher taught me that at school when I was fourteen. Made me bloody sit on the top of a desk on a bloody barstool – bloody terrifying it was due to a wonky leg – the stool, that is, not me or the teacher.' They both laughed. '"Always look at something in a different way to anyone else", he would say. And he was right.'

'I'll try it,' she said, and meant it.

'You should. In all aspects of life's rich tapestry.' Isaac drained his now cooling coffee and looked right at her. 'That scar. Tells a story?'

'Yes.' Glanna felt no urge to elaborate, and he didn't press her. There was a silence as she finished off her drink too.

'"Thou shalt see my scars and know that I had my wounds and also my healing."' Isaac's voice was quiet as he took her cup from her.

'Tagore?' Glanna asked.

'You're not just a talented artist, are you, Miss Pascoe?'

Glanna blushed then became animated. 'I have your print. You know, the dolphins in *Safety in Numbers*? When they are *not* showing off. It's what I have personally renamed *Quiet Dolphins at Penrigan Point*. They are just below the clear surface. I love it. It has pride of place – and also, get ready for this: my mum has the original of your *The End of the Land As We Know It.*'

Glanna noticed the artist stiffen, and his expression alter, before he quickly went back to the way he had been.

'Oh, she does, does she?' he said casually. 'I wondered where that had ended up. It was my first huge landscape, you see . . . but we all need to eat when we start out, don't we?' He pulled at his beard. 'I never got any prints done of that one either. We live,' he cleared his throat and looked to the floor, 'and learn.'

'You wished you hadn't sold it, you mean?'

He didn't answer.

Sensing a change in the atmosphere, one she didn't understand, Glanna gabbled on, 'It has such a good home. I remember Mum buying it when I was a teenager, and it is still one of my favourite paintings ever. I've always wanted to meet you so I could ask who the woman is, her arms out like Kate Winslet in *Titanic* but right at the edge of the cliff. So romantic.'

'I think you are OK to go now.' Isaac's voice was blunt. 'We were in the eye of it, but the storm has passed.' He removed the fence panel and tickled Banksy under the chin to wake him up.

'Yes, of course – thank you.' Perturbed at the man's alteration in mood and energy, Glanna stood up in as dignified a way as she could from the milking stool, then put Banksy's filthy harness and lead back on.

As she was thrust out into the unexpected sunshine, still wearing Isaac's knee-length sweater, Glanna turned to say goodbye and ask for her clothes back, but the door to the secret studio was already closed.

Chapter 17

The following Friday morning, eager customers in cars and on foot were streaming up the hill to Ferry Lane Market.

'Harry's Honeysuckle Honey has hummed its way here today,' Alicia Jarvis shouted from The Sweet Spot, the homemade fudge and honey stall that had been run by her family for many years. 'Clear and golden, perfect to cover your crumpets.'

'I'd cover that crumpet all right.' Charlie Dillon's thought came right out of his mouth, causing his wife Pat to swipe him around the head with the cloth she was using to wipe down the outside till.

'You have to push everything, don't you?' Her chubby face reddened. 'Oh God, don't answer that either.'

The bald gangster-looking man kissed his wife on the forehead. 'You know I only have eyes for you, my love.'

'Yeah – and everything else for the others,' Pat Dillon harrumphed and, wiggling her big square bottom, she headed inside their shop to collect another box of lemons.

Grinning to herself, Glanna left the gallery and strolled over to Monique's Café, where she'd arranged to meet Jen for breakfast. Her friend was already there and gestured Glanna over to the table she had reserved, saying, 'I've ordered you a macchiato.'

'Fabulous, thank you. You OK?' Glanna threw a copy of *Country Lives* down on the table.

'Yes, mad week, sorry I haven't seen you. Jack and I have been office hunting. How was your Monday walk? I hope you got home before the storm broke.'

'No, thanks to me, poor old Banksy and I got caught right in the middle of it and . . . well, I've been meaning to message you too.'

Glanna desperately wanted to discuss what had happened, with losing Banksy then meeting Isaac up on the cliffs and being taken into the secret cave, but her promise to respect his privacy had been given and she would not betray him.

'I've been in a bit of a state due to Sally Jefferson pulling out, but I've rearranged the gallery and put some of the items in the window, and I'm really pleased with the way it looks now.'

'I'll pop in tomorrow with Markus and have a look around. You can talk us through your ideas.'

'Oh, he's here for the weekend, then? That's a turn-up, isn't it?'

'Yes, he's driving down this afternoon. I'm glad the weather is good, so I can show off Hartmouth looking at its best.' Jen then confided, 'Guess what? He's only developed a sudden phobia of chickens of all things – allegedly. Meaning we can't stay with Dad and Pearl now.'

'I suppose you can't blame him for not wanting to shack up with the outlaws,' Glanna replied, amused.

'Crafty, isn't he?' Jen picked up a menu from the holder in front of her. 'He's booked the Penrigan View Hotel instead, so I'm not complaining. It's got a lovely spa and outdoor freshwater pool.'

'Look at you, Miss Fancy Pants, and I assume that's a good thing, that he's making the effort?'

'Yes. I will get my way of luring him down here full-time eventually, just you wait and see.' Jen took a sip of her frothy cappuccino and opened the magazine. 'I didn't put you down as a *Country Lives* reader, Glanna. The Countess of Newham, look at her! Lucky cow to be living in a pile like that. I want my hair like hers too. Must be extensions, surely.'

Glanna laughed. 'She's actually as rough as a badger's arse. Her family have pots of money, which they made in the betting shops they ran in Bristol. She used to be my best mate at the Crowsbridge Convent; we travelled the world when we left school. I think the *Daily Mail Online* would be more interested in some of the stories I could tell about her. God, we had some fun!'

'Are they all her kids?' Three young girls dressed top to toe in Prada smiled rather snootily back from the top of a haybale.

'Yep, think she's pregnant with another one too. "At last, a boy" is the story. She always loved being the centre of attention.'

'Being an earl hasn't stopped the husband from being

pig ugly though. Don't you find that with most titled gentry?' Jen observed.

'Can't say I've taken much notice of them, nor they of me.' Glanna tried to decide what to have for breakfast from the cafe menu as Jen flicked through the pages of the article.

'So why *did* the stunningly gorgeous twenty-something marry the ugly millionaire landowner aristocrat?' Jen said bitchily.

'Oh, like I said, her family are loaded too, so it's got to be true love, hasn't it? I remember how well they got on, from the moment they met. She seems happy, from the outside anyway, and I hope she is . . . Carmel was a good friend.'

'You don't speak to her now, I take it?'

'No. Whilst she was busy popping out kids like peas, I was in London cuddling up to a bottle of vodka as my companion.'

'Well, it's not your companion now, and you know where she is if you want to hook up with her again. Hey – maybe she can leave the kids with the nanny and be our sixth life drawing artist-model.'

'Position filled this morning.'

'Tell me more. Another man to make up the numbers, pretty please?'

'Yes, Gideon Jones, he runs the antiques stall. His wife died a couple of years ago, so he moved down here from Cardiff for a new start. They used to holiday here evidently. So that's me, you, Gideon, Mrs Harris, Hayden from the ferry and Sadie Peach. A good mixed bunch, it should be fun.'

At that moment, Linda Harris appeared with her order pad. 'Sorry to be nosy but did you just say that Gideon Jones is joining us at the art club?'

'Yes, he is.' Glanna felt slightly weird knowing that this woman was now having sexual relations with her father. According to Fred, Linda was under the impression that nobody in the town knew, and Glanna was more than happy to keep it that way, especially as she was to be the woman's art teacher for the next six weeks.

Linda Harris looked around to make sure nobody else was in earshot. Her voice fell to a whisper. 'Does that mean he'll be taking all his clothes off too?'

'Yes, that's how we will work for the time being, Mrs Harris. My idea is that by each of us posing in turn for one of the six sessions, we will all get to learn more about the body. And no one needs to take off all their clothes.' Glanna thought that in comparison with her slim and elegant mother, the plump woman might have lacked her looks and style, but she certainly matched Penelope Pascoe on the libido front.

The cafe was now filling up fast with market-day customers. Breda came out from behind the counter to start clearing the empty tables. 'Linda, hurry along now, please,' she said. 'You can see how busy we are.'

Ignoring her boss, the woman carried on. 'Let's hope they're his own clothes,' she said archly. 'Rumour has it that he used to dress up in his wife's things and make her call him Zoe.'

'If he's only been here two years, and she's dead, how on earth do you know this, Mrs Harris?'

'I've worked here for years, you know that,' the woman said, bridling. 'They used to stay at the Dolphin for their holidays and come in here for their pasties. This place is like Reuters, news on tap 24/7 if you listen carefully. Apparently,' Linda Harris looked around furtively to check no one else was in earshot, 'his you-know-what is so big that when he got together with Erica – you know, the busty secretary from Penrigan Rugby Club – she was so overwhelmed at the sight of it that she passed out,' her voice fell to a whisper, '*before* he even got her up the stairs, if you get my meaning.'

As Glanna and Jen were picturing the scene, Breda Brady tried not to make her storm over to their table too obvious. Through gritted teeth she said in her thick Irish accent, 'Gossip is the devil's telephone, Linda Harris, so best you just hang up now and come and do some work, don't you tink?'

Linda Harris pretended to put an imaginary handset down on the table as Breda disappeared. 'Well, that told me.' She then picked up a menu to fan herself and winked. 'I for one can't wait until Tuesday. I feel hot and bothered at just the thought of it.'

'LINDA!' Breda shouted from behind the counter.

'On my way,' Mrs Harris breezily called back. 'Now, what can I get you lovely ladies? And please don't even suggest a cream horn.'

Stuffed full of a bacon sandwich and buzzing after two of her favourite macchiatos, Glanna strode purposefully back to the Hartmouth Gallery, ready for what she hoped would be a busy market day. Sadie was starting at ten as the summer season was Glanna's busiest period, even more so than Christmas. But before she herself returned to start work, she had one more thing to do.

When she reached the crystals and jewellery stall, she took a deep breath. It felt good to have made a decision like this without having to ask anybody their opinion. She was doing this for herself, another step in her recovery.

Star Murray greeted her with a grin. 'You want it, don't you? I knew you would.' The petite blonde's grin was contagious.

'Yes, I do. I got soaked to the skin up at the cliffs the other day and just to get into a warm car and not have to wait for a bloody taxi would have been SO much better.' Memories of her embarrassment at tugging down Isaac's huge green jumper as she got in and out of one of the branded Hartmouth Cars cabs with Banksy flooded her mind. She had felt so angry at the big man for shutting her out like that, without so much as a goodbye or giving her back her own clothes, that she hadn't even begun to think how she might retrieve them. If it meant she had to see Isaac Benson again, she wasn't sure she'd want to go through with it.

'Three thousand for the car, you said, didn't you?' she said, collecting herself.

'Jack said if it was to go to someone I knew, then to knock a hundred pounds off, so two-nine is fine. I'm just happy it's going to a good owner. Aw! I love my little car, will be sad to say goodbye to it.'

'Well, Banksy and I will do our very best to look after it. He will appreciate it as much as me after a long walk, I'm sure.'

'Where is the little fella today?'

'Sunbathing in the front window, I expect. We had early walkies before the market got going as he's a bit like me, he doesn't like crowds.' Glanna raised her eyes. 'Breda is averse to having pets in the cafe so I left him at home.' She reached for a card from her bag. 'Let me scribble down my number and you can text me your bank details. Is a bank transfer OK? Or I can do cash later, if you'd prefer.'

'No, just send it over on Internet banking when you're ready, that's fine, and I'll let you know when I've got all the paperwork out, et cetera, and you can come and get the car. It hasn't got to move far now, has it?'

'Great. Thanks, Star. You've made it so easy.'

'Yes. For all of us, I reckon. Me and Mr Murray need to pull our fingers out now and get a lovely little family four-door number. How dull. The joys of parenthood, eh?' The second-time mum made a face, then turned her attention to a customer who had picked out a necklace from a display of birthstone crystal jewellery which glittered on a navy blue velvet jewellery stand.

Glanna had just walked around the side alley to the

back of the gallery and let herself in when there was a knock on the front shop door, where the sign still read *Closed*. No doubt an eager customer was standing there, chancing their luck that she might open early. Huffing with annoyance, she went to open up, and on realising it was a uniformed delivery man she felt relieved. Dealing with customers wasn't really her forte. In fact, if she could hide behind an easel and paint or draw all day, she would be far happier than actually having to sell her creations and those of her fellow artists too.

'Glanna Pascoe?'

'That'll be me.'

The scruffy-haired man in front of her passed her two separate packages, which she put down, then held out his tablet, saying, 'Sign here, please.'

Locking the door behind her, she looked perplexed. One of the packages was a huge canvas by the feel of it under the brown paper in which it was wrapped very badly, and the other was a small soft parcel. She thought that all her orders had come yesterday, and she certainly hadn't ordered something of this size as there was no space for it.

On opening the small parcel first, a tingling sensation such as she hadn't felt in a long time went right through her. For inside, neatly washed and ironed, were the jeans and T-shirt she had been wearing on her Monday walk. She fished out a scribbled note on a crumpled piece of paper.

I was rude, 'Yes, you were,' Glanna said aloud, *and I'm*

sorry, the note continued. 'So you should be,' she sniffed. *I hope the contents of the big package will help things along after being let down by Sally Jefferson. Take the prints with my compliments and I'll have the original back when you've found another artist for the window. Want to come to see my studio? A week Monday at ten. I will meet you at the gate to Kevrinek (my house). Banksy is welcome. Yours, Isaac Benson*

Glanna hungrily tore the brown paper off the bigger package and gaped in disbelief. For there in front of her was the framed original of *Safety in Numbers,* the very same painting she had the print of upstairs. Propping it up on an easel in the middle of the gallery, she stood back to look at it in awe. Now, at close quarters to the original, she could make out all of the details. Could revel in the intensity of the colours, lit by the magical Cornish light which had brought artists to these parts for so many years. She saw the sheen on the dolphins' backs, the turbulence of the ocean, the frightening beauty of the stormy sky and the ruggedness of the Penrigan cliffs. The care and detail that this incredible artist had put into his work was just amazing. Glanna was in awe.

An envelope with DO NOT BEND in red paint was stuck to the back of the canvas. She opened it carefully to reveal a stack of prints of the very same painting. There were ten of them, limited editions numbered in pencil in the bottom right corner from 291 to 300. All, of course, signed by Isaac Benson. A Post-it note in Isaac's erratic writing: *I won't be offended if you sell them for £300 each.*

Glanna gulped and put a hand to her heart. She did the maths. £300 x 10 equalled the money she needed for her car, leaving a spare £100 which she could put towards the insurance. Plus, having such a great artist's work in the window would attract so many more visitors too. Maybe the Star Murray magic had rubbed off on her today too, for it felt like all this was a dream coming true.

A knock on the front door startled her. It was Sadie.

'Hi, Sadie,' Glanna greeted her, opening up. 'We need to get a wiggle on. I want this large canvas in the window, so we have to move the other things out and up.'

Sadie stared at the painting on the easel, and then stared some more before managing to say, 'Jesus! Is that what I think it is?'

'Sure is.'

'That must be worth a fortune! What did you do – sleep with him?'

Glanna smiled, and as she went to the gallery window to start handing the contents out to her young assistant, she mouthed silently, 'Not yet.'

Chapter 18

Sunday night and Glanna lay in the deepest bubble bath she could have run without getting in and spilling the water over the sides of her big copper freestanding bath. She loved the fact that the owner of the flat and shop, a social media entrepreneur also in her late thirties, had had such a great design eye, as the kitchen and bathroom were exactly to Glanna's taste. She was surprised that as it was a long-lease rental it should have been fitted out to such a high spec, but the agent had told her that the owner's plan was to eventually retire to Hartmouth, and that this was her pension. The higher the spec, the higher the rents and the greater the financial rewards and all that.

The Friday and Saturday market days flew by with lots of sales and happy customers. Five of the Isaac Benson limited edition prints had not surprisingly sold already, and the shop had been constantly brimming with customers, due to the pull of *Safety in Numbers* in the window and also the eclectic *Seascapes in All Seasons* exhibition that Glanna had not only marketed well but had displayed so enticingly around the gallery.

On learning of the excitement around her gallery,

Henry Hall, the general manager of the Dolphin Hotel, had also popped down and selected five paintings from just one artist with which to adorn their recently refurbished dining room. Glanna had sold one of her own rainbow prints too – a view from the Crowsbridge quayside back over to Hartmouth, where it looked as if the rainbow was actually ending right on top of the roof of Frank's Café.

All in all, it had been a very successful weekend, topped off by her picking up the car from Star and being able to pay her without even touching her savings. She had already managed to organise the insurance too, which cost nearly as much as the car due to her driving history. This had hurt, but she knew she deserved it, and at least being able to pay this via monthly direct debit had softened the blow.

Having a car again would be both scary and exciting. The fact it was a little convertible too was a wonderful bonus, especially in the summer when she could cruise around the Cornish country lanes. Having a car would also open her life up to more adventure. She and Banksy could discover new areas to park up and walk in, and it would also make it easier to visit her mother at Riversway. Which she really must do soon. She had avoided Penelope recently and, as much as her mother annoyed her to the brink of white-hot anger on occasion, Glanna noticed that Penelope had seemed generally sad the last few times they had spoken. Despite everything, she was still her mother and Glanna did love her.

Of course, being able to drive to Isaac's home would be so convenient. The thought of it had not left her mind since reading his note. It all seemed so surreal, as if she had wished it to happen, and it had. She suddenly splashed her feet around in the bath like a little girl and counted the days down in her head until the following Monday. 'Eight more sleeps,' she said out loud as she had done as a child when Christmas was approaching.

As she topped up her bath with more hot water, her thoughts turned to Oliver and how happy he would be that she was driving again at last. It was the kind of big life event where normally he would have been the first person she would have called. She also suddenly recalled that dreadful moment in hospital coming around with her head in pain from having stitches in the huge cut above her eye, two black eyes and the worst hangover she had ever experienced in her entire life. She thought both her ankles were broken, but they were just badly bruised. She had opened her eyes to her dad's face, his expression full of fear. Penelope, not being able to cope, had sat in the waiting room drinking excessive amounts of bitter-tasting lukewarm coffee from the vending machine. Glanna touched her scar. Isaac had mentioned it. Isaac understood.

Her accident had been the final wake-up call to end her drunken despair. It still amazed her, and she had talked to Myles about this in depth: where, in the attic of the human psyche, did you suddenly realise that you had to put a halt to your addiction, or get away from an awful relationship, or just generally sort your life out? When did you suddenly think more of yourself than the situation you were in, or the drug of choice you were so reliant on, in order to pull yourself out of such a desperate situation and want to start living a clean, happy and fulfilling life again?

She cringed at how close she had been to getting her life back on track before falling so spectacularly off the wagon, purely out of fear of falling in love with someone who really wanted her and her babies. God, her self-sabotaging streak had a lot to answer for in the story of her life. Thank goodness she was well on the road to recovery now. It had taken a long time, but it felt good to be making progress. And despite her mixed-up feelings, she did hope that Oliver was happy; he had certainly looked it.

Wearied by her thoughts, Glanna lay back in the fragrant bubbles and, putting a hand down between her legs, began to touch herself. Since shagging the ugly barman, the only other time she had had sex – and sober sex at that – was after the London wedding at which she had been the photographer. The bride's brother, who was the hottest man in the room, had drunkenly flashed his hotel room-key number at her and she had followed him to the lift. It had been a perfect one-night stand, giving much-needed gratification. But since then, nothing. Yes, she was living in a quieter area and there were fewer available men to fancy, but perhaps she had started to change on that front too. If the right 'brief encounter' came up, maybe she would take it, but now that she was beginning to love herself just that little bit more, it was hard to explain but she felt her body was more sacred to her and she didn't feel so inclined to put out to just any old Tom, Harry or Dick!

Sex had been such a huge part of her life pre-Oliver, but her therapy with Myles was showing her that it had been linked to her need for attention – the attention, perhaps, that she hadn't received from her mother. It was a coping mechanism, like taking a drink or a long drag on a joint or a cigarette. And as long as somebody wanted to fuck her, she felt that she was needed and it would take her emotional pain away.

But whatever stage of life or love a woman was at, she could still fantasise, couldn't she? Taking a deep breath, Glanna shut her eyes to imagine walking in on a naked Oliver and Isaac in the cliff cave. The two very different but equally handsome men, completely naked, began making love to her in turn . . . and then with a shudder she felt her body flood with happy hormones as she realised that making love to herself could be just as fulfilling as sharing the joy with someone else.

Chapter 19

'You all set then, love?' Fred Gribble tinkered with one of the spare easels his daughter had got off eBay. Glanna began busily attaching a few sheets of drawing paper to each, then undid a pack of willow charcoal and placed a couple of sticks in the attached trays, plus a pack of coloured chalks and a 4B pencil and a rubber. Banksy was lying quietly with one eye open in his basket.

'I think so, Dad. Actually, would you mind bringing the portable aircon unit up from the shop? It's boiling up here, even with both windows open. I thought it would have cooled down slightly by now.'

'Everyone will be stripping off, eh.' Fred Gribble winked. 'And are you sure I can't stick around? I mean, it is Linda who has offered to get her kit off first, isn't it?'

'Dad! I think you've seen quite enough of our Mrs Harris, don't you?' She grinned as Fred trotted off downstairs chuckling naughtily to himself.

Glanna plumped up the two cushions on the chaise longue which she had positioned at the front of the room ready for the first life drawing model. She was lucky that the main bedroom of her flat was so large. When she had first seen it, she realised it would be perfect to convert into her art studio. With its huge south-facing sash windows, the light was perfect. All she and her dad had to do was put down a temporary flooring over the wooden one and paste some wallpaper lining paper over the paintwork so that she could splash it with as much paint as she wanted without worry. They had also set up a table in the corner next to the basin unit that had already been there for all of her paints, small tubes of which sat in rainbow colour order, along with a variety of brushes, pens, pencils and water containers.

Glanna had been perfectly happy to take the spare room as her bedroom since, in her eyes, art took precedence over sleeping, and with its white fitted wardrobes there was still enough room for a double bed.

As she was placing her own canvases to one side of the room, her dad appeared with the cooling unit and plugged it in.

'I'm seeing Mum on Friday night. She's cooking me dinner,' Glanna told him as she carried on setting up the drawing stations.

'You mean Mrs Maynard has been summoned to the kitchen?'

'No, Mum has assured me she's doing it herself – a salad of some sort. Is she OK, have you seen her?'

'She seemed to be limping a bit when I saw her but she brushed it off as nothing, you know what she's like.'

'Oh, maybe that's why she's sounding more miserable than usual then. Plus, of course, suspecting that you are seeing someone else has completely thrown her.'

'Did she ask you about it, then?'

'Yes, she did. I said nothing but I know it's really bothering her.'

'Not enough for her to tell me to my face though, eh, Glanna? You know how much I adore your mother, but what more can I do? I waited years for her to see what was right in front of her, but she still prefers much younger men who buy her expensive gifts. Now, I have to make the best of what life I have left and I am having fun with Linda.'

'I don't know how you can do that if you profess to love Mum so much, but I'm glad you are getting on with it.'

'Fun can be fun without feeling, you know.'

Glanna's face dropped at her father's innocent words. She had, after all, been the Fun Without Feeling Queen, and her biggest faux pas had been made at the expense of her relationship with Oliver.

Fred Gribble beamed. 'And at least Linda appreciates my humour.'

'Take care with all these hearts on the line though, won't you, Dad? And that includes yours.'

As Fred tutted at Glanna's comment, there was a ring on the back doorbell. Glanna checked the camera on her phone, then brushed down her baby-pink sleeveless jumpsuit. Her hair was neatly pushed back with a black and white polka dot knitted headband, and she had chosen her thick black-framed spectacles to match her ensemble.

'Good, good, it's Linda. Show her up, Dad, and thanks for helping me. Shall I see you on Friday when I go over to Riversway?'

'Maybe. I hope it all goes well tonight, my darling.' He stopped before heading for the stairs and turned around. 'I'm super-proud of you, you know.'

Glanna gulped. 'Clear off, Dad, and no sneaking back in, you hear me.'

♡

Linda Harris had chosen to be the first of their group to pose, so had come early and was now sprawled out across the pale blue chaise longue. She had without a doubt the prettiest of faces, with the softest of skin. Pink-cheeked, blue-eyed and rarely without a friendly smile, Glanna could see what her father liked about her. The woman's curly dark brown hair had been tonged into neat ringlets for the event. With one arm above her head, she showed off her voluptuous 38E breasts and a big tummy which was surprisingly firm. The mauve silk sheet she had brought to lie on covered her lower regions, and her dressing gown was close at hand for the break times. Glanna had fussed around so that one of the woman's legs hung neatly over the sofa and the other freshly pedicured tiny trotter-like foot poked out from under the silk on the other side.

It was 7 p.m. and the other budding artists arrived one by one.

'Stunning!' the young Sadie Peach exclaimed.

'Jesus,' Jen directed at Glanna as she poured herself an iced elderflower cordial from the glass jug on the table at the front of the class.

'Look at the tits on that,' Gideon Jones mouthed to a grinning Hayden.

'I'm ready!' Mrs Harris shouted cheerily from where she was draped.

Chapter 20

It had been a perfect summer evening to go horse riding with her mother in the grounds of Riversway. A long overdue and unexpected treat that Glanna had loved every minute of.

'Good boy, Blake.' Glanna dismounted the huge grey stallion and patted his wide and sweaty neck. 'I forgot how much I enjoyed doing this. And the smell of these gorgeous beasts.' She stuck her face into the horse's cheek, and Blake whinnied and pushed himself towards her. 'I really must come over here and ride out more often.'

'You're going to have to help me off, dear,' Penelope Pascoe said hesitantly, her face somewhat pained. Glanna guided her mother down off the other majestic creature, Krystle. The smaller sixteen-hand chestnut mare was now tapping her hoof as if to say, 'Come on, I'm ready for my stable now.'

'What's up, Mum? Dad said he'd seen you limping again.'

'It's nothing. Must have pulled a muscle. Don't fuss, Glanna.'

'It's clearly something.'

'Oh, very well. I did Google my symptoms and it could

be my hip as my leg does give way sometimes too. I'm terrified I might need a replacement.'

'Oh. I hope not, Mum.' Glanna was concerned. Then, collecting herself, she said firmly, 'Ring the surgery on Monday – that's the sensible thing to do. It could be something as simple as a sprain, and if it's not, well, we will deal with it.'

'Talk of the devil.' Penelope Pascoe immediately stood upright and brushed her tight beige jodhpurs down. 'Freddie, darling. I haven't seen you for ages.'

'I've been busy, that's why, keeping your ladyship's garden in order.' Fred Gribble looked comfortable in his baggy shorts and fitted T-shirt.

'And someone else's by the sound of it, dear,' were the words that fell out of Penelope's mouth. There was a little silence.

'We had a great ride.' Glanna cut the sticky July evening atmosphere.

'Your mother always did like *a great ride*, didn't you, Pen?'

'What is this, some kind of *Carry On* film?' Penelope Pascoe dropped the horse's rein, her face reddening with anger.

'We used to love watching those together, didn't we?' Fred said quietly and without waiting for a response, took the reins of both horses and started walking them towards their stables. Then, with feelings of pent-up rage, he suddenly whipped around and said in a calm but firm voice, 'What is it that you want, Penny? What is it that would really make you happy? Because from where I'm standing there is nothing on this earth that would satisfy you.'

Penelope, taken aback by this passionate outburst, then matched it. 'I want to get away from this place, travel around the world, see the seven ancient wonders of it. Ride horses in the sea, climb the Sydney Harbour Bridge, swim with dolphins, see giant tortoises in the Galapagos Isles and watch flamenco danced by gypsies in Seville. I want to travel and explore, before it's too late.'

Her words hung on the air long after she had finished speaking.

A silent Fred, now shaking his head in exasperation, carried on slowly walking the horses towards the stable.

'Dad, join us for dinner?' Glanna called out, trying her best to remain upbeat.

'No. You two need to catch up and I need to sort the horses out.'

The two women sat at the huge table that Fred Gribble had lovingly made all those years ago in the grand dining room at Riversway. This high-ceilinged space had always been Glanna's favourite as the full-length windows offered the perfect light for her to sketch. The French doors lay open to the immaculate lawn and glorious view down the garden to the water; a chicken Caesar salad and two glasses of fizzy water sat in front of them. Birdsong filtered through from the countless trees in full green leaf, and the sight of boats making their way along the estuary, their passengers enjoying the balmy summer evening, completed the picture.

'The bloody kids are on holiday now; so shrieking is all I hear when the wind is in the right – or should I say the wrong – direction,' Penelope Pascoe huffed, still slightly discombobulated from Fred's earlier comment and her inability to deny the strong feelings that had rushed through her.

'Thanks for "cooking", anyway,' Glanna said with a wry smile.

Her mother managed a smile back. 'It took me ages to open that packet of salad, but I did have to take the skin off the breasts.' They shared a rare laugh together. 'How are you, darling? I feel as if I haven't seen you for ages.'

Glanna looked at the magnificent Isaac Benson oil painting hanging on the wall in front of her. Should she mention him? No, she had promised, and despite his rudeness, the depth and sincerity of the man had made her vow not to betray his trust.

'I am actually really good, thanks for asking.'

'Please do note that I am drinking water in front of you. I find it so hard not having my evening carafe of red, but it's not about me now, is it, Glanna?'

'Oh Mum, I've said before that you can drink what you want; it's not a problem any more. And as I was saying, I'm feeling great – quite happy actually.'

'Good, good. Well, apart from you having had that stupid short fringe cut in, but the colour is nice, and are those new glasses?'

Glanna put her hand to her forehead. She had asked Sadie if she could cover whilst she had her hair cut earlier and loved the new trendy style and colour combo that Jason, the stylist from Salon X, the hairdresser's at the bottom of Main Street, had created for her. It had taken her a while to trust somebody new, always having gone to some ridiculously expensive celebrity hairdresser when in London. But Jason had come with a five-star recommendation from Myles and, despite her therapist having no hair of his own to mention, she had trusted his judgement and rightly so.

'If you are going to throw comments like that around, Mother, some people might say that you are too old for long hair.'

'And I would just reply, "Jane Seymour, darling".'

'She paints, you know,' Glanna added, 'and one of her middle names is Penelope.'

'Look at you, dear, the font of all knowledge, of sorts. Anyway, whilst you're here, have you thought any more about your birthday party? Would you want it on the actual day – it is on a Saturday, after all. I've got a quote for a marquee already.'

'Like I said before, I'm not sure I want a big do.'

'Oh. That's so disappointing. It's a huge event – four decades, darling. Amazing you're still here really, when you think of the past. And it's too long since I've had a proper celebration here at Riversway. Please don't spoil my fun, you know how I love a good party.'

Glanna took a slurp of her fizzy water to wash down the words of pain and annoyance that were sitting on the tip of her tongue.

Penelope Pascoe was on a roll. 'Jilly St John-Davis told me you have some Benson prints in the shop.'

'Er, did she now?' That woman misses nothing, Glanna thought. 'And, yes, I thought I'd take the plunge and invest in some – and it was worth it. How are you anyway, Mum? Aside from the dodgy hip.'

Penelope finished her mouthful and aligned her knife and fork. She had hardly eaten anything. Glanna recognised her mother's face twitch in a way which meant that the stiff upper lip had to be maintained despite it wanting to wobble. She took a drink of her fizzy water and cleared her throat.

'Allow me to offer you some advice, dear daughter. Take a thousand naked pictures of yourself now. You may think, Why on earth should I do this? Who wants to see these pert boobs or magnificent thighs? That chiselled chin or wrinkle-free skin round those lovely big brown eyes of yours.' The cawing of a seagull interrupted her flow, causing her to sigh. 'But believe me, one day when you get to my age, you will look at those photos with much more appreciation and say, "I really was quite a beautiful specimen of a woman."'

'Mum, what's wrong? You are still a very attractive woman, if that's what you are getting at.'

'In whose eyes, dear, in whose eyes? Anyway, this is not a conversation a mother should be having with her daughter.'

'I disagree. I can't remember the last time we actually had a true and honest one of those, to be fair.'

Penelope Pascoe sighed. 'I don't think your father loves me any more and I actually don't know what to do with that.'

'Oh, Mum. Who just arrived the minute we had finished riding, to take care of the horses, eh? That would have taken us ages. I told him we were having dinner tonight.'

'He also looked after them in that storm.' Penelope Pascoe was thoughtful. 'Plus he saved the pool from being damaged and the gladioli from snapping.'

'See? Love is about actions. It's not what you say, it's what you do. And if you asked him, I don't think the reason he has hung around for over forty years would have anything to do with the size of your tits or arse.'

'Do you have to be so crude, Glanna! And your father was caring for the animals, not me.'

'Was he really?' Glanna responded wisely. 'And showing you care is not a weakness, either. Maybe you should try it sometime. Dad is the best thing that will ever happen to you, and I actually refuse to tell you that, ever again. So, you either quit moaning about him, do something about it or move on. Because I hate to be the bearer of bad news, but he is doing just that.'

Penelope Pascoe harrumphed. 'I can't imagine she's a patch on me. Who is it?'

'Why don't you ask him?'

The older woman frowned. 'That is your advice, is it? And when exactly, Glanna, did you become the guru on love?'

Glanna said sadly, 'Never,' then added in a whisper, 'I saw Oliver. He has a baby now.'

'Oh darling. Well, it was only going to be a matter of time, wasn't it? He's a handsome man, that one, and I did tell you he'd be snapped up in a jiffy the moment you refused to have his child.'

Glanna took a deep breath. Her mother would never change, and she wasn't sure if she would really want her to. But saying aloud what she felt about the mess of her own parents' relationship had made her think about Oliver and her feelings for him. She was treading water at the moment, with regard to love. And maybe she should be giving herself a taste of her own medicine – swallowing the reality that it was time to forget about him and move on, just as he had rightly managed to do, so readily, without her.

Chapter 21

The following Monday, Glanna linked up Spotify to her car radio and began to sing loudly and out of tune to her *Best of Bowie* album. It really was a spectacularly scenic route through the country lanes of Hartmouth to Penrigan Head. Rolling fields to her right and, when the tall hedgerows and hand-built granite stone walls allowed, glimpses of the sea to her left.

Although time had allowed logic to prevail that her crash had been a consequence of being drunk and nothing to do with her prowess as a driver, she had still been slightly hesitant when she had first got into the little Smart car. But once she had got used to the controls and a few miles under her belt, Glanna had pushed the awful memory of the accident to the side and remembered just how much she used to enjoy driving. She had never really liked the Alfa Romeo Spider that she had crashed. Had hardly used it, in fact. It was just another glitzy accessory taking up an expensive resident's parking place outside her London flat. But now, to own another convertible, which she had bought and paid for herself, and to be able to drive it with the top down in this great weather and with the lovely views all around her made for a new and so much better experience. With the quieter roads and thanks to her work with Myles, a much quieter mind, she felt no fear, was now in control of herself – so why wouldn't she be in control of a car too? For many reasons she felt suddenly liberated. Banksy too had found his place, sitting upright on the passenger seat next to her, his leathery wet black nose to the air and his soft black ears flailing around in the breeze.

Feeling a mixture of fear and excitement, Glanna slowed down as she entered the long lane that led up to Kevrinek, Isaac Benson's home. It was as if she was going on a first date, with no idea how the conversation would go or what on earth was going to happen. Normally, she would have felt a bit put out by the arrogance of the man, who on his invitation to see his studio today at ten, had omitted to include a phone number, so there was no way she could decline. It was as if he presumed she would be so honoured by the invitation that she would grab at this chance – be there like a shot. Though, he had presumed right, Glanna thought to herself. She would have crawled the twenty miles on her hands and knees to get here, if there was no other way.

Glanna pulled up to the metal gate midway down the lane and breathed in the clear sea air. Steep banks rose either side of the little Smart car, covered in wildflowers of differing colours and species. It really was a gorgeous day, not too hot to get sweaty but warm enough to feel a comfortable heat on her face. Banksy was also basking in the sun, in his usual regal manner. She was just checking what time it was, when she saw a battered old Land Rover with Isaac Benson's massive physique in the driving seat reversing towards the gate on the other side of it. She grinned at the sight of Beethoven sitting in a matching upright position to his master in the passenger seat. As the gate slowly started to open Isaac, without turning around, stuck his big arm in the air and gestured for her to follow.

They pulled into a huge courtyard surrounded by outbuildings and stables. A long lawn, with stepping-stones through the middle, led to the granite farmhouse she recognised from the television documentary and the attached modern glass-fronted studio facing the rugged coastline, custom-built on to the side of the old building, made for an interesting mix of architecture.

Isaac jumped out of his vehicle and came to open her car door.

'You got my note, then?' he said with a welcoming smile. His teeth were very white and perfectly clean, Glanna noticed. And she loved the fact that at fifty-five his man bun really suited him. Isaac then went round to Banksy to fuss him, and let him out of the passenger side.

'He can run with Beethoven, he'll be fine,' he told Glanna. Sure enough, the two dogs sniffed each other then set off to the freedom of the fields. 'It's a stunning day, isn't it? The dawn light was incredible. Please, follow me.'

As they walked towards the old farmhouse, Glanna

saw that the television had not done justice to this remote and magical setting. Luscious green fields rolled down towards the cliffs' edge, and beyond, the blue-green water was being hit by the sun, causing myriads of gems to shine. All around was Nature at her best. And the weather was calm today, unlike the destructive storm of a fortnight ago. Even the distant horizon was currently free of any boats. It was so quiet up here that all she could hear was the sound of seabirds and the distant movements of the sea.

'I assume from the stables that you have horses?' Glanna asked politely.

'Just the one, at present. Beauty. He's in the back field today.'

'Aw. I have Blake, he's a grey. My mother keeps him at her place.'

Isaac didn't respond. 'Here.' He opened a low side door to his studio and ducking his head, ushered her in before him. 'Welcome to my world.'

'I feel very honoured to be here.' Glanna looked out of the glass wall down to the sea. She was quiet, absorbing the spiritual quality of the room. Eventually she said, her voice low, 'This is the most inspiring space I've ever stood in. The light is incredible.'

She turned to look at the rest of the big room, liking the mess of the place, the orderly disorder: this was how a real studio should be. Scattered with finished and unfinished works, the old flagstones splattered with oils of every colour. A huge canvas was set on a horizontal easel in the corner, with the beginnings of one of Isaac's recognisable landscapes. The easel she had noticed during the TV programme was, she noticed, still covered in a black silk drape. As for the light . . . the incredible soft light had attracted artists through the centuries, including the group that became known as the St Ives artists. Patrick Heron, Christopher Wood, Barbara Hepworth the sculptress and more recently the likes of Francis Bacon, Terry Frost and many, many others . . . all had come here seeking it.

A huge, dark green beanbag was positioned in front of the glass wall.

'Oh my God! I love this – can I?'

Isaac smiled and nodded as Glanna, in childlike manner, threw herself on to the beanbag and looked out at the amazing vista.

'I call it my think pad,' Isaac informed her.

'I can see why. This is like some kind of film set,' Glanna enthused. 'It's too beautiful for words. I can see why you paint these views, they are truly breathtaking.' More than that, the whole experience was making her yearn to paint, and to paint well.

'Coffee?' Isaac held up a jug of steaming black liquid. Glanna caught a whiff of the caramelised, almost nutty smell.

'Do you have milk?'

'The girl doth get fussy.'

'Er, sorry. It's OK, I can . . .'

'Glanna, you have to get used to me. I'm joking, it's

me who owes you an apology. I said it on the note I wrote you and after this I won't ever say it again, but I behaved badly in the cave. And to leave you to walk down the path with just my old jumper on was inexcusable. Eccentric I know I can be, but ungentlemanly, not normally.'

'I said the wrong thing,' Glanna put in.

'No, your innocent comment evoked a memory, that's all. Right,' the man's voice became brisk. 'I have some milk, warm and fresh from the cow.'

Glanna was surprised at his confession and also relieved that he didn't blame her. They were friends again. Despite also itching to ask what was under the black silk cloth on the easel across the room, she wisely chose to say merely, 'Cows too? You have quite the menagerie, with Beauty and Beethoven and now a herd of cattle.'

'No, the cows aren't mine, they are two fields along. I was up with the larks this morning so I climbed over the fence and sneaked a quick udder-squeeze into the plastic cup from my Thermos, before the farmer called them down for milking.'

Glanna heaved herself up off the beanbag, laughing. 'Now *that* I would have liked to see.'

Isaac handed her a plain white bone china mug full of milky coffee. 'I don't have any sugar, I'm afraid,' he said, 'but the milk may well be a bit sweet.'

'Just like me.' Glanna took a sip and sat down on the high stool next to a wooden workstation splattered with paint.

'I'll be the judge of that.' The man's unexpectedly familiar comment in his strong Cornish accent made Glanna feel a little giddy. His aura appeared to take up as much space as his body. So much so that she already didn't really look at him physically, but at Isaac the person as a whole. Something which was never usually that instant for her. She felt a weird sense of warmth and comfort in his presence.

'Thanks so much for the loan of the dolphin canvas,' she told him. 'I love it so much and it has caused quite a stir in the market, and not just with the art buffs. My window looks the best it ever has. You are very generous. And are you sure about the prints?'

'I am never not sure of anything I do,' was the man's reply. 'You needed a leg up; I gave you one.' He picked up some binoculars and stared through them. 'There they are.' He handed the binoculars to Glanna, who saw Beethoven and Banksy charging up and down in the field beyond. 'They'll be tired tonight, that's for sure,' he said.

'I just hope there are no rabbits,' Glanna said. 'Banksy can be as quiet as a lamb one minute, then he sees a rabbit or anything move and he's off like a shot. And will have no hesitation in killing it.'

'I hadn't even thought about dinner tonight, so I don't mind. Rabbit stew it is, then,' Isaac said straight-faced. Glanna wasn't sure if he was joking or not. 'Come on, let's go for a walk and catch up with them.' Selecting a bone-handled walking cane from a tall hand-painted urn by the low studio door, the big man marched outside.

'So, you've lived here all your life, then?' Glanna asked as they strolled through the fields towards the clifftops.

'Yes, I was born in the main house. There's plenty of space in there so as a family we didn't get on top of each other. Some folk think it's strange – that we never left our parents, that is . . .' His voice tailed off.

'And your sister?' There was a long silence, which Glanna filled. 'They showed a photo of her on the programme. Does she still live here too?'

'Kind of.' Isaac took an intake of breath. 'Anyway, enough about me, what's your story?'

Glanna obediently took her cue to move on. 'I studied Fine Art at the Slade, where you went.'

'Brilliant, how did you find it?'

'I loved it. I got a first.' It was the first time that Glanna had openly said that with pride.

'Ah. A dark art horse in our midst. Well done, you. That's a great achievement.'

Glanna sighed. 'It makes me sound like my life was so sorted, but the truth is I was a complete and utter spoilt little madam. I started the course well after leaving school. I wasn't the student eating beans on toast and working in a bar to fund myself. No, my dear mummy thought I needed to do something with my life, so insisted I apply to university, and when I got in to UCL, she threw money at me so that I completed the course.'

Glanna looked Isaac in the eyes. 'I'm surprised I actually went through with it, but in the end it was art that saved me – and still does, I think. Thank God for talent, as if I had had to study anything that involved my memory, I'd have been knackered. In those days I could barely remember my own name. I had travelled extensively and drunk extensively through a lot of my earlier life, and after university. It caught up with me in the end, and I spent time in treatment. I see now that I wasn't very well, Isaac. But with the gallery and my rediscovered love of painting, I'm getting there now.'

'Nobody looks back on life and remembers the nights they got plenty of sleep, do they?'

Glanna smiled ruefully. 'I guess not.'

'Your scar was a result of that old life then?'

She rarely opened up to a nigh-on stranger, but this time it felt easy and natural. 'I crashed into a stationary car, drunk. Luckily it was only me who got injured but the incident caused a lot of pain and worry to my parents, I know that. I don't drink now.'

'The alcohol tasted better than tears back then, I bet.'

'Wasn't it Tennessee Williams who said that if he got rid of all his demons, he'd lose his angels too?'

'I paint to keep mine at bay, Glanna. We all have them. It's the way we manage them that counts.'

'I didn't manage them that well, clearly.'

'But you are now, and at least you've lived it, girl.'

'Wasted a lot of it too.'

'Regret is the only waste of time, in my opinion. Only regret the things you don't do, I say. And there's a whole future ahead of you now, to not regret anything.'

'Isaac Benson! I love that logic.'

'Not just an internationally renowned painter, eh?'

They were both laughing, when suddenly Isaac's face dropped. Noticing the two dogs in the distance, he shouted, 'No!' and began running full tilt towards them. Knowing that Beethoven wouldn't hear and fearing it was Banksy getting too near to the cliff's edge, Glanna was soon in hot pursuit.

Red-faced and ribs heaving on catching up with him, she put her hands on her hips and bent to regain her breath. It was then she noticed that Isaac was holding Banksy by his collar and that there was a pile of recently dug earth behind her pet.

'He was digging,' Isaac managed. Beethoven lay happily panting on the grass next to his master's feet.

'Er, yes, he quite often does that, picks up on a strong animal scent and burrows like crazy. What's the harm? You frightened the life out of me.'

She looked up, saw Isaac's crestfallen face and then, kneeling down to stroke and quieten Banksy, who was quivering, she put her hand over her mouth. For there, sitting amongst the long grass near to the cliff's edge, was a plain wooden cross with a small brass plaque attached to it on which were etched the words: *Fly free, Sweet P, fly free.*

Saying nothing, Glanna clipped on Banksy's lead and brought him to sit down beside Beethoven, where he settled up close to the deaf sheepdog, gaining comfort from him just as he had in the cave. Isaac meanwhile, looking utterly distraught, stood staring at the cross.

Instinctively, sensing the pain emanating from the big man, Glanna then put her arms around Isaac's huge chest and hugged him as tightly as she dared. When he hugged her right back, she sighed deeply and pushed her face into his soft cotton checked shirt. They stood there, embracing, for what seemed like forever. The sea breeze dancing around them, the sense of Isaac's inexplicable loss stronger than the midday sun. Like Banksy with Beethoven, the warmth and security that Glanna had felt with Oliver and now with Isaac, enclosed her again, like two big kindly hands cupping her soul.

Chapter 22

'Thank you so much for seeing me tonight instead of tomorrow. Art Club is for the next five Tuesdays, so we only need to rearrange one more.'

'It's fine, Glanna. You know I always try to be flexible, if I can. So, what's going on with you?' Myles Armstrong took a mouthful of water from the tumbler next to him. 'Are you sure you don't want a drink?' He fanned himself with a coaster. Beads of sweat were forming on his high, smooth forehead.

'No, thanks. I had a cup of tea before I left home so I'm fine, thank you.' Banksy, exhausted from running round the fields of Kevrinek, slept soundly at her feet, emitting soft little snores now and then. 'Well, I'm fine on the thirst stakes anyway.'

'Oh, go on.'

'This is totally confidential in here, isn't it?'

'Glanna, you know it is.'

'Fine, fine, just checking. I went to Isaac Benson's house.'

Myles was excited with what might be coming but of course didn't show it. 'OK, and that's a good thing, isn't it?'

Before she could stop herself, Glanna just came out with it. 'I think he could have buried his sister in his garden. Well, on his land, near the cliff edge, that is. Don't you think that's a bit weird?'

'People have humanist funerals a lot around here, and as long as you register the death and gain approval from your local authority, it *is* legal.'

'I know that, but in the documentary, there was no mention that his sister was dead.'

Myles remained unshocked. 'So did you ask him about her?'

'No. Banksy was digging up earth, Isaac went mad, and then I saw her cross. It just said *Fly free, Sweet P, fly free.*'

'P? What was his sister's name? I forget. I watched that documentary too and she was in it, wasn't she?'

'Hmm, actually yes, I rewatched it when I got in and there was a reference to her, but not her name. They just put up a grainy picture of her riding on a horse. Odd. So, I searched the Internet and amongst the huge coverage around Isaac Benson's art achievements, I managed to find an article from way back, and it said his sister is called Elizabeth.'

'Did it say she had passed away?'

'No, nothing at all.'

'So why do you think it's his sister?'

'Where is she, if it's not her? And surely it would have been in the press if something had happened to her. My gut is telling me something's not right – and you have always told me to follow my gut. Maybe he killed her?'

'Glanna, come on. Your imagination does have a habit of running away with you. We've talked about you watching that. And why on earth would you come to that assumption?'

Glanna thought for a second. 'He acted in a strange way when I asked if his sister lived there too. He just said, "kind of".'

'"Kind of" can mean anything. Maybe she lives half there and half with a partner or something. And surely with his fame, it would have been documented, locally at least, if she had died.'

'Myles, I know you always tell me never to assume anything, but what do you really think?'

'I'm your therapist not a clairvoyant, Glanna. Communication is key. Why don't you just ask him? I'm sure there will be an explanation to both the mystery grave and his sister's whereabouts. I very much doubt there's a murderer in our midst and if you do believe that, you are being very brave.' Myles smiled. 'How are you feeling though? It has obviously rattled you.'

Glanna frowned. 'I'm all right. The whole of the few hours I was there was like a dream, mostly a good one. In fact, it was amazing to be in his company.' She became animated. 'And I don't know if you've walked by my gallery lately, but I have one of his original oils in the window and he gave me, literally *gave* me, ten of his limited edition prints to sell, as Sally Jefferson had let me down.'

'How kind is that?'

'I know. I have so much to tell you. I used the money I made from selling the prints to buy a car.' She beamed.

'Wow, that's a big step, well done.'

'I know. It's Star Murray's little convertible Smart car. It's perfect, not too fast, and I just love both the freedom and the fact that in this weather I can roll the roof back. This little fella loves it too.' Deep in doggy dreamland, Banksy remained both mute and motionless as she leaned down to stroke one of his ears.

'And how did you feel when you first drove it?'

'I wasn't as scared as I thought I might be. Driving here is a breeze compared to London roads, although saying that, some of those single-track lanes scare the jeepers out of me. You know what? I enjoyed it, Myles. My accident was a long time ago now. I do think waiting to drive was a good thing though. It dulled the memory of all that pain and guilt.'

'Feelings can still linger inside if we don't talk about them.'

'Yes, I know,' Glanna said quietly, then with excitement again: 'He has a cliffside cave too – Isaac, that is. He paints from it as the view from the open side down to the Point is so amazing, and he quite often catches the sight of the dolphins there in all weathers.' She suddenly felt slightly guilty. Even though she was telling Myles, who she did in fact trust with her life, the words had passed her lips. The secret was out.

'He's quite a man, isn't he, this Isaac Benson?' Myles said, mirroring her earlier mood.

'Yes, he really is. He's as deep as the ocean – and you know how I like my men layered. We hugged. Who'd have thought that the once sex-mad Glanna Pascoe would enjoy a hug. It felt so right. It was after I'd seen the grave and it was a really wonderful, emotional moment.'

'So, you obviously didn't ask about the grave, but did you talk about the hug afterwards?'

'No, we didn't need to. Words were not necessary. I did feel a bit odd being there after it, so I said I had to leave. He walked me back to the car and opened the gate for me, but he has asked me over again, this Wednesday.'

'Are you happy about that?'

'Yes, I think so. Sadie said she is happy to cover for me, so it doesn't affect the gallery.'

'But how does it affect you?'

'What do you mean?' Glanna cocked her head to the side.

'As in, what are your feelings telling you about him?'

Glanna pushed her glasses back on to her nose. 'Oliver had layers too. It's hard to even think of falling for someone else. And I don't know if that's what it is leading to anyway. It was just a hug, after all.'

'Have you heard from Oliver?'

'Why would I?' Glanna almost snapped. 'He knows I have a gallery in Hartmouth now, Myles. It wouldn't take much to find me if he really wanted to.'

'Do you want him to find you?'

She sighed heavily. 'It's over and I have to face it. I actually was at Mum's the other evening and thought just that. I've wasted too much time. I have to move forward with my life.'

'And how is that decision sitting with you now?'

'Oh Myles, give me a break. It's too early to tell. I'm doing my best, OK?'

'Don't bury anything though. Feel it as it comes up.'

'I will,' Glanna said. 'And sorry for being short with you. I do think I am getting somewhere, wherever that may be. Even chatting with Mum doesn't feel quite such a chore these days.'

'You are right – you are doing so well.' Myles smiled kindly. 'That sounds promising about your mum too.'

'Well, I say not so much a chore, she's still a bloody nightmare. Maybe I can bat off her comments more easily than I used to be able to. She's pining after Dad and won't admit it. Throwing around acerbic comments about Oliver leaving me, and Dad being with another woman. She's cross because I won't tell her who this woman is, and her hip is playing up. Bottom line is, I think she's lonely.'

'It sounds like there have always been a lot of secrets or things unsaid in that family of yours.'

'I know, but it's not my place to tell her, is it?'

'It must be hard when your dad is asking you not to say anything and your mother wants to know what is going on. It is very unfair on you actually, Glanna.'

'You're right. I'm going to tell them again to sort out their own bloody problems. I've had enough of it all my life.' Her voice quivered. 'I just want them both to love me.'

Myles wanted to punch the air in triumph. His patient really was beginning to understand the long-term effects of her dysfunctional upbringing on herself and the choices she had made in the past.

'I felt proud though as I did stick up for myself and said that a big party for my fortieth with all my mother's friends was *not* what I wanted.'

'And what did she say?'

'She said I always did spoil her fun. I managed to bite my lip at that stage. *Her* bloody fun! What about me? I matter too.'

'Of course you do and you need to start believing it all of the time now.'

'I know. I do feel I am thinking it a bit more, now, though. Mum has never liked the way she looked, even though she's bloody gorgeous. Thankfully, she hasn't passed that insecurity on to me, which is a start. I can see now that believing that people like what's inside of me too – that's been the problem.'

Myles spoke softly. 'It's got nothing to do with other people. I keep saying it: you have to like yourself.'

'You know you asked me before why I didn't want children.' Myles nodded. 'I have thought long and hard about it, and it came to me that it's because I don't want to be like my own mother. Imagine if I was as awful as her, feeding my kids with money and visions of grandeur instead of love. I'm not even sure she actually *likes* me when she's not playing me off against Dad. And if my own child ended up in therapy, I just couldn't bear it.

I'd feel I had gone wrong. And with my mental health being as it has been, there is no guarantee that a child of mine would be happy and well adjusted.'

'The only guarantee with anyone's life is that we shall die.'

'Blimey, let's jolly this up, shall we?'

'That's a fact, and it's well worth remembering. Also, coming to accept that people you love are not up on the pedestal you first put them on is hard, isn't it?'

'Notwithstanding all of that, why is *all* this so hard? Therapy, I mean.'

'Because if it was easy, everybody would be brave enough to do it. Now look, from what you've told me, it sounds like Isaac enjoys more than your company.'

Glanna blushed. 'Thirty-nine going on nineteen is what I feel like at the moment.'

'That's good, isn't it?'

'Why on earth would he want someone like me though?' She frowned in bafflement.

'Glanna. What have we just talked about? He's a human being who happens to be a great artist, not God Almighty.'

She tipped her head back and laughed. 'What were you saying about not being a bloody clairvoyant? He actually said that very same thing, in a roundabout way, too.'

'Well, there you are, then.' Myles smiled. 'And there we are, then, too. We need to finish up now, Glanna.'

'Thank you, as always.' Glanna tickled Banksy awake and slipped on his lead.

'I hope your life drawing classes go well until we meet again. And with regard to Isaac, there is no rush with anything.' Myles stood up. 'You know where I am if you want to come before the month's out. If not, I'll see you the last Monday in August.'

Chapter 23

Oliver Trueman turned off his alarm, slowly opened his eyes and put his face into the neck of the curvaceous redhead by his side, murmuring, 'Sorry, gorgeous, but we need to get up.'

His bed partner groaned. 'What time is it?'

'I know, it's early but I promised Clarence's mums that I'd be there for nine as they are going to look at a wedding venue. I did warn you.'

'Is it always going to be like this?'

'Yes, for a while, it is. He's my son, Suzanne, and a huge part of my life.'

'Surely once his mums are married, it will be different?'

Oliver didn't reply, just rolled out of bed and headed to the shower. Tipping his head back into the steaming water, he sighed. It had been an easy decision when his good friend Katie, an English teacher at the school he was working at, had asked outright if he would father a child for her and her lawyer girlfriend, Ellie. They had often discussed his desire to have children too and how he worried that he wasn't getting any younger after Glanna upped and left. He had gone away for a walking weekend alone to think it through, but to him there was no downside. He would get the child he had always longed for with a woman who would never leave him as they would always be good friends. It had seemed a natural and clear arrangement that they would all be involved with the little one's life. And that it could only enhance the upbringing of the child with the amount of love that would be surrounding it. And when Clarence had arrived, the outpouring of love they had all felt for the little smiley bundle of joy cemented their decision and more.

What he hadn't realised was that it might not be as easy to have a relationship with someone who didn't quite understand the arrangement. He had met Suzanne at his Bikram yoga class a couple of months ago. She was great and they had been having fun, but deep down he knew that she wasn't Miss Right and her last comment had made him realise that she wasn't even Miss Right Now. He needed to find somebody to complement both him and his lifestyle and the truth was, since seeing Glanna at Tate Modern, he had been unable to stop thinking about her. She had looked so good, healthy and as attractive as the day she had walked out on him. There was a strength about her too, that hadn't been there before. Maybe being apart had been what was needed, and maybe the reason she hadn't shown up at Paddington could have been as simple an explanation as she had overslept and missed him and then missed her train. As he had thought before, perhaps she had lost his number or she surely would have contacted him to explain. The last thing he wanted to do was halt her visible progress, but he needed to talk to her. Needed to tell her how he was feeling. Because if he didn't, he knew he would regret it for the rest of his life.

His dear late mother's last words to him had been, 'Follow your heart, son, because it always knows.' She had then squeezed his hand and, surrounded by all of her immediate family, had died with a look of joy on her face.

Showered, with a small white towel around his middle and with Bessie Trueman's wise last words whirling around his head, he went back through to the kitchen to find an already dressed Suzanne putting her high-heeled sandals on in a rush to leave.

As she hurried for the door, Oliver placed his towering frame in front of her.

'We need to have the "it's not you, it's me" talk, don't we?' she said shakily.

With a sad look in his eye, Oliver bit his lip and nodded slowly.

Chapter 24

Glanna smiled around the room. 'So, welcome everybody, to our second life drawing class. I have spoken to you all before about how we are a mixture of old and new in the knowledge and experience of art. But if we vote with our hearts, and choose the drawing or painting that appeals to us most, however basic, we can't go far wrong. Mistakes can, in fact, be the making of a picture. We are all learning our craft and no one of us is better than the others. Having said that, let's congratulate young Sadie here for winning the first round last week.'

A ripple of applause went round the room and Sadie Peach, with her pretty little oval-shaped face and long fine brown hair, glowed with pleasure.

'It was a unanimous decision, Sadie,' Glanna went on. 'Your sketch of Linda was full of character. Plus, the use of just three coloured chalks made it all the more striking in its simplicity. Well done.'

Glanna, looking very much the artist in her black and white spotted dungarees and cerise hairband, addressed the group again. 'I've put all of our masterpieces on the back wall for us to take note of what we felt went right and wrong last week. Last time was a bit different as Linda wanted to be in her pose before you all arrived.'

'Yeah,' Mrs Harris called out. 'I didn't want to frighten you all by uncovering my old growler on our first go.'

'Wouldn't be the first time you've got that out in public, I don't dare say,' Gideon Jones said in far too loud a voice to Hayden, who was now discreetly googling the word 'growler'.

'Oi, you.' Mrs Harris lowered her eyes across at both men, then gave a huge wink to Glanna. The latter tried not to cringe at the thought of Mrs Harris's unkempt lady parts and, even worse still, her dad entertaining them.

Glanna cleared her throat. 'Black and white is the theme for today. We are going to be just using the charcoal sticks that I've put on your easels. For those of you who are new to this, let me show you the basics of how this adaptable tool works.' She pulled her easel around to face the group and drew a black line down the piece of A2 paper. 'You will see how the point creates a broad line which is good for outline. And if you use the side, it makes the line even thicker. You can use your ring finger to blend' – she demonstrated – 'and don't be afraid to layer either, to get a darker colour. I am not looking for perfection in our two hours, just a good use of the charcoal and as much as you can complete of today's model. There are a couple of putty erasers on the side table should you need to make use of those too. Be prepared, as it can get very messy.'

The new artists picked up the liquorice-coloured sticks

from their easel trays and gazed at them. 'Before Gideon gets into pose, let's have a lightning-quick practice to get a feel for how charcoal works. I would like you to draw this.' She pointed to a straight vase containing a sunflower that she'd put on the windowsill behind her. 'Now go for it! Do as many sketches as you can in five minutes!'

When her phone alarm went off, Glanna clapped her hands together. 'OK, how was that?'

A murmur of positive acknowledgement went around the room.

'Excellent. Before you get yourselves a clean sheet of paper, I just wanted us to do a quick introduction as to who we all are. I should have done it last week but we kind of got off to a hasty start. I'll go first.'

'*Ach-y-fi*, I hate all this happy-clappy bullshit,' Gideon Jones said under his breath, whilst rubbing his charcoal-blackened hands furiously together to try and clean them.

Glanna cleared her throat. 'My name's Glanna Pascoe, I have lived in Hartmouth for nearly two years and I run the Hartmouth Gallery here. I am also known as the Rainbow Painter due to my love of painting rainbows. I have a dog called Banksy, who is asleep right behind me.'

Glanna then pointed across to Sadie, whose quiet voice matched her petite frame. The girl's right arm was fully tattooed with letter symbols near her wrist, while a beautiful floral pattern encompassing a sea horse spiralled from her upper to her lower arm. There wasn't a section of her ears that wasn't covered in piercings. She also had a tiny sparkling diamond in her nose.

'I'm Sadie Peach,' she said. 'I'm in my final year study-ing Art and Design at Penrigan University. I work here for Glanna during the holidays and on market days when I can.'

Hayden sat up from slouching and wondered why he had never noticed this pretty girl sitting at the easel by his side. 'Peach, that's a nice name. OK, everybody, I'm Hayden Spargo.' The five-feet-eight teenage lad ran his hands through his floppy blonde fringe. His face was square and chiselled, and he possessed the maturity of someone much older than his years. 'I'm nineteen – and before you hear it from anyone else, I spent six months in Penrigan Young Offenders. My mum, she's on her own and never had much money, see, and I wanted to help her out. I broke into some-one's house when they were away and stole one of their tellies 'cos ours had broken and Mum was upset. I'm not justifying my actions, but they were rich, could afford it. I paid back every penny I owed, I promise you. But I've always loved art. Drawing in my bedroom helped me when my old man left home and dumped me and Mum. So now, I'm currently working on the Hartmouth ferry for Billy Dillon to get some money together before I start studying at the Brighton University of Art and Design. I want to become a famous artist, like the Benson fella whose painting you have in the window downstairs. Then I can buy my mum whatever she wants.'

There was a round of applause from the group, at

which he said helplessly, 'I don't deserve that kind of reception.'

Glanna smiled at him. 'Yes, you do. You're turning your life around now. Well done, Hayden, for being so honest with us all. That took courage.' The teenager shuffled nervously in his seat.

'I've painted that ferry many times,' Sadie said meekly. 'Some are in the gallery downstairs if you're interested, Hayden.'

'Yes, Joe Moon commissioned one of Sadie's paintings to give to your boss Billy and his wife Kara as a wedding present,' Glanna told him.

Hayden nodded. 'Fair play, I will check them out later.'

'So, Gideon, are you going to make us all giddy by showing us your parts?' Linda Harris announced.

'Let him introduce himself first.' Glanna was beginning to realise how annoying the woman was when you spent more than a hello/goodbye in the cafe with her. She really hoped it was just a fling with her father, as with both Linda *and* her mother in her life, it really would be too much to bear.

'So, I'm Gideon Jones. Last time I looked I was sixty-something. Thank the lord for hair dye, is all I can say.' His dark curly hair still looked very natural if this statement was true. His Welsh accent was faint, his voice lilting. 'I'm originally from Cardiff and have run the antique stall here in Ferry Lane Market for two years now, since my wife died. I have two lovely grown-up boys, Rhys and Cabe, who are still in the Valleys with their families, and they are happy there. So, I thought I'd try a hobby like this life drawing class here, as it's quite lonely when you've spent your whole life with someone, and they bugger off early. We wanted to retire down here to the sea, me and my Cheryl. My boys think I'm mad moving away, but I wanted to stick to our plan, you see.'

'Aw. Thanks for sharing that with the group, Gideon, and I hope this class brings you some comfort and new friends to boot. Now, if you want to get up and get yourself ready behind the screen, Linda can tell us all about herself.'

'Not much to tell, is there really. I'm Linda Harris, a widow also, and I use buckets of hair dye.' The group laughed. 'I have an ancient cat called Darlington. I'm younger than Gideon and work in Monique's, the cafe formerly known as Tasty Pasties. I've been there as long as I can remember. I too wanted a hobby, plus what's not to love about looking at a man's flaccid or erect penis? I can't get enough of it, speaking for myself, that is.'

While the others couldn't quite believe what they'd just heard, Jen burst out laughing, saying, 'Flaccid is a suitably horrible word for, in my opinion, quite an ugly and useless state, don't you think?'

'Oi,' Gideon Jones piped up. 'I knew there would be trouble with a four-to-two ratio of females to men! Come on Hayden, stick up for me.' The man fell about laughing at his own poor joke.

'*Jen,*' Glanna said far too loudly in an attempt to restore order. 'I nearly forgot about you. Your turn.'

The woman grimaced. 'Hi. I'm Jenifer Moon. I was born and brought up here in Hartmouth, and my dad and sister still live here. Nowadays I live half in London with Markus, my boyfriend, but spend as much time down here as I can as I run an accountancy business here with Jack Murray, husband of Star who has the crystals and jewellery stall in Ferry Lane Market. I've always fancied myself as a bit of an artist, but after last week's disaster, I'm thinking maybe fancying pigeons may be a wiser hobby.'

A little laugh went around the group interrupted by a Welsh-accented, 'I'm ready,' from Gideon Jones, who was now behind the screen that Glanna had put in front of the chaise longue she had decided to use for all poses.

'OK, charcoal at the ready, everyone.'

'Ta-da!' Gideon Jones declared as Glanna pulled back the screen hiding his decency. The sight of him even shut Linda Harris up. For in front of their startled eyes, in the complete all together, aside from a pair of oversized dark sunglasses and a copy of the *Antiques Times* which had begun to slip down his thighs, was a smiling hairy-chested man, with equally hairy legs and groin area, sagging deep purple testicles and the longest penis that any of the group sitting in front of him had ever seen.

Chapter 25

'Cheers.' Glanna held up her bottle of Peroni Libera and clinked Jen's wine glass. 'Thanks so much for helping me clear up.'

'My pleasure. And I literally thought we were going to have to sweep Mrs Harris up from the floor when she saw Gideon spread out on the chaise longue like a porn star.' Jen took a sip of her wine as she and Glanna sat in the Ferryboat's estuary-facing garden enjoying the balmy July evening. 'I couldn't believe the raw natural talent of Hayden, but I'm not surprised old Linda won; she didn't take her eyes off his nether regions for the full two hours. I don't think she missed the replication of a single hair.'

Glanna laughed loudly. 'Maybe Erica from the rugby club really did pass out. My poor dad.'

'Oh my God, too funny. And what do you mean, your poor dad?'

'Between you, me and the gatepost, he is having the time of his bedroom life with her.'

'No way that he's seeing Mrs Harris!' Jen made a face.

'Way! I can't bear the thought either. My mother knows he's seeing someone, but I can't bring myself to tell her who it is. She'd be mortified that he dares sleep with someone who works in a cafe. And someone with curves, to boot, while no carbohydrate dares pass her lips.'

'Well, if he's happy that's the main thing. What do you make of it, Glanna?'

'Dad tells me it's just a fling, so I can deal with that. I still want to bang my parents' heads together though; it is so obvious they should be together. Anyway, enough of that.' Glanna took a drink of her non-alcoholic beer. 'What's going on with you?'

'Well, Jack and I have found an office above the Hot Wok in Main Street. The rent is very reasonable and it's perfect for what we need. We move in in September. I hope you approve of our name: we are calling ourselves Murray Moon Accountancy.'

'Ah, that's really nice, and has Markus made any more noise about moving down here?'

'No, but we had a really lovely weekend when he came down though. I can highly recommend the Penrigan View Hotel. Food, sea views, bedrooms, all amazing. It's kind of not so bad spending half of our time together. We actually agreed that we get more quality time together that way, if that makes sense.'

'Perfect sense. I think the days of married life and two point four children are so last century now. Women don't need men like they used to with regards to them providing for us, and there are so many alternative ways to have kids now, aren't there? We don't even need a committed partner for that. Separate bedrooms and bathrooms are becoming the norm, I hear.'

'Don't you think as much as that is empowering, it's also quite sad?' Jen chipped in.

'No, I truly don't. The number of women of our grandmothers' generation who stayed married for the sake of the children and their own survival is pitiful. Live, laugh and love, I say. What's the point of being miserable?'

'Which brings us nicely on to you and Oliver.'

'Hmm. I've got my head around the fact that it's over.'

'Really?'

'Yes. He is clearly happy. The woman he is with looked really lovely and he has what he always wanted, a child. My knocking on his door now would only bring me further heartache and I don't need that, especially now I feel my mental health is in such a good place.'

'Well, at least you have made the decision not to pursue him. I think that coming to a decision is half the battle. We all agonise over decisions but once they are made, I for one always feel better. The die is cast and the inner turmoil ceases.'

'Yes, I still hanker after what could have been – but no doubt that will ease with time.'

Jen finished off her wine and looked out at the view. 'It will. This place . . . it's so bloody blissful here. Can take your mind away from anything.'

The harbour-wall fairy lights and those around Frank's Café glittered against the still, dark water of the estuary, matching the star-laden night sky. The seafaring sound of yachts' halyards clanging and the flight of seabirds heading for their clifftop perches made for a perfect relaxing late-summer evening.

'I er . . . well, there is someone else taking my mind off things actually,' Glanna decided to reveal, 'but Jen, you have to promise not to say anything when I tell you.'

'Oh my God! You dark horse, Glanna! Tell me everything with immediate effect. Actually, let me get us another drink first. Another fake beer?'

'Can I be even more weird and get a cup of tea, please.' A bit anxious that she was about to tell her friend of her secret trysts, Glanna looked out across the water, deep in thought. Isaac had let her in to his world because he trusted her to keep his privacy. She could see why he wouldn't want anyone to know about his cave, but she had also learned that it was important for her to discuss her feelings, and telling Jen the bare bones of what was going on wasn't akin to getting a megaphone and telling the whole of Hartmouth about him, was it?

Jen came back to the table with the pot of tea for one and another glass of wine on a tray.

'I've brought sugar if you need it. Come on then, Glanna, spill the beans. I want every single detail – and if whoever it is is as well-endowed as Markus or Gideon, can you please ask if he's up for a threesome.'

Chapter 26

Isaac had already reversed up to the gate in his old Land Rover and was waiting for Glanna when she pulled up in her Smart car, the roof up. The weather was dull and quite cold for August, and she could see he was wearing the green jumper he had lent her a couple of weeks ago in his cave. She loved the fact that he used his clothes to cover him, not define him. There was not one ounce of 'look at me' about the man, but far more 'learn from me', which in Glanna's eyes was now far more attractive. As before, she could see his hand rise in the signal to follow him.

Banksy sat up straight and put his nose out of the crack in the window, excited at the prospect of seeing Beethoven and being able to run free like before. It was all quite surreal, Glanna thought. Here she was, following the man who had seemed like an enigma to her for so many years, to his home, his studio, his life.

'How are you today?' he asked as they sat in his studio. He poured her a coffee and added the warm cow's milk. Despite the sun not being out, his glass-walled studio was still full of light and felt airy.

Relieved that there was no embarrassment after 'the

hug' or reference to it, she signalled towards the bean bag. She had made a pact with herself that if he didn't mention it, she wouldn't either. It was what it was – a moment of intimacy between two people who liked each other and needed each other at that moment.

'Do you mind?' she asked.

Isaac smiled. 'Fill your boots.'

Glanna plonked herself down on to the huge squishy cushion, looked out and sighed. 'I could literally sit here forever. I defy anyone to tire of this view.'

'I agree. I think the joy of it is that it is always as different as it is the same. The tides are always turning, the seasons come and go, the skies are refashioning themselves by the minute. It's the cycle of life. Nature at her best.'

'Nature . . . Just one word for all of this beauty doesn't somehow feel enough.'

'You are very sweet,' Isaac said matter-of-factly.

'I have my moments.' Glanna struggled up in as lady-like a fashion as she could manage and went to sit opposite the big man on a high stool at one of his two work benches. She took a sip of coffee. 'I could get used to this fresh milk. It makes for a delicious cup of coffee. Thank you.'

'My pleasure. It gave me an excuse for another early-morning walk.' He took a drink. His tone then changed. 'So, if you have time, I was thinking we could maybe walk the cliff path and go to my cave today. It was on a day like this I caught the – what did you call them? "The quiet dolphins", I think you said.'

222

'Well remembered, and I'd love that. I am going for afternoon tea with Mum, so I have a good few hours to spare.'

'Good. OK. Well, let's finish our coffees and head off.' Banksy and Beethoven appeared at the window as if to say hi, then charged off again towards the open fields.

'I'd never have to walk him again if I lived here,' Glanna said dreamily. 'He loves it. And I'm so sorry about the other day – you know, the digging.'

Isaac put his hand up to stop her. 'She's known me for two minutes and she's already moving in.'

Glanna blushed. 'Ha! I didn't mean—'

'I'm teasing you. Now come on, let's get cracking. What have you got on your feet?' And when Glanna held up her right foot: 'Walking boots, blimey, you are learning.'

'After the other day I'm surprised I haven't got full waterproofs, wellies and a lightning conductor stuck to my head.'

Isaac laughed to reveal his strong white teeth. He was even more handsome when he looked happy, Glanna thought.

'Shall I call for the dogs?' Glanna offered, then: 'Oops. Not that Beethoven will hear.'

'No, don't worry, there's someone in the main house today who can keep an eye out for them.'

'Oh my God, you were right. They are here already.' Glanna sat at the entrance of Isaac's cave studio, her legs crossed, comfy on the blanket he had put down for them both. Two dolphins had swum into full view far below, just as the sun started to peer through the cloudy sky and streaks of blue became visible too.

'The beach is not very full, see,' Isaac explained. 'They like the peace as well as the company, I'm sure.'

'A bit like you,' Glanna added intuitively.

'Yes – and much like all of us, I think. We all need some down time, whether we are an introvert or an extrovert. Our minds need to settle. That's the trouble with this mad world of Internet and intrusion. Unless we are wise, we don't ever switch off.'

'That's why moving to Hartmouth was therapy in itself. Without adding social media to the mix, London is a constant social circus itself if you allow it to be.'

'I can only imagine.' Isaac nodded then went on: 'My father was a very calm man. He taught me that peace is the result of retraining your mind to process life as it is, rather than as you think or wish it should be.'

'And are you always peaceful?'

'Most of the time.' Isaac was thoughtful for a second. 'I've not had a mobile phone long. My agent insisted in the end. Was sick of my lack of email response and me pulling my landline out of the wall when I didn't want to talk to her. Saying that, I still turn my mobile off whenever I fancy.'

Glanna noted, 'It's a strange dynamic that your work is so public but as a person you are so private.'

'Look at them,' Isaac interrupted her. The dolphins were now swimming at speed up and down the beach, showing off to a small family group who had spotted them in the shallows. 'They can't help themselves.'

'Is that why you did the documentary, because you felt the urge to show off a bit?' Glanna asked daringly.

'I hated every minute of it.' His voice was gruff.

'I don't understand.'

Isaac jumped up from the floor. 'Come on. Let's get on and paint whilst the dolphins are fresh in our mind's eye.'

'One minute more.' Glanna stared out to sea. 'I gain energy from this whole perfect vista and the sun is coming out now.'

'I can pull your drawing board to the entrance. By the way, dolphins swimming along with the ship is a sign of good luck as they are considered a sacred friend of fishermen,' Isaac stated.

'I didn't know that.'

'Yes. There is nothing bad about a dolphin. They always have the welfare of man in mind and their presence indicates that you are under their protection. They have kept a lot of sailors' hearts lifted on many a perilous journey, I'm sure.'

'I feel safe with you,' Glanna suddenly blurted out as she followed Isaac back into the high-ceilinged rocky retreat.

'How very dangerous,' Isaac retorted, opening his rucksack to take out his painting supplies.

'What do you mean?' Glanna's voice had a sudden element of fear.

'One of the great myths in life is that you need others to be happy, safe and loved, et cetera. I believe it's much better to rely on yourself – not in a selfish way, might I add, but in an emotional way. Saying that, I enjoy you, Glanna. I enjoy both your company and *your* energy.'

Glanna smiled. 'And I you and yours.'

'Milking stool or floor? We need to feel as uncomfortable as we can.'

Experiencing a sudden flashback of her recent bath-time fantasy, Glanna stuttered, 'The floor, please, definitely the floor.'

They reached the end of the cliff path.

'I'm really impressed with what you did today.' Isaac guided her through the kissing gate that signalled the entrance to his land.

'Thank you. That's what I love about art, there is always so much more to learn. I can't wait to put it on my wall.'

'Actually, could I have it for my own gallery? I really like it, especially that you sneaked in a huge rainbow and there wasn't even one there.'

Glanna thought her heart might burst out of her chest with pride. 'I felt I had to, it fitted with the moment. Dolphins and rainbows together. What's not to like?'

The big man smiled at this woman's childlike ways. 'Oh, and make sure you sign it for me before you go too, please. As you know, we must always sign our work.'

'Yes, of course.'

On reaching the spot where they had hugged, Isaac stopped, allowing Glanna to look again at the small cross on the big grave with the words *Fly away, Sweet P, fly away.* He pulled a picnic rug out from his rucksack.

'Let's sit here for a bit, if you have time.'

'You don't have to tell me anything,' Glanna said without thought, sitting down on the rug next to him.

'I want to.' Isaac took a deep breath. 'She was my sister's pony, Patience, but Lizzie always used to call her Sweet P. We all loved her. She was piebald. Black and white patches, you know.' The big man rubbed his eyes. 'My big Beauty was prancing around in the field as he does and by complete accident he kicked back behind him and caught Patience's foreleg.'

'Oh no.' Glanna guessed what was coming. 'Not broken, I hope?'

'Sadly, yes. As you know, there is little chance of recovery if a horse breaks its leg, there is only one solution. And so Patience had to be put down.'

Glanna thought back to the grief she had felt pulsating through Isaac's body the week before at this very spot.

As if reading her mind, he told her, 'But I wasn't crying just for the horse, Glanna. This is not where this awful tale ends. I was crying for my Lizzie too.' His voice cracked slightly as he checked his watch. 'You need to get off to Riversway. How about you come to me next Monday lunchtime? We can talk more then.'

'But . . . you're upset.'

Isaac stood up. 'Like I said, we can talk more then.'

Chapter 27

'Oh, hello, darling, I've made us tea, shall we take it on the terrace next to the croquet lawn? Could you be a love and carry the drinks? Mrs Maynard is just putting together some sandwiches and cakes for us.'

'I'm right behind you, madam.' Louisa Maynard appeared at the French doors, carrying another tray of delicious-looking goodies.

'Super yes, we can go in convoy. I hope you brought your swimmers, Glanna,' Penelope said. 'The pool is a perfect temperature for an afternoon dip. Amazing how it's got warm all of a sudden. It was positively Baltic this morning, but that's coastal weather for you. Where have you been anyway?'

Glanna lowered her voice for her mother's ears only. 'I went to see Isaac Benson.'

'What? *The* Isaac Benson?' Penelope Pascoe repeated loudly.

'Shh, Mother. Yes,' Glanna's voice reverted to a whisper, '*the* Isaac Benson. He's been showing me some new techniques on my Monday days off.'

'I bet he has.' Penny's eyebrows rose.

'Mum, we are not all like you, chasing men like a

greyhound with a rabbit. Anyway, I'd rather you didn't mention this to anyone. I thought you'd like to know because of your picture in the dining room. He's a lovely man and he is making me smile. And that's all I'm saying on the matter at the moment.'

They reached the terrace by the croquet lawn with its perfectly smooth mint-green grass and the gorgeous views of the estuary waters it offered between the trees.

Penelope made an *oomph* noise as she sat down at the ornate garden table with its matching seats and comfy patterned seat-covers. Mrs Maynard placed the tray of treats in front of her and smiled sweetly.

'I hope you enjoy the afternoon, the pair of you,' she said. 'I'll be off now, Mrs Pascoe. My Derek's taken the car to be fixed and I said I'd meet him at the garage.'

'Of course. I'll see you Friday. Thank you.'

The woman waddled back up the hill to the main house.

'Can you deal with the sunshade, please, darling?'

Glanna fiddled with the large cream fabric umbrella to make sure it covered them both.

'I noticed your limping is worse,' she said.

Penelope sighed. 'Yes. I went to see my surgeon and had an X-ray last week, and as I predicted I do need a new hip. I mean, anyone would think I was an old woman.'

'Sixty-nine is hardly old, these days.'

'That's precisely my point. If this is crumbling now, what else is going to give up on me? By the time I'm seventy-five, I'll be like the bloody bionic woman.'

Glanna replied calmly, 'I imagine you will be going private?'

'Of course I am. The operation is already booked for the 9th of this month. I think they should put in a gold one, the amount of money the private medical insurance company has had off us over the years.'

'So, what does having a new hip involve, then?'

'One, maybe two days in Penrigan Pines, and then around six weeks – six whole weeks, Glanna! – when I can't bend, turn over in bed, even go to the bloody lavatory without some special disability seat! I'm mortified by the whole thing. I thought of asking Mrs Maynard if she might help me, but you know what a gossip she can be, and I'm not sure I want half of Crowsbridge knowing what colour underwear I have on or worse still, the embarrassment of having to be cared for so intimately.' She shuddered.

'You could get a nurse in or carers who don't know you, that might be easier.'

'Don't be ridiculous, dear. I am not allowing strangers anywhere near my lady parts.'

'It hasn't stopped you before.'

'Enough! And I mean it, Glanna. That's all behind me now. I literally can't bear looking at myself, let alone someone else being given the pleasure.'

'Oh Mum. Well, I will help then.'

'No, Glanna, I wouldn't dream of it. I'm your mother and I'm supposed to care for you. Even though I've made a bloody pig's ear of most of that too. I mean, whoever imagines that their only daughter will become a filthy addict.' At this, Glanna bit her lip and took a big sip of tea. 'And you have the gallery to run,' the woman continued fussily. 'No. I won't hear of it.'

'You could ask Dad.' If looks could kill, Glanna would have been dead and thrown in a field of pigs to get rid of the evidence. She was, however, undeterred. 'He has seen you in every state possible, childbirth included. You know he would help you.'

Penelope slumped down in the chair, gesturing as she declaimed, 'Why me? Why me, Glanna? I've kept myself fit, I try to eat the right things. And you know what this means. I won't be able to arrange your fortieth birthday party – not properly, anyway – and I so wanted to do that for you.'

There *is* a God, Glanna thought, then said aloud, soothingly, 'We will work it all out, don't worry.'

'Well, if I can't arrange a big do, I want to get you a special present. Think what you'd really like. Something you've always wanted.' Penelope put a hand to her forehead and murmured dramatically: 'Because now my body is falling apart, who knows how many more of your birthdays I shall be able to share with you.'

Chapter 28

Glanna sat on her comfy cream sofa above the Hartmouth Gallery, with Banksy's head resting on her knee, playing lovingly with his ears. Fred Gribble sat in the armchair opposite, fish and chips on his lap as he ate them out of their greasy paper wrapping with a wooden fork. 'Are you sure you don't want some of this?' he asked his daughter, his mouth full.

'No, it's OK, thanks. I had a huge afternoon tea with Mum. I'll have a snack later. Dare I ask what you're doing over this side of the river at this time of the evening?'

'Well, I was supposed to be seeing Linda, but when I got there, she came to the door with just her dressing gown on and said she was so sorry, but it must have been something she'd eaten. She said a bad stomach had just hit her so I couldn't possibly go in.'

'Oh, she seemed fine at art club last night. In fact, she won. Her charcoal sketch of Gideon Jones was surprisingly good actually.'

'Naked, was he?' Fred enquired, stuffing a couple of chips in his mouth.

'As the day he was born, apart from a magazine and a pair of sunglasses.' Glanna couldn't help but laugh. 'There was me, thinking that this would be a serious course for budding artists, but it is turning into a bloody sitcom. I am enjoying it though.'

'Good, you seem brighter than you have done for a while.'

'Ah, I dare say that's down to the fact I've met someone I enjoy spending time with.'

'A man someone?'

Glanna gave the giggle of a little girl. 'Very much a man. It's Isaac Benson, in fact, but nobody knows. Saying that, you do now, and I did mention it to Mum and Jen, but I trust you all, so that's fine. It's all top secret as he likes to keep his private life that way. We paint and chat and I like him.'

'Well, just be careful. He's quite a bit older than you, isn't he?'

'Yes, but age isn't an issue when I'm with him. Art is a complete leveller and anyway, I'm not a kid any more, Dad. I can make my own decisions and mistakes.'

'And I've been around the block and back again enough times to know that a man of his age and stature won't be looking for anything other than a fling with a younger beautiful woman.'

'Dad! Stop being so old-fashioned. I'm nearly bloody forty – and it's not like that anyway. We are just friends.'

'Well. As long as you are happy, then I am too.'

'I am – and I'm also very glad that you've popped in

tonight as I wanted to talk to you face to face about something else important too.'

'If telling me about Isaac Benson is not enough.' Fred grinned. 'But joking aside, that sounds ominous. What's going on, my love?'

'I'm fine. It's not me, it's Mum.'

Fred jerked and nearly spilled his fish and chips. 'Oh my God, what's wrong?'

'Nothing serious. It is her hip though; she needs a replacement and I suggested you might care for her for the six weeks after the operation.'

'I can't even imagine the height of the dramatics.'

'Yes, it is pretty bad. She is at the "why me" stage at the moment.'

'I see.' Fred thought about it. 'The problem with that is, the snotty attitude she's bringing to my table at the moment, there's no way I am going to move in and be at her beck and call. Can you imagine? I bet she'd have a bell and everything. There would be no peace for the wicked.'

'You are seeing someone else, so that does give her reason to be grumpy.'

'Glanna, you're talking to me now and this is not a secret to you but aside from Karl Muller, who we both know about, there have been tens if not hundreds of lovers who have graced the bedrooms of Riversway. Look at me – I have *one* relationship, which is hardly a relationship to be fair, and she goes crazy on me. I had to make a stand.'

'That's all true, Dad, but you know what she's like.'

'But maybe that's not enough any more. I love her, Glanna, but I loved her before we started covering up her rudeness with the "knowing what she's like" tag. I've had enough.'

'Maybe she's got worse because of you not being around her so much.'

Fred Gribble stabbed four chips on to his fork with force.

'You don't see it, nor does she, but I'm like a silent angel around that woman. She doesn't know half of what I do for her.' He chewed the chips, swallowed them, then took a long drink from his can of lemonade resting on the side.

'Love has a lot to answer for, doesn't it?' Glanna said thoughtfully, while Banksy snuggled further into his mistress's lap.

Fred Gribble tutted. 'When did you say the operation was again?'

'A week tomorrow. And I do know what you do for her, Dad. Just you coming to help with the horses the other day, that was so sweet of you.'

He smiled. 'Who am I trying to kid with all my bravado?'

Glanna pushed out her bottom lip. 'Well, it's certainly not me.'

'She's having it done privately at Penrigan Pines, I assume?'

'Of course.' They both laughed.

Fred wrapped his leftover chips up in the paper and headed for the kitchen to dump them in the bin.

'I will tell you one thing though, dear daughter of mine. It's that true love doesn't feel any different whatever age you are.'

'Please don't say you're in love with Linda Harris already,' Glanna joked.

'Yes, we are getting married next Thursday and would like you and Banksy to be maid of honour and page boy respectively.'

'Imagine!' Banksy leaped down, allowing Glanna to stand also. She went to her dad and put a hand on each of his shoulders. 'Maybe the only way to love anything is to realise that it may be lost. How would you feel if you were told that after today, you'd never see Mum again?'

He pulled away from his daughter and, with tears in his eyes, choked, 'I would rather be dead.'

'Oh Dad. That's the sweetest and saddest thing I think I've ever heard you say.'

'I hope one day you feel love like I have for your mother for all these years.'

It was Glanna's turn to feel her eyes moistening. 'I did, but I let it fall through my fingers and it's too late now.'

'Oliver?'

Glanna's face was confirmation.

'Come here, you.' The Cornishman held out his arms

and, just like he had done when his daughter had needed him before, and not caring if she was nine, nineteen or thirty-nine, he wrapped his arms around her in a warm and comforting hug.

Chapter 29

'Bugger.' Glanna had just locked up when the gallery phone started ringing. Banksy looked up at her as if to say, 'Come on, Mum, it's walkies time, so will you please stop faffing about.'

'They'll leave a message, love, and it's your day off, isn't it? Nothing is so important it can't wait a few hours,' Pat Dillon offered. She'd been passing the gallery and witnessed Glanna's dilemma.

'You're right, especially when my Morning Macchiato is also calling.' Glanna grinned. 'Have a good day, Pat.'

'Yeah, looks like it's gonna be a scorcher. They say flaming June, don't they, but it's turned into a red-hot sizzling August this year. But we mustn't complain, eh. It'll be bleedin' Christmas before we know it and we'll be shivering our tits off.'

As Glanna and Banksy headed up Ferry Lane, the gallery answer machine kicked in. Oliver had found the landline number of the Hartmouth Gallery from the Internet.

'Glanna, hi. I hope this is the right number – anyway, it's Oliver here. You remember, Oliver Trueman, the tall, dark, handsome one from London? Draws a bit, chats a lot?' Oliver held his hand to his head and groaned silently. He was

239

prattling rubbish. He should have waited until she picked up. But he was mid-message now, so he had to keep going. *'Right, yeah. It was a shame we didn't get to talk a few weeks ago, and I'd still really like to do that. So, um . . . maybe next time you're in London, we could meet or er . . . I could come down to you. So – please call me, Glanna. I'd love to see your gallery and Hartmouth, your new/old home-town. The best number to get me on is this one.'* He relayed his number then, with a deep intake of breath, hung up, took a drink from his coffee cup and looked out of his apartment window. He'd done it, the ball was in her court. He would head off now for his shift at Brightside House, and afterwards he would check his phone to see if she had replied.

He was relieved by how well Suzanne had taken the news that he wanted to split up. They had seen each other since then at yoga, and they had spoken as friends. He had always said that he was after something casual, not wanting to commit to anything whilst Clarence was in his early stages of development. But as he had found with women in the past, they would agree to that, but when it came to the goodbye bit, the crunch, they weren't able to handle it.

Not including Suzanne, he'd had two short flings since he and Glanna had split and yes, both occasions had been great, but had also allowed him to compare them to what he'd had with her. Their sex life had been amazing – explosive at times but also tender and caring. To Oliver, it had been the true definition of 'making love', and now that the initial excitement of having a new baby around had faded, and he had settled into a routine and normal life again – well, as normal a life as him sharing his son with his two mums could be – he found he missed Glanna and everything she represented. His little boy was lovely, and he did feel that Clarence had filled a missing piece in his jigsaw of life, but it had become obvious now that there was still one huge, Glanna Pascoe-shaped gap and if he didn't take action to try to fill that too, he would forever regret it.

♡

'Car going all right?' Star, a soapy sponge in hand as she washed the front windows of her shop, shouted across to Glanna.

'Love it, yes, thanks. And it's perfect for this weather.'

'Kara asked me to check which flowers you want for this month,' Skye Bligh reminded Glanna as she watered the hanging baskets which adorned the front of Passion Flowers.

Glanna walked over to her. 'Oh yes, I'd forgotten about those. Could you do blues and whites, do you think? Are cornflowers in season? I have no idea. I like the idea of a sea theme if that is at all possible.'

'I can do that, no problem.' The young girl bent down to fuss Banksy. 'He really is the quietest dog I know. Kara's dad's dog, Bob . . .' she broke off to giggle. 'Try saying that after a pint of the Ferryboat's cloudy cider. He may be old, but he's a boisterous mutt, that's for sure. Oh yeah, and whilst I remember, Kara said that when I saw you to let you know she is literally over the moon with the wedding photos. Ha! I only just got her pun there. She will thank you personally, but she's run ragged with the twins at the moment, as you know.'

'Good. That's lovely to hear and yes, my Banksy does tend to fade into the background like his namesake, but you wouldn't recognise him when he's ready to chase something. He killed a chicken the other day when we walked past Broomfield Farm. The poor thing was just pecking around innocently with all the others when off he shot – it was horrible to watch. It's not as though he isn't well-fed.' Glanna looked down at Banksy waiting patiently at her side. 'I had to go and pay the farmer, and I felt dreadful, so guilty. Yes, this one's definitely got hidden depths.'

'Well, they say the quiet ones are always the worst,' Star said, causing both herself and Glanna to laugh heartily.

♡

'I thought a picnic under the big oak tree in the top field would be perfect on a day like this. I hope that is all right?' Isaac greeted her as Glanna got out of her car in the stable courtyard, Banksy by her side. It was the first time he had not met her at the gate, which had just opened automatically on her arrival.

'It's a great idea. And I'm not dressed for any kind of cliff walking today. Here, I brought a bottle of zero-alcohol fizz, it's so refreshing in this heat.' She reached for the chilled bottle from her bag and handed it to him.

Isaac took in her long, multi-coloured summer dress with its thin straps and her gladiator sandals. Her long silver earrings in the shape of feathers hung from her tiny earlobes. Secretly, Glanna had never been fond of her attached earlobes, had always wanted them to be the free kind, with a soft plump lobe, like her mother's.

'You look just like a rainbow angel,' Isaac told her, his confidence growing in the company of this beguiling younger woman. Not only did she possess talent and intellectual curiosity, she also possessed those rare things: empathy and emotional intelligence.

Banksy and Beethoven ran backwards and forwards as the couple strolled across the green field towards the cliff top. Isaac carried a large bunch of sweet peas in one hand, a huge cool box in the other, and had his battered old rucksack slung over his right shoulder. They talked easily now, Isaac laughing at her tales of the recent life drawing class and expressing concern about her mother's hip. He was chatting about the date in late September that had been set aside for the hanging of his exhibition at Tate St Ives. Unfortunately, as all the leaflets and advance publicity had long since gone out, it was too late to officially rename it *A Sense of Porpoise* as Glanna had suggested. They had laughed about that. The show was titled instead *Dolphins in Depth*. In it were displayed paintings Isaac had chosen from his collection that focused on dolphins as a main or minor subject, and it was clearly stated on the publicity material that a maximum percentage of any sales of catalogues, post cards and gifts related to the exhibition would be donated equally to the Worldwide Wildlife Fund and to Headway, the brain injury charity.

'Wow!' Glanna exclaimed on getting a full view of the ocean below. 'I don't think I've ever seen such an intense blue. I feel I need to capture it.'

'Go on, then. Have you brought your watercolours?'

'I'll just take a photo for now, it's fine. And that sky too . . . there's not a single cloud. It's almost as if there's no horizon today, as the sea and sky blend together. Isn't it beautiful, Isaac? And aren't we so lucky?'

Isaac smiled. 'Yes, we truly are.' He shrugged off his rucksack, took out the faded blue picnic rug, put it on the ground, and laid the cool box on top of it.

Whilst Glanna was adjusting the camera on her phone to get the best angle, Isaac walked over to Patience's grave, knelt, and placed half of the sweet peas gently down on the earth mound.

'Sweet peas for Sweet P,' Glanna said quietly.

'Sweet P is what Lizzie called her, which made sense, as dear sweet Patience was just so very patient and understanding with Lizzie. Me and Sis would plant the seedlings together in the secret garden at the back of the house and when they came into bloom, without fail, Lizzie would pick a bunch and bring it here weekly.

Anyway, come on, let's get this picnic lunch on the go. My stomach's rumbling.'

At the smell of food, Banksy and Beethoven bounded up and, after a good drink from the bowls Isaac had thoughtfully brought, along with a bottle of water to fill them with, he tossed them each a bone treat to chew on, and they collapsed panting in the shade of the tree next to them.

Glanna had decided that she would wait until they were sitting munching on their picnic before she tackled the sister-shaped elephant on the clifftop. Considering he was a self-confessed *cookaphobe* (his words), Isaac had excelled with a shop-bought ensemble of her favourite egg mayonnaise sandwiches on white bread, pork pies, crisps and little pots of coleslaw and salad. He had even put in plastic flutes for the 'champagne', plus mini-pots of ice cream wrapped in ice blocks for dessert. Simple but perfect fare for a hot summer's day, sitting on the pinnacle of Penrigan Head with a gentle breeze and the murmur of the sea beneath them.

It was time. She jumped in: 'So does Elizabeth – I mean Lizzie – live here with you, then?'

Isaac drained his champagne flute and laid it on the grass next to the rug they were sitting on. He cleared his throat and took a deep breath. 'Elizabeth Anne Benson is my sister's name. That was our mother's name too, so Lizzie was always Lizzie to avoid confusion. She's ten years younger than me and was born with learning difficulties. We all managed just fine and she never knew she was any different from anyone else. Because she wasn't. When she reached her twenties, our doctor suggested she go into a home to be cared for, but our parents insisted that they would look after her until the day they died. I promised to carry this on when they had both passed away.'

'That was so selfless of you all.'

'It didn't feel like that. Lizzie was very much loved. I arranged for female carers to come in every day so that she was kept comfortable. Aw, she was such a friendly girl. She liked nothing more than me leading her around the fields on Patience and watching me paint in my studio. Beethoven, too, was her soulmate. She would spend hours with him on the beanbag when the weather was bad just looking out at the view, doing jigsaw puzzles and colouring on a little table I would set up for her.' He was wistful for a second. 'She always did love colouring.'

'Oh, Isaac, did she pass away, then?'

'No. No, but she might as well have done.' Isaac stumbled on his words. 'When Patience had to be put down, Lizzie was beyond consolation. Very slowly, she gradually became more accepting. Together we planted the sweet pea seeds and looking after the flowers did help her a lot. What's more, I started to take her to a stables near here for rides twice a week on one of the docile ponies there. It helped to keep her fit and I didn't want her to lose the pleasure of riding. She liked all of the ponies, and I intended to ask her to choose one that I would buy and keep here for her. But I was taking things slowly. I hoped we were both coming to terms with the traumatic loss of Patience. Glanna, I hadn't really begun to understand how my sister's mind worked. I can see now that she believed Patience might wake up – I don't know why or how she thought that, but Lizzie could have some very restless days when her mind ran away with itself.' He paused and braced himself. 'She sneaked out of the house one night and came down here in the pitch dark. It had been raining, the route down to the cliffs was treacherous. We will never know if she slipped or whether she jumped.'

'Oh, Isaac. I am so sorry.' Glanna put her hand on to his knee.

'It was truly awful. The morning she went missing, I let the carer in as normal and the woman found my sister's bed empty. We raced around the house, searching for her, and then it hit me. I knew exactly where she would have come to. I have forever blamed myself.'

'Why? It sounds like it was just a dreadful accident.'

'It was my fault for not locking the front and back doors at the top, where she couldn't reach. The whole thing was my own bloody fault! If I could turn back time then . . .'

'Oh my God, Isaac, no! You cannot blame yourself.'

'She survived,' he went on in a low, hoarse voice, 'but she lives a life of hell in my opinion. She had head injuries and now my bright girl, my beautiful bubbly sister has to have twenty-four-hour nursing care. We don't even know if she recognises me. She's full of so many tubes and drugs that sometimes I wish the tide had taken her away.'

'So, she's here, at Kevrinek?'

'Yes. I wouldn't have her anywhere else. I had a wing converted in the main house with a specially adapted bed and equipment, and in answer to your question of before, the reason I got the film crew in was because, although I obviously have the capacity to earn a lot of money from my paintings, that sort of private care is not cheap.' He sighed and suddenly looked a lot older. 'And if, God forbid, anything happens to me before her, I want to leave a substantial trust fund so that this level of care can continue. The programme-makers paid very well, plus I left it open that I can invite them back anytime. The PR around it has reminded people that I exist, which has at least done wonders for my career.'

'I can't even imagine how difficult all of this must have been for you.'

'The only thing I'm pleased about is that the accident happened after Mum and Dad died. They would have found it hard to cope with this extra level of sadness.'

'And do you cope?'

'I have to.'

'So, you can never have a holiday?'

'I haven't for years, but her nursing staff, they are truly angels, the lot of them. They say that they and she would be just fine, if I did want or need to go away for a while.'

'I'm sure they know what they are doing,' Glanna said softly.

'They do, but I make a point of saying good morning and goodnight to Lizzie every day, and I talk to her in the usual way about normal day-to-day events whenever I have time to go and sit with her. I don't know if she's even aware of my presence, but if she can hear and understand, it might help her to feel safe. I would hate her to be frightened.'

Glanna put her hand on Isaac's arm. 'That's massive.'

'Real love *is* massive, Glanna.'

He reached for his rucksack and handed her the remaining sweet peas. 'In Victorian times these symbolised thanks and gratitude, and were given as a token of appreciation for the lovely time the giver of them had had with their host.'

'Is that so?' Glanna said, changing her position on the rug. 'The host? That means I should be giving them to you. These are beautiful, and I'd love to think that maybe these came from seeds that you and Lizzie once planted before her accident. Thank you for sharing your story. I am truly sorry for what you and Lizzie have been through.'

'As the saying goes, life will always throw us lemons, and you can forget about any notion of making lemonade. It fails to add that some might be great big heavy fuckers.'

They both laughed.

'I can't believe the time; we've been out here hours. I'd better get these flowers in water before they wilt.' Glanna put her hand on his thigh. Without thought he picked it up and kissed it gently. Looking deeply into his enigmatic green eyes, she then reached up for his mouth. His long beard felt funny on her face, his lips felt plump and as soft as velvet. They kissed, a two-second linger, and it was Isaac who pulled away first.

'I'm sorry.' Isaac stood up, Glanna followed. Beethoven let out a little bark and Banksy suddenly got up and started sniffing around the pair of them.

'Don't be,' Glanna replied. 'It was my fault – I shouldn't have done that. I just assumed it would be OK.'

'I'm really sorry,' Isaac repeated.

'Is it because of Lizzie you don't want a relationship?' Glanna surprised herself at her boldness in asking.

'Partly. I can't risk being distracted from my work, not at the moment when I need to achieve so much for her.' He then said gruffly, 'I was in love – once; the woman broke my heart and then my trust by selling some ridiculous story to the press, saying that I was asexual. After that, I didn't paint – I couldn't – for two years.'

Glanna was deeply shocked. 'Why would anyone want to hurt you like that?'

'Money does funny things to some people. It wasn't even as if she was the injured party. It used to be that today's news was tomorrow's fish and chip paper, but the bloody Internet put paid to that.' He sounded bitter.

'What a betrayal,' Glanna said. There was a pause.

'Let's not break this friendship we have,' Isaac said more brightly. 'For a good one can be everlasting.'

'It's a deal. By the way, Isaac, whilst we are talking so candidly, do you mind me asking what is under the black silk cloth in your studio? I saw it on the documentary and it's still there and—'

'It's Lizzie – well, half of Lizzie.'

'I did wonder.'

'The only painting I have of her is the one your mother owns. It actually comforts me that I know where it is now. I wanted to remember her like that again. Whole. I painted that way before she fell. I wanted her to look free and happy, gazing over the bay that she so loves – and now she just looks trapped and sad. I tried and tried to paint her again, but working from photos I just couldn't capture the magic of her essence. So it sits there half finished as I can't bring myself either to finish it or throw it away.'

Glanna put her hand on the man's arm. Isaac reached for her hand and held it.

'Like I say, sometimes those lemons are as big as whales.' He looked at the sky to suppress his emotion then went on, 'I really like you, Glanna, you are a great woman. In fact, I was only thinking the other day that you are not only a talented artist, but you're beautiful, bright and charming, with buckets of empathy too.'

Glanna felt tears stinging the back of her eyes. 'That is the nicest thing anyone has ever said to me in my entire life.'

'Good. Because it's all true. Now come on, the sun will be going down at this rate, these dogs will need feeding, and Beethoven and I need to say goodnight to Lizzie.'

The sun was setting as they reached the gate at the middle of Isaac's long drive. He had followed Glanna down in the Land Rover to ensure it shut behind her properly. She stopped as she got close to it and started fiddling with her ear.

'You OK?' he shouted.

'These dangly earrings, the wind caught one and it's flown back and stuck in my hair. I need to get it out before I can drive. *Ow.*'

Isaac got out of his vehicle, came towards hers and leaned over the open roof of her little Smart car to try and help her release the earring. Just as he put his face close to hers to ease the strands of hair out of the clasp, there was a sudden flash and commotion in front of them, the sound of footsteps running back down the drive, then the screeching of a car heading off at speed.

'What was that?' Banksy was barking louder than Glanna had ever heard him bark before.

'That's what happens when you take your eye off the security camera,' Isaac said grimly. 'I take it you haven't told anyone you've been visiting me?'

'Er . . . no, of course not,' Glanna lied, feeling sick to her stomach with deceit.

'Because the last thing I want is another blasted fabricated story about my private life out there.'

Chapter 30

Glanna sped through the country lanes, the wind in her hair, David Bowie in her ears. Banksy lay curled up in the footwell, tired after his running exploits with his new sheepdog pal.

Glanna had a lot to think about. She had realised that Isaac was both famous and infamous as a recluse – but not to the extent that anyone would care if he was seen with a woman or not. It had pained her to lie to him but she knew that of the few people close to her – her mother, her father, Jen and Myles – none of them would have broken her trust and gone to the press. And anyone looking more closely at the photograph would be sorely disappointed when they realised that Isaac had just been freeing an earring from her hair. Whoever it was, if they'd wanted the real action, they should have been clever enough to spot them on the picnic rug earlier that afternoon.

Poor Isaac, it had really rattled him. He hadn't even waved her off, just wished her a curt goodbye and driven off at speed to the main house in his beloved Land Rover. She lifted her hot face to the breeze as she accelerated, and tried not to think about it. What if it was the press and a story did get out? But Isaac Benson helping her to free an earring was hardly a story. Nor was a woman at his gate: after all, she could have been anyone. A friend of his sister, a nurse. And it wasn't as if they were having a relationship, was it?

Glanna thought how much she was enjoying owning Star's little Smart car. It was on warm evenings like these that driving a convertible was pure joy. And living in such a beautiful area suddenly made total sense. Putting the worry of what had happened to the side, she inhaled the rich smell of a farm, the whiff of manure preferable, she thought now, to the polluted streets of London. And when the one-track road widened, she was exhilarated by the lack of traffic and of speed cameras, and the freedom to go at her own pace.

Like the hug he had given her before, today's kiss had felt just as good, but she respected what Isaac had said. And what a bitch of a woman to have made trouble like that for him in the past! Glanna was surprised that she hadn't spotted that article during her search for news about his sister. But with so much coverage – there were pages and pages of items about the artist – it was probably buried way down the list. It had felt so nice to have human contact again, lip to lip, and the gentleness and caring of him freeing her earring; he had been so close that she could feel his breath on her cheek. He hadn't disregarded her feelings; he had been honest and open. Not unlike Oliver had been, and right now it was suddenly thoughts of Oliver that filled her brain. The kiss was proof that she clearly wasn't over him. Glanna acknowledged that, even if she had wanted to let the whole beauty that was Isaac Benson into her heart, that all-knowing, all-seeing organ of life and love would not have let her. She had agreed with Jen just the week before about how freeing it was to make the decision to let Oliver go, but she had been deluded.

Oliver Trueman was still very much in her heart and mind.

Glanna drove slowly up Ferry Lane, loving the familiar sights. She adored it here. The market, whether quiet or busy, day or night, season by season, took on its own character and she loved glancing in the shop windows to see the displays that had kept locals and tourists coming back to this historic place, year after year.

As she turned the car into the back of the gallery to park up, the security light didn't come on, and in the glare of her headlights she could see that the top of the stable door that led into the back kitchen was swinging open. Her heart began pounding. If she were to call her dad it would take an age for him to come to her – and maybe there was a simple explanation. A power cut maybe, or perhaps she'd just forgotten to turn the light on or lock the top door? Surely Hartmouth was a safe place . . .

Telling Banksy to 'Stay!' inside the car, she was just reaching in the boot to find the big torch that Fred had insisted she keep there for emergencies when she felt a presence behind her. It was a figure in a black hoodie, and she screamed out loud.

'Jesus, Glanna. It's OK. It's only me – Hayden.'

'Oh my God, you scared the shit out of me! What are you doing here at this time of night?'

'I've just moved into Kara's rental flat above Passion Flowers. It was too much hassle getting to work every day from the mobile home park where I live with my mum so I'm officially a neighbour now. I've just been to Costsmart to get some beers.'

'Good, good,' Glanna dismissed this hurriedly. 'OK, have you got a second? I need some help. Look,' she pointed. 'My security light is off and the stable door is open. I'm worried I may have been burgled.'

'Oh no. Glad I'm here in that case.'

'Should I call the police, do you think?'

'No, no. Leave your headlights on and give me that torch. Banksy should stay in the car whilst we investigate. I'll cover you but follow me, so I know where I'm going.'

With her heart beating wildly, Glanna did as she was told. When they reached the door Hayden made a point of opening it wider to see if he could see anyone or anything before they ventured inside.

'Maybe don't touch anything in case of fingerprints.'

'OK, Miss Marple.' A fearless Hayden laughed as he flicked on the light in the kitchen.

Glanna then turned on the gallery light and looked all around. 'Everything seems to be in order down here,' she told him. 'Can we go upstairs now?'

They made their way up to her flat and studio, Hayden leading, Glanna continuing to turn lights on as they went. Again, everything seemed untouched.

They went back downstairs, with Glanna feeling relieved and also a bit foolish.

'Maybe I did just leave the top of the stable door open, Hayden, and the breeze caught it because – look, I must have also pressed the back security light switch off by mistake. The outside light has to be on to activate it.' She switched it on and the backyard area lit up brightly.

'Mystery solved, then. Nothing more than a careless mistake.' The young lad grinned at her.

'Thank you so much though, Hayden. I couldn't have done that on my own.'

'Glad I could be of service. I'm really enjoying the life drawing, by the way. Not only am I having fun, but I am learning a lot too.'

'I'm so pleased to hear that – and welcome to your new home. Right, I'd better get Banksy out; he'll be going crazy in the car wondering what the heck is going on.'

Hayden cleared his throat. 'Glanna, er . . . if you're nervous I am happy to spend the night here. I can sleep on the sofa or somewhere.'

'That's so sweet of you, Hayden, but I'll be all right. I've got your number and you're minutes away if I do need you.'

'Yes, make sure you call me anytime, if you're worried at all.'

They said their goodbyes. Hayden picked his carrier bag of beers up from the ground and ran up the stairs to his new flat. Seeing his mistress come out, Banksy leaped out of the car and immediately ran to pee against the storage shed.

He then followed her inside and drank thirstily from his water bowl. Glanna patted his head, saying, 'Silly Mummy thinking she'd been burgled.'

Going through to the gallery again for a final check that the front door was locked securely, she then gasped loudly in horror. In her haste to make sure everything was as it should be, she had missed the front display – and there in the window, instead of Isaac Benson's original oil painting of *Safety in Numbers*, was nothing but fresh air.

Chapter 31

Glanna awoke to the sound of loud knocking on her back door. Sleepily checking her phone to see the time she groaned and, with the recollection of what had happened the night before, she groaned some more. Groggily, she pulled on her silk dressing gown and headed downstairs.

'I'm coming,' she shouted. She peered at her video doorbell to see who her visitor was, but there was no image showing. 'Who is it?' she called as she reached the door.

'It's me, Jen. Quick, let me in. Where's your doorbell anyway? What's happened to it?'

Glanna poked her head out of the door. 'Oh. It's not there. Has it fallen on the ground? Those things are screwed on normally.' Then it hit her. 'Oh, for crying out loud. Looks like that's been stolen too.'

Jen frowned, repeating, 'Too? I only got your message to call you this morning. And you said it was urgent, that's why I'm here so early. Are you all right? What's going on?'

'Jen, give me a second to wake up. The last time I saw this kind of six thirty, I was high on cocaine or in a Premier Inn with you.'

An even sleepier-looking Banksy sloped down the stairs for his morning wee. 'Go up, Jen, put the kettle on. We won't be a minute. Tea for me, please. Strong and sweet.'

A little later, with Banksy now on his bed in front of the window and Jen cradling a mug of coffee in the snuggle chair opposite Glanna, the two women began to talk.

'Jen, something serious has happened. The Isaac Benson original was stolen from the window last night.'

'Oh my God! I didn't even notice or see that the window was smashed.'

'It's not. They got in and left via the back by the look of things.'

'What did the police say?'

'Oh Jen, I didn't call them. You know how private a man Isaac is, and I felt I should talk to him first. It is the kind of thing the local newspaper would pick up on straight away and he doesn't want any kind of negative publicity at the moment. I decided to sleep on it. I did try and call Dad, but he didn't pick up. And then you. I then just turned my phone off and went to sleep as, to tell you the truth, I couldn't bear to face the reality of it all.'

'Weren't you scared, sleeping here?'

'I figured they'd got what they wanted so why risk coming back?'

'Are you insured?'

'Yes, but I remember Mum saying something about insuring high-value single items separately, and I never really had anything of such great value as this to insure, so I've no idea if I'm covered or not. Anyway, I can't even be thinking that far ahead.' She took a sip of tea. 'It was a relief that Hayden was around, I have to say.'

'What was he doing here?'

'He luckily happened to be walking past just as I got home last night. He's moved into Kara's place above her shop.'

'Oh, she didn't mention it.'

'He's only just got the keys. He was sweet last night actually; said he'd stay if I was scared.' Glanna's face then lit up. 'Of course! I know what to do. I'll check my doorbell video footage. Whoever took the front of it will have had to walk through to nick it.'

Jen frowned. 'Surely if they are professional thieves they would have thought of that – but yes, look now, quick.'

With shaking hands Glanna checked her phone. 'Oh my God! Look at this!' She held the phone up to Jen's face. 'It's just one person, I'm thinking a man, in a dark hoodie with his face covered.' She could see the shady figure walking down the back path towards the door, then the picture went black. 'It looks as if he is limping. He must have turned the outside light off once he had got in the door because it looks like it came on in this footage.' Her voice lowered. 'Hayden was wearing a black hoodie.'

'Surely he wouldn't have put himself at the scene,' Jen said wisely. 'The police could have been here already or anything.'

'S'pose, but he was quite happy to leave his fingerprints on the door and elsewhere. But then I guess if he wanted to cover his tracks, he would do that. Do you think he really is going to art school in Brighton?'

'It's a lot of trouble joining a life drawing group just to case the joint, isn't it?'

'Not for a forty-grand painting it's not, and he told us himself he has form.'

'He seems so nice though,' Jen said innocently.

'I bet Jack the Ripper seemed so too, once.' Glanna plonked herself back on to the sofa, then gazed up at the ceiling, deep in thought. 'The lock wasn't damaged.'

'That's the trouble with a stable door. If you had left the top door not locked properly, it's easy to pull open the bottom,' Jen said sensibly.

'You sound like my dad! He's always going on about my lack of security. Hmm. What a bloody mess,' Glanna said mournfully.

'What are you going to do? Is there anything I can help with?' Jen drained her mug of coffee. 'Personally, I think you should call the police.'

Glanna put her hand to her forehead and shut her eyes.

'I can't face the art class tonight. Can you pop in on Gideon and Mrs Harris and say it is being postponed to tomorrow and see if they can make it?'

'Of course. And if they press for a reason?'

'Just say you don't know but that I've promised that in future it will be happening every Tuesday as originally planned. Sadie will be here at ten, she has her own key, so I will just message her, and I can text Hayden and tell him too.'

'I wonder what he'll think is going on.'

'If he's guilty let him squirm. I will just say the whole incident has shaken me and I have things to sort out.'

Jen unravelled her legs from under her, got up from the snuggle chair and checked her watch.

'It's seven thirty already, so I'd better go back to Bee Cottage and get ready for work. You know where I am.'

'Thanks so much, Jen, I really do appreciate it.'

'What are you going to do now?'

'As difficult as this is going to be, I need to go and tell Isaac before the bloody *Hartmouth Echo* get hold of this. It would be front-page news for them.'

Chapter 32

'There's no point in sugar-coating this. Your dolphin canvas has been stolen from the front window of the gallery.' Glanna took a sip of the warm milky coffee Isaac had just handed her. Beethoven was snoring in the corner of the studio. The morning sun was causing shafts of bright light to hit the floor and Isaac had to put his hand up to shield his eyes for a second.

'Was anybody hurt in the taking of said object?'

'No.'

'OK, then. Did you call the police?'

'No. I wasn't sure if you'd want the intrusion.'

'And you were right. Do you have any damage to fix?'

'No, the thief was very professional.'

'And you are obviously insured?' He rubbed his beard. 'Saying that, without calling the police, you probably wouldn't be able to claim anyway.'

'Shit, I didn't think of that.' Glanna paused. 'Isaac, can I just say, you seem very calm for a man who has just potentially lost a hugely valuable painting.'

'It's a material object, Glanna. If you look at it dispassionately, it is a white board with a few splatters of paint

265

on it. And that painting has no particular sentimental value to me.'

Hearing this, Glanna felt a rush of relief. She loved this man's sense of reality and rationality.

'And truth be told, I'm actually quite excited.' Isaac Benson grinned his big-teethed smile. 'You see, there's something I haven't told you. After I didn't know where my *End of the Land* painting had ended up – one of mine that I *did* have an affinity with – I vowed that this would never be the case with any of my other paintings.'

'I don't understand.'

Beethoven gave a little whine of contentment as the sun reached his sleeping body.

Isaac became animated. 'Every time I produce one of my large paintings, I put a tiny GPS tracking device within the canvas. I even tracked one to New York the other day.'

'Oh my God, that's amazing.'

Isaac reached in his pocket for his mobile. 'Let's see where *Safety in Numbers* has ended up now, shall we? We'll soon catch that scoundrel.'

Glanna moved to the man's side. He smelled soapy and fragrant, not unlike Christmas tree pine needles. She felt small against his six-foot-six bulk. She liked that. Felt a physical warmth exude from his manliness. His uniform of faded T-shirt and well-worn long shorts were now so familiar. They both looked eagerly at the screen, waiting to see where the tracker would pinpoint the painting.

'It should flash its location as a red dot.' Isaac held his

phone up. 'The signal is terrible in here. Damn, it looks like the battery's about to go too.'

'Well, it's stayed local, at any rate.' Glanna's heart was racing as Isaac put the phone in front of them again.

'Yes. I see . . . it's in Crowsbridge, by the look of it.' He tutted loudly. 'Bugger, the battery has died. Let me plug it in.'

Trying not to show the sense of panic that was now flooding over her, Glanna checked her watch. 'Oh no, look at the time,' she gabbled. 'I'd better go. Poor Sadie has got Banksy and needs to open up, and I hadn't quite finished redoing the front window.' She hated lying but this was serious.

'Do you want me to see you to the gate?'

'No, no, just open it if that's OK.'

'I'd put that roof on, if I were you. Rain is coming, I can smell it in the air.'

'You're funny. My dad does that too – smells the weather.'

'Maybe it's a Cornish thing. And as for funny, I'd much rather peculiar.' Isaac laughed. 'I'll find out exactly where the painting is pinpointed, and we can work out a safe plan of retrieval.'

As Glanna headed down the narrow lanes as fast as her little Smart car would allow, she felt physically sick. For not only was the missing painting in Crowsbridge, if she wasn't mistaken the red dot was showing its location in the grounds of Riversway, her family home! Thoughts began to rush around her head. The house sat on acres of land so there could be any kind of explanation. Fred Gribble loved her too much to cause her such worry, and as for her mother, Penelope might be difficult but stealing from her daughter was beyond the realms of even her possibilities, surely? And for what motive, anyway?

Chapter 33

Glanna pulled into the gallery at speed to be greeted by a concerned-looking Jen.

'Jen – what are you doing here?' Glanna demanded, her heart sinking. 'Has something else happened now? Why aren't you at work?'

Wordlessly, Jen got in the passenger seat, handed her phone to her friend and watched as Glanna's expression went from concern to shocked disbelief.

'*Benson, Banksy and the Mystery Blonde,*' she read aloud. Then went ashen as she continued to scroll down the piece.

Acclaimed Cornish artist and recluse Isaac Benson, 55, well known for his dramatic landscapes, was spotted yesterday kissing blonde beauty and owner of the Hartmouth Gallery, Glarnar Pascoe, 39.

'They couldn't even spell my bloody name right!' she seethed. 'He is going to be so mad at me. He was so adamant that his private life was to be kept, well, just that!'

During the recent WCTV documentary entitled The Tradition of Art in Cornwall, *when questioned about his love life, Benson had cagily quoted Picasso, saying 'Art is the lie that enables us to realise the truth.' A source told the* Daily Shout *that the couple have been seeing each other for a few weeks now and are getting closer and closer. Convicted alcoholic Pascoe moved from London to Hartmouth two years ago, following a serious accident whilst drunk and narrowly escaping a term in jail.*

'No! No! No, No!' Glanna felt tears stinging her eyes. 'Why did they have to say that?'

This certainly turns on its head the claims of asexuality from an ex-partner of the artist. Banksy the whippet, Pascoe's pet, was also spotted at Kevrinek, Benson's impressive sea-facing mansion – a sure sign that she will soon be moving in. Nursing staff were also spotted entering the property, adding further speculation that Benson's sister Elizabeth, who has not been seen in public for several years, has been suffering from some kind of mystery illness. Benson's brand-new exhibition, Dolphins in Depth, *will be at Tate St Ives from 25 September.*

Glanna's face had gone from ashen to red. Her expression was pained. 'I don't believe this is happening. Fucking hell! We weren't even kissing – he was only trying to untangle my earring from my hair. It's just the angle they've got us at. Oh, Jen.'

'I wanted to categorically tell you I have *not said a word* to anyone, not even Markus. You said it was confidential and OK, we haven't known each other long, but I'm no gossip, Glanna, I can promise you that. I'm here for you, mate. Whatever you need to do I've got your back.'

'Thank you, and thanks so much for coming straight to me with this.' Jen put her hand on top of her friend's.

'It will all work out, don't worry.'

But Glanna wasn't listening to any voice of reason. 'This is like my worst nightmare in one go. Do you think the painting being stolen is connected?' Glanna put a hand to her aching head. 'Isaac is going to be furious. He trusted me. If it was just about me and him, he'd probably deal with it, be able to ignore it – but the reference to his sister will destroy him. She has round-the-clock nursing care because she is brain damaged from an accident. He doesn't need this kind of intrusion. *Fuck!*' she nearly screamed in frustration. 'How can someone make up so much bullshit from one photo that is not even the truth? And I have worked so hard on losing that alcoholic tag since I arrived here.'

'Well, that's the tabloids for you.'

'Throwing in Banksy's name too, just to get such a sensational headline, I bet the real one is delighted – not!'

'Who else did you tell, Glanna?'

'Just Dad and Mum. Grrr. I'm so angry with myself. I

know Dad wouldn't say a word so it must be my mother. I actually fucking hate her, Jen, I hate her with a passion for doing this! I don't know why I opened my mouth. How stupid was that? I felt I was getting closer to her. All I said was that I had been going to his house on a few of my days off and that we were just friends. I can just imagine her spilling it all in multicoloured exaggerated delight to bloody Jilly foghorn St John-Davis, who no doubt will have told someone else until the Chinese whispers would have eventually got into the hands of whoever this bloody reporter is. I'm surprised we are not getting married and moving to the Bahamas. Oh Jen, what the hell am I going to do?'

Chapter 34

Oliver sang as he made his way into Brightside House then, on reaching the Activity Room, he checked his phone again for messages. Tuesday morning and still nothing from Glanna. From memory, when they had met in Tate Modern, she had told him she took Mondays off, so maybe she was just busy catching up with work and had not yet got around to checking her answer machine. In this new age of technology, who even used landline answer machines anyway? Saying that, he recalled that Glanna hadn't been that good at checking her mobile phone messages when they were together. To be fair, communication in general had never been her forte.

Why oh why hadn't he insisted that they exchange numbers when he had seen her? Deciding that he would try her one more time if she hadn't responded by Friday, he began setting up the room for his art group. Then, with a few minutes to spare before everyone started arriving, he reached in his bag for his iPad, switched it on and was about to check his emails when an art-related news headline flashed up and caught his eye.

Benson, Banksy and the Mystery Blonde. Intrigued to see what the two famous artists had been up to, he began to read. When he got to the photo he looked once, looked again and then, on putting his face right up to the screen and realising that the mystery blonde in the white car kissing the great artist, Isaac Benson, was none other than his own Glanna, he swore loudly.

'She'll be furious they spelled her name wrong,' he said aloud, his heart now slowly sinking. No wonder she didn't feel the need to return his call last night. On reaching the bit where it described Glanna as an alcoholic, he exclaimed aloud again, 'No, no, *no*, poor Glanna!' She was obviously making great progress down in Hartmouth, and he knew just how much this ugly tag would upset her.

A frowning Oliver finished reading the article then turned off his iPad. He could have dealt with Glanna's insistence not to be with him, and even if she was with another man, he would have maybe continued to vie for her affections. But this wasn't just any other man. This was Isaac Benson they were talking about here. A great artist and one whom his ex-love had particularly admired from afar for many years. He hoped that she knew what she was doing, that her feelings were being reciprocated. The last thing he wanted was for Glanna to get hurt but if she was happy, as difficult a pill as it was to swallow, he had to be happy for her too.

Sighing at the realisation that he would have more hope of finding a pot of gold under a rainbow than winning her back, with a heavy heart and a forced smile, Oliver Trueman started to greet his addiction group one by one.

Chapter 35

'Trust me for calling it sizzling August the other day – I've bleedin' jinxed it. Rain's forecast for later,' Pat Dillon addressed Glanna as she opened up the front door to her fruit and vegetable shop. 'Good for the farmers though,' she said wisely, and waddled heavily back inside.

Glanna had come outside to see how the two paintings looked that she had hastily arranged in the window as a stopgap. Sadie would be here to open up in ten minutes. She had left the girl a note instructing her to work her magic on a display of Sadie's own choosing from the *Seascapes in All Seasons* pieces, as Isaac Benson had requested his painting back for his own exhibition. OK, it was just another lie – but the last thing she needed was the whole of the market knowing what had happened. She also tasked Sadie with looking after Banksy, which thankfully the young girl loved doing, so Glanna didn't feel it too much of a liberty to ask her.

She was just getting in the car when her dad phoned. 'You OK, love?'

'Er . . . yes, why wouldn't I be?'

'I missed your call last night. Are you sure everything's

all right? And where are you going? I can hear you walking.'

'You've seen the article, Dad, haven't you?'

'Yes. Linda sent it to me.'

'Oh Dad.' Glanna tried not to cry. 'Everything is such a mess, and somebody broke into the gallery last night and stole Isaac's painting and—'

'Oh darling. Have you called the police?'

'Not yet.'

'Why not?'

'Because that will cause further local press interest which will then go to national interest, with this story running, and they are likely to put two and two together and make five thousand and – and as for Mum, I hate her. I hate her for breaking my trust.'

'What do you mean?' Fred sounded shocked at her fury.

'She's obviously been showing off to her fancy friends that her daughter has been hanging out with a famous artist. You know how much they all admire the painting she has in the dining room. I can just imagine her doing it. What a bitch!'

'Calm down, love. Just . . . calm down. The fact is, the story has got out and we need to see a way through this to stop you feeling so stressed and to protect Isaac from any further damage. Have you spoken to him yet?'

'That's where I'm going. I've only just left his place as I went there to tell him about the painting, but now he has to hear this bombshell too. Oh Dad.' Her voice was full of panic. 'What if he's seen it already? He is going to be so angry.'

'It's not your fault.'

'It *is* my fault, for opening my big mouth.'

'Do you think it's wise to go to him right now?'

'What do you mean?'

'Well, if you visit again it could stir up more press interest – and from what I can gather, that is the last thing you want to happen.' His voice changed. 'Glanna, you told me you were insured. You *are* insured, aren't you?'

'I don't know without a police report. That's not the point though, Dad. That painting is an original. It will never be recreated in exactly the same way, even from a print. It was a masterpiece, Dad. And now it's gone and will probably be sold to some foreign art dealer somewhere for thousands of pounds – and for what? It was to be at the heart of Isaac's exhibition in St Ives next month too. I am SO bloody angry.'

'I'm coming to you on the ferry now.'

'No, don't do that. I'll talk to you later.'

'Is the gallery secure?'

'Yes, and that's the thing: there was no sign of a break-in. I do have video footage of a man in a black hoodie approaching the door though.'

'You do? What can you see?'

'I can't make out his face but he looks quite short and has a bit of a limp going on by the look of it.'

'A limp, really? Shit! I'm surprised it picked up on that level of detail.'

'Until it was ripped off the wall, it did, anyway.'

'The bastards!'

'Exactly.'

'Another brownie point for your mother, I have to say. She insisted you got that type of security doorbell.'

'Please don't even mention her name to me at the moment. This is possibly the single worst thing she has done to me in my life.'

'Oh, darling.'

'Dad, something strange too. Isaac has a tracker on all of his paintings and . . . well it's showing that it's in the grounds of Riversway.' Fred sneezed loudly.

'Bless you.' There was a brief silence. 'Dad, are you there?'

'Yes, yes, I'm here.'

But he was being evasive and Glanna felt a sudden flash of alarm. Could one of her parents really have crossed a line and stolen from her? And if so, why? She let out a huge sigh. 'I'll talk to you later, Dad. I need to be alone with my thoughts for a while.'

♡

A steady drizzle of rain had begun to fall when Glanna drew up at Isaac's gate for the second time that morning. She had once found it kind of sweet that he rarely used his mobile but now that she desperately wanted to talk to him, it was downright inconvenient not having his number. Not that he would pick up anyway, especially if he had seen the article already.

Bracing herself, Glanna reached for the intercom button. By not giving her the gate code, he obviously hadn't trusted her fully yet, and now that this had happened, it proved he'd been right. Why, oh why, had she opened her mouth to her mother? This had taught her once and for all to keep things to herself, that the whole world didn't need to know her business. If she were Isaac Benson, she wouldn't trust her again either. It would take bridge-building of the Millau Viaduct kind if they were ever to get to the same level of friendship again. But a friendship they had built, and she was sure they could work through this, if he would just allow her to explain.

After five rings of the intercom, she was just about to give up when the deep familiar voice of Isaac Benson said in firm but level tones, 'It takes a lot for me to trust and I distance myself from people for a reason, Glanna. Please never come here again.'

'NO!' Glanna shouted as the buzzing noise of the intercom went dead. 'I'm so sorry, I made a mistake. We all make mistakes; you have to forgive me. Please hear me out.'

Putting her window up, she laid her head back on her seat and shut her eyes. How could she have put this kind and thoughtful, extraordinary man in such a predicament? He, who had suffered so much loss. Here he was, minding his own business in this remote setting, creating art that gave pleasure to so many people . . . and yet he was now tainted by some ridiculous gossip. He had enough on his plate to deal with, with his dear sister Lizzie, let alone unscrupulous journalists trying to encroach further on his private life.

Turning on her engine, she was just about to reverse all the way back along the narrow drive when she caught sight of a car reversing towards her. The vehicle suddenly stopped. On seeing the driver approaching on foot, a large camera in hand, Glanna was suddenly overtaken by rage of a kind she had never experienced before. She leaped out of her car and started to run at the figure. He was a lot older than she imagined any kind of paparazzi might be. She also recognised him, but for the life of her couldn't remember from where. Her shriek of, *'You stop right now, or I will report you to the police for trespass!'* was lost on the now strengthening wind – and within seconds the man had turned on his heels and was speeding off down the drive as fast as his green Mini Cooper would allow him.

Chapter 36

Glanna hastened into the gallery to find Sadie laughing and chatting away to Hayden. The lad handed her a bunch of pink roses. 'It must have been quite a shock last night. I got a bunch for you and another for the lovely Miss Peach here.'

'Thank you,' Glanna said without a smile.'Face of an angel, mind of a devil, that one – you be careful.' Having directed her misplaced anger at Sadie, she immediately dashed up the stairs followed by Banksy, who had jumped out of his basket in the gallery on seeing his mistress.

'Glanna, Glanna!' Hayden called until she appeared at the bottom of the stairs. His voice was tight. 'If you are implying that I had something to do with last night, you are very much mistaken. That's the trouble with admitting your mistakes. You get tarred with the repeat offender brush! I'm going.' As he stormed towards the door, Glanna noticed a bandage around his knee.

'Hayden, come back!' But he had already set off down the hill.

'What's going on?' Sadie asked, bewildered.

'I will tell you everything soon. Did you see Hayden last night?'

'No, why?'

But without answering, Glanna said, 'Sorry, I have to go out again. I need to catch the ferry to Crowsbridge.' She clipped on Banksy's lead and added, 'Lock up early, if you like. I so appreciate your help – and Sadie, the window looks really fab. Thank you.'

Glanna was just driving away when Sadie came running out the back and waved at her to stop, calling, 'I forgot to give you a message. Somebody – I think they said their name was Oli—'

'Text me the details!' The Smart car was already bowling down the hill and Glanna's voice carried back up to the girl.

♡

With the sun back out, the roof off and the wind blowing through her hair, Glanna disembarked from the *Happy Hart* ferry at Crowsbridge Quay, then drove on along the coastal road towards Riversway. Banksy, delighted to be in his favourite seat with his favourite person, lifted his head as his ears flailed behind him.

Glanna, however, was having trouble controlling her dark thoughts. To lose Isaac *and* Oliver would be too much to bear. It had taken a lot for her to win Isaac's trust – and then she had gone on to immediately betray him. What the hell had she been thinking, letting certain people know that she was seeing him when she *knew* he guarded his privacy so fiercely? Didn't he have enough to deal with, with Lizzie's ongoing health problems?

And what the hell was the painting doing here at Riversway?

Still fighting with her logic to not let a guilty parent scenario be a reality, Glanna's mind was buzzing with confusion, rage and foreboding. Maybe someone had dumped it in a bush or something, since there were plentiful grounds and places to secrete it. But whatever the situation, the fact was that the painting had landed up at her mother's house. She was terrified that Isaac might find out and then decide to come and get it back in person. Glanna shuddered at the thought of what Penelope, with her zero-empathy filter, might actually say to upset him.

Thinking about the article again brought up more waves of red-hot anger. So much so that, by the time she drove up the long tree-lined drive and reached Riversway, she was on the verge of exploding. Thoughts of the missing painting were, for the time being, forgotten.

Her mother was lying on a sun lounger by the side of the swimming pool when Glanna marched down the lawn towards her. Banksy had taken himself to stretch full length just inside the open French doors of the dining room.

'There is low and then there is very low,' Glanna said, her voice a growl.

'Darling, what on earth's the matter?' Penelope Pascoe winced as she sat up. A floral turban protected her long chestnut-coloured hair from the sun. Huge dark sunglasses covered most of her face. She was the only woman Glanna had ever come across who wore full make-up when she sunbathed.

'Who did you tell about me seeing Isaac Benson? WHO?' Glanna screamed.

Penelope Pascoe took off her sunglasses to look at her daughter in surprise. 'Glanna, calm down. I may not be perfect, but I am the mistress of discretion when it comes to affairs of the heart. You should know that. Now tell me, what is it? What has happened?'

'It had to be you! I told Dad and Jen and I know I can trust them.'

Penelope Pascoe for once looked shocked. Her voice when she spoke was shaky. 'I'm your mother. You can always trust me.'

At that moment Mrs Maynard seemed to appear from nowhere. 'Did you want any sauce on your chicken this evening, Mrs Pascoe?' she asked, then turned to Glanna. 'Oh, hello, Glanna, how are you? You have to be careful what kind of sauce you are dealing with round here, don't you?' She laughed, causing a gap in the back of her teeth to show and her heavy breasts to wobble.

Glanna said innocently, 'What exactly do you mean by that, Mrs Maynard?'

'That article about you and that artist fellow. Lucky you. He looks right handsome, he does. Bet he's got a few quid too.'

'What article? What are you talking about?' A perplexed-looking Penelope clocked the look of anger that she had seen many a time on her daughter's face. 'And what time is your Derek picking you up today, Mrs Maynard? Soon, I hope. You said the Mini's been fixed and you need to pop off early again, didn't you?'

'What colour is your Mini, Mrs Maynard?' Glanna asked. Adrenalin was now running through her veins.

The woman's face dropped. 'What's that got to do with the price of fish?' she said sulkily.

'It's racing green,' Penelope told Glanna. 'I used to have an old MG exactly the same colour.'

'It was you, wasn't it?' Glanna's voice resumed its growl-like tone. Mrs Maynard retreated, looking alarmed, and started making her way back up the garden as quickly as her overweight frame would allow. 'You overheard us the other day and thought you'd spread the word.'

The woman stopped in her tracks. 'You folk with your fancy houses and all this money, we just wanted a little bit of cash towards our retirement, that's all.'

'So, you thought you'd go to the press with half a story and cause misery in two people's lives just for your own financial gain, did you? That's sick!'

'You're fired,' Penelope screeched, getting off the sun lounger and advancing towards the woman. 'Never come near this house or my family again, or I'll call the police!'

'You can't get rid of me just like that,' Louisa Maynard shouted back, her face bright red.

'I just did. I will pay you until the end of the month,

now *clear off*. No housekeeper of mine breaks my trust or upsets my daughter.'

Penelope Pascoe sat down again, took a sip of her glass of water and smiled sweetly as if nothing had happened. All she said was: 'Do you believe me now, dear?'

At that moment there was the roar of an engine and the splattering noise of gravel flying around up at the house. Glanna could make out a quad bike.

'Who the heck's that?'

'Oh, it's your father's new toy. Well, old toy – it's been sat in the top garage for years. He got it going last week. Fell off the bugger at the weekend and hurt his leg, he told me. Surprised to see him on it, actually.'

Glanna waved but, seeming to ignore her, he whizzed back off round to the front of the house. She then sat herself down on a garden chair, feeling quite dizzy with it all.

'I'm so sorry, Mum. For not trusting you.'

'Well, yes, it was rather dreadful of you. But let's face it, I haven't always been the best of mums, have I?' Penelope cleared her throat. 'So . . . darling, I'm going to hospital on Thursday. I'm terrified, but the procedure needs to be done.'

'Did you speak to Dad about looking after you?'

'No, of course I didn't.'

'So, what are you going to do?'

'I will manage. Well, I might have done with Mrs Maynard to feed me. Anyhow, I shall be moving myself downstairs to the estuary-facing guest room. There's a walk-in shower with an en suite in there. I can hobble about on my crutches. I'll be fine.'

'Are you sure? You told me yourself it's hard to look after yourself for a few weeks after a hip replacement.'

'Let's see how I manage, shall we, and if I do have to get some kind of nurse in, I will. I wonder if you can request their age, gender and sexual orientation? I was thinking maybe two heterosexual males, around thirty-five.'

Glanna managed a smile as she stood up. 'You really are incorrigible. On that note, I'm going to pop down to my old studio to see what's been left in there. I might be able to use some of the stuff for my new art club.'

The truth was, Glanna badly needed space and time to calm her racing nerves and to think all these developments through. It was all too much – getting close to Isaac, followed by his rejection, the burglary at her gallery and how shaken she was by that and by the mysterious hooded figure, making her feel unsafe in her own home, the vile actions of the treacherous Maynards, her fury at her mother, the missing painting . . . She gave a long and shuddering sigh and, as if sensing her distress, Banksy ran down from the house to be by her side. Her best friend, love emanating through his soft coat and entering her bloodstream.

'Spiders and memories are all you'll find in there, I should imagine,' Penelope said. 'It's been a long time.'

'Yes, too long . . . and Mum?'

'Yes, dear?'

'You know you asked me what I wanted for my fortieth birthday – well, could I have a print of one of Isaac Benson's paintings, please? I have *Safety in Numbers*, as you know, so any of his others would be great, especially the ones with dolphins featured. What I really would have loved is a print of your *The End of the Land As We Know It*, but the original is just that, the original, as it was before he got any prints made up of his work.' For a second, she thought of confiding in her mum how Isaac longed to have the painting back, as it was the only record of Lizzie as she once had been, before the accident. Then common sense reasserted itself. She would not betray him again.

'Gosh, that makes it all the more special, then. I'll have a look and if I can find any of his prints anywhere, darling, of course. Although you could just ask your boyfriend for one . . .' She caught herself up. 'I know, I know, it's none of my business.'

Glanna's face fell. 'As I said before, he's not actually my boyfriend – and after this little episode, I don't think he will ever speak to me again.'

'Give it a few days,' Penelope said softly. 'He will calm down.'

Reaching for her phone to show her mother the offending article, Glanna realised she had left the handset in the car. 'If you can be bothered to read the trash, it tells all and sundry that we are an item. The fact was, poor Isaac was untangling an earring from my hair and not snogging my face off as the amateur photo from Derek bloody Maynard with his antique camera implies.'

'Of course I will read it, but don't get it all out of proportion, Glanna. As long as you both know the truth.'

Glanna relaxed slightly. 'Thank you, Mum. Right, I'm going to drive down to my favourite old haunt. Do you need anything before I go?'

'No, I just need to get upstairs and start getting my things together for the hospital. Actually, Glanna,' Penelope Pascoe paused for a second, 'could I trouble you to take me there? I was going to ask your father, but it makes me feel sick to think he's touching another woman's private parts at the moment. Really sick.' Her face distorted beyond recognition.

'Mum, of course I will. Thursday, you said, didn't you?'

'Yes. I need to be there for eleven.'

'I'll be here for nine then.'

Making a mental note to let Sadie know she needed to hold the gallery fort again, and throwing an awkward kiss on her mother's cheek, Glanna whistled to Banksy and walked round to her car. She was just heading down the track to her old studio when a text from Sadie buzzed in. Glancing at it quickly, Glanna slammed on the brakes in shock: for staring back at her from the screen were three simple words followed by a number: *Oliver Trueman called.*

Chapter 37

With Banksy at her side, Glanna pushed open the door to the art studio that her father had built for his only child, wanting her to have a place of her own where she could work undisturbed. And this, her first ever art studio, had been a happy place. It was a basic wooden hut with electricity provided, but Fred Gribble had also supplied a couple of easels, plenty of shelves, a table for paints and tea-making, and her special 'squidgy chair' as she used to call it. She could sit in it and look out over the estuary for inspiration or to drown sorrows of some sort or other.

Fred had kept everything as it was the last time she had been down here, after her split from Oliver and just before she had thrown herself into taking over the Hartmouth Gallery. It felt kind of spooky with the art table and furnishings now covered in waterproof sheets that looked a bit dusty. A few cobwebs hung from the rafters and, despite it being summertime, there was a distinct whiff of damp in the air.

She went over to the huge canvas which was propped against the end wall and carefully removed its covering. The canvas looked as pristine as when she had painted it in her teens. It was the largest painting she had ever tackled at that stage. Depicting the same view from this window, it showed a dreamlike rainbow overarching the boats and the world going by on the estuary, its colours illuminating the sudden peace that falls over everything after a storm. This was where she would sit and sketch, totally absorbed. Before her demons had fully taken hold, when everything had seemed possible.

Glanna stood and admired her work, a smile on her face. Hey, not bad for a teenager! She had forgotten how she used to sign her work with *G Pascoe*, whereas now she would sign off with a simple swirly *Glanna* in the bottom right-hand corner.

Stepping back in decades was weird. So much had happened to her since those early days. Had she ever really been happy? She thought back to the many times she had played at this very river's edge with Carmel, running in and out of what they called their 'summerhouse'. While Fred kept an eye on them, they were allowed to go swimming and to play here, and occasionally he would take them out in *Ups & Downs*, Penelope's little old white boat that he had conscientiously maintained and which was still sitting on the jetty in front of her. Glanna gave another smile, a less innocent one, recalling the night when she had shagged her teacher in that very boat.

They had been careless days, when you didn't look to the future, just lived in the moment. She and Carmel had been allowed to spend the night down here too. Both on camp beds, scaring the life out of each other as they tried to sleep amidst the spooky night sounds of owls and foxes, and thinking every little thing was a spider or a beetle climbing on their bed. And how about those midnight feasts of stolen crisps, bars of chocolate and tins of condensed milk, slurped up by the finger scoop. Her childhood had been happy then, and also when she first went off travelling with Carmel. Her late teens and early twenties had been exciting and freeing, fun and drunken, with many a male conquest and story to tell. She sighed. It had only really started to go horribly wrong when the drinking had got serious; when she had tried to drown the demons caused by an absent mother and warring parents with both vodka and denial.

Throwing open the two front windows and pulling back the plastic cover to reveal her now faded squidgy chair, she sat down on it and saw the dust fly. Banksy sniffed around these new surroundings before leaping up next to her, his warm body close to hers. Taking in the peaceful vista, she let all her worries float away. A brief shower had given way to a deep blue sky hanging over the still expanse of the wide estuary. She searched for a rainbow but couldn't find one, and then was distracted by a packed pleasure boat that was slowly making its way from Penrigan Pier to Hartmouth, with the chitter-chatter of excitable children and tired parents on board. A lone heron was sunning himself on an orange buoy.

Filling her lungs and her soul with fresh air and hope, she reached for her phone and wrote a message to Oliver.

Hey, it's Glanna. I got the message. You called, are you OK? She sent it straight away to the number Sadie had texted her.

She jumped at his immediate reply: *All good, thx. Was just checking to see how you are and maybe we could meet for that missed coffee one day? x*

Glanna stuck out her bottom lip. Dear sweet Oliver, simply glossing over the fact that she had stood him up. She then made a little groaning noise. He was so casual. 'One day,' she repeated in a sarcastic voice. 'Why not today?' She had kind of hoped he was missing her the same way she was missing him – badly. But he was just being true to his usual caring self: simply checking in with her, was all. She so wanted to see him, but now he had his baby and a girlfriend, she wasn't sure if she could bear going through the heartbreak again. She now wished she hadn't even started the message. Had instead carried on holding on to the feelings of what could be, rather than the reality of what *was* – knowing that if she saw him and knew he was happy, then they would never get back together.

Sighing, she tapped out: *Not planning on coming to London anytime soon but yes, when I do, I will let you know. Good to hear from you*

Debating whether or not she should put a kiss on the end she paused, then added a smiley face.

Back in London, Oliver read the message and wanted to cry with the pain of it – but who was he to get in the way of her happiness, the happiness he had craved for her the whole time they were together and beyond. He had tried to reach her; it hadn't worked but he hoped she would keep to her word, and that they could meet in the future.

The voice of his beloved mum filled his mind: *'Follow your heart, son, because it always knows.'* She had been so right because, as much as he tried to pretend that he could get over Glanna, he couldn't. An invisible cord connected them, and whoever else he had met in his life since, that cord had not broken. And like cream, thoughts of Glanna had always risen to the top of his mind. The best cream he had ever tasted . . .

Back in the painting hut, as if sensing his owner's anguish, Banksy licked his mistress's hand. He then jumped off the chair, trotted over to the rainbow painting and disappeared behind it, leaving just his tail visible. It lifted in the air and started to wag, hitting the rainbow painting each time with a brief thwacking sound.

'What are you up to, Banksy boy? Have you found a mouse, or are we playing hide and seek now, mister?'

As he darted out of the other end, his tail still aloft and wagging to and fro, Glanna got up and went over to peek around the edge of the big painting: what she saw there made her freeze. Hurriedly, she began manoeuvring the rainbow painting round to prop against another wall, fully revealing what someone had hidden behind it.

There, in front of her dazzled eyes and in all its glory, was the missing painting. If only those three mysterious-looking dolphins lurking beneath the surface of the dark Penrigan Head waters could talk!

Gleeful and also a little scared at discovering it, she felt the urge to call Isaac straight away, but then waited a moment to think things through. It was a very tricky situation. The fact was, Isaac had said he never wanted to talk to her again. And this, along with the undeniable fact that the precious item had been found on Pascoe property, thereby implicating her family, made her decide otherwise. Hurriedly, she began to search the back of the missing canvas. Eventually finding a tiny tracker hidden near the edge of the frame, she dug it out with her fingernails then took it outside and threw it as far as it would travel into the moving water.

Sitting then on the riverbank, as Banksy scurried in the trees around her, barking at squirrels and chasing birds, she frowned in concentration. Only a handful of people knew this wooden hut was here. Or so she believed. It was some way from the main house, but was just about visible from the estuary and accessible from the jetty. The Pascoes had never felt the need to lock the door of her little studio. Hayden, for instance, could have spotted it from the ferry – but if his motive was money, surely he knew that her parents lived here and there was a chance the painting would be found before he could sell it? No, that theory didn't work. And if the Maynards had taken it, the last thing they would do is to hide it on Penelope Pascoe's doorstep!

The mystery was deepening, as was her despair at the thought of losing Oliver and never seeing Isaac again.

Going back inside the studio, Glanna rummaged around until she found a small pad of art paper that was still dry enough to write on. Thank heavens she always carried a pen in her bag.

If Isaac wasn't going to listen to her, she would write him a letter to explain.

Chapter 38

'So sorry that I had to postpone last night's class, everyone, but we are here now and will be for the next three Tuesdays.' Glanna wasn't in the mood for the life drawing class tonight, but she had made the commitment and would stick to it.

'Busy with your new fella, I expect?' Gideon Jones said in his Welsh accent. 'Maybe now I know that you like an older man we should go out for a drink.' He gave her a salacious wink.

Glanna smiled sweetly. 'No disrespect, Gideon, but if I did still drink, I think the amount of alcohol I would need to sleep with you would actually kill me.'

Good-humouredly, he took the remark and waggled his hand at her.

While Sadie put her hand over her mouth to suppress her laughter, Linda Harris leaned over and whispered to Glanna, 'That Isaac fellow is so tall and handsome, Glanna, and see how big his feet are. You know what they say about big feet, don't you?'

'Big shoes?' Glanna replied with despair in her voice.

'Not as big as mine,' Gideon called out, overhearing,

and he winked at Linda, adding far too loudly, 'And you should know, my pretty.'

When she had recovered from a renewed bout of mirth at this, Sadie said, 'I definitely have an older-man crush on Isaac Benson.'

'You need to be careful what you read in the papers,' Glanna said firmly. 'They're full of stupid lies and made-up stuff, sent in by morons.' Like the horrible Maynards.

'But you were kissing him?' Sadie challenged her.

'Yeah – and right hard on the lips, by the look of it.' Linda was almost salivating at the thought.

'You are both so wrong. Right, I am going to teach you about angles today, then you might understand.' Glanna moved behind her easel. Her hands were shaking as she adjusted the paper that was pinned up there.

'No Hayden tonight, then?' Linda asked.

'No, he's not coming any more.'

'That's a shame. Did he say why?' Glanna sighed.

'Frightened to strip off, was he? Too much competition, eh?' Gideon said crudely.

'I think Glanna knows why,' Sadie replied curtly, the smile wiped off her face.

Glanna put a hand through her hair. 'Something cropped up for Jen and she has had to go back to London tonight too, so it's just the four of us. I don't know why I am bothering with this really.'

'Who do you think stole the painting, then?' Linda asked, arranging her own pencils and charcoal on the easel tray.

'*What!* How did you know about that? It was confidential!' Glanna exploded.

Sadie was shuffling by her easel, looking uncomfortable.

Glanna bit her lip and said no more. Who was she to be cross at Hayden for telling people? She had virtually accused the lad of stealing – and with no proof.

Last night, she had told her dad the whole story from beginning to end.

Fred had agreed to move the stolen painting carefully back to the main house and lock it in a downstairs room. He had encouraged Glanna that, as she had enough stress going on at the moment, he should not get the police involved, but instead get it back to Isaac as soon as possible. She could then try and make her peace with Isaac, using the excuse of taking the painting back to him, knowing he needed it for his upcoming exhibition.

'So, whose turn is it to be our model for tonight, then? I've forgotten.' Glanna, wishing she was anywhere but here, tried to keep herself upbeat and take control of the class.

'It was Hayden's,' Gideon stood up, 'but I don't mind doing it again. I stole a prop off Linda last night actually, to make it all the more exciting.' He produced the biggest pair of crotchless sparkly red women's knickers Glanna had ever seen in her life. 'Ta-da! I thought I could make use of the "-less" bit.'

'God forbid,' Glanna said under her breath, adding quickly, 'No, thank you, Gideon. Please put those things away. And anyone who doesn't want to take our life drawing class seriously can *leave right now.*' There was a silence as everyone heard her anger. For all she cared, the lot of them could clear off for good and all, Glanna thought. In a tight voice she snapped: 'Sadie, will you oblige?'

Sadie was feeling guilty for talking behind Glanna's back and also sad for the woman, who she liked and who had always tried to help her.

'Of course,' she agreed immediately and went behind the screen to change. The pretty student had always planned to pose lying down with her back to the group, so the artists could learn about the curve of the spine and the way the hips rose and blossomed from it.

If Gideon started on his stupid smutty remarks, the girl decided she'd leap off the chaise longue, chuck some paint at him and ask Glanna to ban him in future. But Gideon, who knew he'd gone too far this time, was keeping his head down.

'Let's draw,' Glanna said, despondently.

Chapter 39

The next day, Glanna pulled up at Riversway and reached for the bag of magazines and chocolates she had bought for her mother to take to the hospital with her. As she was shutting the car door behind her, her dad pulled up next to her on his quad bike.

'You need to be careful on that thing,' Glanna told him. 'There have been loads of reports of accidents on them, and Mum said you fell off it last week.'

'Phooey. It's just a graze and anyway, what does she know?' Fred replied cheekily.

Penelope Pascoe appeared at the door, pulling a huge case on wheels. 'I know more than you bloody think I do, Freddie Gribble.'

'Mum, you're only in for two nights max, aren't you? And I don't think that case will fit in my car!'

'But I need to look the part for all those doctors.'

Fred shook his head slowly from side to side.

'And what are *you* shaking your head at?' Penny snapped. 'I shall say just two words, *Linda* and *Harris*! Really, Fred, is that your level?'

'How did you . . .?'

'Louisa Maynard knows when the Pope takes a shit!'

Penelope Pascoe winced as she thought back to the painful and familiar feeling of loss and hurt she had experienced on reading the heartless text from her ex-employee, gleefully updating her of her Freddie's exploits.

'It's none of your business and it's over now anyway,' Fred fought back.

'Oh.'

'Yes, she's with the owner of the antique shop now, and from what I hear, I'm unable to compete in more ways than one.'

'Oh,' Penelope Pascoe repeated. Then, rallying herself: 'Well, you probably deserved each other. Two of a working kind.'

'STOP IT!' Glanna suddenly shouted. '*Just stop it*, the pair of you! Please stop tearing each other apart. It's obvious Dad still loves you and you love him too, Mum. So why are you two not together?'

'I'm here now because I know she needs me.' Fred's voice was shaky.

'Glanna is wrong, I don't need anyone.' Penelope Pascoe wasn't ready to give in.

'Well, *I* need *you*.' Fred held his head high.

'Oh? And when did you realise that – before or after you got it together with that fat old cow? Just get out of my hair, will you!'

Looking defeated, Fred went to walk away.

'Are you just going to let it go like that, Dad – that easily, when clearly it's not what she wants?'

'She's forever saying she needs her space.'

'And she's forever fooling herself and you.'

'Who's "she", the cat's mother? *Ow.*' Penelope put a hand to her side.

Fred's face was pained at Penelope's discomfort.

Glanna's face went as red as a beetroot. 'So, you're going to give up again, are you, Dad, just walk away like you always have? If you're not going to fight for her, maybe you don't deserve her.'

'I stole the painting.' Fred put both his hands over his face.

Glanna gasped. 'Dad! No!'

'When your mother was asked what she really wanted to make her happy, she said she wanted to travel the world. I don't have that kind of money, you know that. So, I thought I'd steal the painting, sell it and then I could do something to please her, for once.'

'I can't believe you'd do this to me.'

Fred's eyes filled with tears. 'Glanna, I know you may never forgive me, but I couldn't see another way. I knew you were insured and I'm so sorry if it caused you any kind of fear.'

'Thank God I didn't call the police.' Glanna felt she needed to sit down as her legs had gone wobbly. 'I didn't want to even consider it would be either of you. I couldn't even fathom a motive. You would have been caught red-handed if the police had been involved, storing it where you did.'

Fred sighed deeply. 'I was confused, desperate, angry all at the same time. Not at you, dear Glanna, but at myself. Having a fling with Mrs Harris really was the last straw, and that is the truth. Penelope Jane Pascoe, I have never stopped loving you from the minute my young eyes met yours.' A visibly moved Penelope limped out of the doorway and, grabbing both of Fred's hands, she held them out in front of her. 'Freddie, ask me again what will make me happy.'

'I'm too old to be playing these games with you now.' His face was wracked with guilt and anguish.

'Just ask her, Dad,' Glanna pleaded, and crossed her fingers behind her back.

Fred sighed. 'So, pray tell me, Penny Pascoe, what *will* make you happy?'

'You,' the woman said directly.

'Just me?' Fred directed his index finger to his chest.

'Just you. It's always been you, always.' Then attempting to get down on one knee, Penelope stumbled. Fred caught her and held her in his arms. 'And realising that I might be losing you when you went off with Linda . . . well, I just couldn't bear it. Frederick Anthony Gribble, will you marry me?'

'Bloody hell,' Glanna said under her breath.

'Yes, I will – but on one condition.'

'Before you even say it, I will be honoured to be known as a Gribble,' Penelope said and laughed.

'I actually think you should get a tattoo of it on your forehead.' Fred kissed Penelope full on the lips, gently lifted her off the lawn and swung her around.

'Careful!' Brushing herself down, Penelope pulled

away then, standing as upright as her hip would allow, in an officious voice she said, 'Right, now that's done, we'd best get me to that hospital. How you expect me to chase you around the bedroom with just one good leg, I don't know.'

Glanna laughed out loud. 'I think I preferred you hating each other.'

'I'll take your mother to the hospital,' Fred said, 'and Glanna, I am so sorry for what I did. It was unforgivable – I can see that now. I must have been going mad.'

'One second, Freddie. I just need to use the loo, before I leave.' Penelope made her way back inside.

'Once I'd found the painting, you could have just told me then.' Glanna was bemused.

'I kept thinking I should just confess, but the thought of the worry and pain I have caused you, well I just kept playing along. I couldn't bear for you to think badly of me, that was why.' Fred squeezed her arm lovingly. 'I still can't believe I could do such a thing to my own daughter. On the plus side, maybe it will soften the blow with Isaac.'

'I doubt it, but at least you and Mum have seen sense, which makes me happier than anything. You're getting married – that's amazing.' Glanna kissed her father on the cheek, tears of joy smudging the lenses of her big glasses. 'And as for the painting, let's blame love, shall we? It usually has a bloody lot to answer for.'

Chapter 40

'Good heavens! I leave you alone for five minutes and there's a break-in at the gallery, Oliver gets back in touch, wanting to meet, you're in the gutter press as a secret blonde mistress, Isaac has disowned you, and your mother and father are getting married.'

'I know, right.'

'That's a lot to take in. How are you feeling? Take your time.' Myles got up to open one of his front windows. The familiar sound of seagulls came drifting in on the breeze. A sleeping Banksy jerked in a dream and let out a little whiffling sound.

'I have to say my heart is like a bloody collage at the moment,' Glanna said eventually. 'So many parts of it are involved in what's going on.'

'What would you say is the biggest part and affecting you the most?'

Glanna replied without thought, 'Oliver – yes, definitely Oliver. And I am of course devastated that I have upset Isaac. He is such a lovely man and has been through so much.'

'What did Oliver's message say?'

'Oh my God, do you know what, with everything going

on I don't actually know. Sadie simply texted me to tell me he'd called and gave me his number. But what does that matter, Myles? He doesn't want me romantically and we know that, so—'

'He took the time to look up the number and to call you at the gallery though. When was that exactly?'

'Um . . .' Glanna thought back. 'Around the time of the break-in.'

'Before the article making the press?'

'Shit, I didn't even think for one second that Oliver might have seen the article.'

Myles stayed quiet.

'But he'd have mentioned it, surely?'

'We are all different, Glanna.'

'Thank goodness.' She thought about it, feeling a jolt of excitement. 'I need to communicate properly with him and not do the dance of – what did you call it – the dance of intimacy or something like that?'

'Correct. And yes, you do,' Myles said gently.

'The fact I upset Isaac is eating away at me too. I wrote a letter to him explaining what had happened, but I have heard nothing back. I even painted him a small picture of a little girl on a horse, with a bearded man leading her, standing in front of the cliffs, with a rainbow behind them. I posted that to him too.'

'Were you drawing you?'

'No, I had his sister in mind. Weird you say that though.'

'Why weird?'

'Because I feel in a way that I am a child with him.

That I could never be his equal. He is too wise and talented.'

'What would he say if you told him that?'

'He would say I was being ridiculous.'

Myles said nothing.

'I don't know what else to do to reach him. Kevrinek is like a fortress. I can't just pull up to his drive and run in and say sorry. And the cliff path that leads to his house is so dangerous and I'm not sure he'd appreciate me sneaking in the back way, after all the damage I've caused already.'

'Give it time,' Myles suggested. 'He will do what he will do and, when he's ready, if he wants to, he will come to you.'

'It's hard, and I hate the fact that I broke his trust.'

'Mrs Maynard overheard. You didn't actually tell her.'

'Yes, you're right and he does know that now, but I shouldn't have told Mum in the first place.'

'You did what you wanted to do. You hadn't signed anything like a contract in blood with Isaac. It was just his wishes.'

'Which is so much worse,' Glanna said solemnly. 'I broke an unspoken trust.'

'Maybe, but you have done all you can from your side, and you can't force anyone to react the way you want them to, you know that. He knows you are sorry.'

Glanna puffed out heavily. 'By the way, I decided to stop the life drawing classes.'

'You did?'

'Yes. I found out that Mrs Harris was having an affair with Gideon Jones behind Dad's back. I had virtually accused Hayden of theft, and because Sadie is soft on him, she's a bit feisty with me now too. And Jen – well, she thought she wanted to do it, but she didn't really enjoy it. So, it all became a bit pointless really. It was quite hilarious though, especially when Gideon started brandishing a pair of Mrs Harris's crotchless knickers.'

Hearing this, Myles visibly flinched.

Glanna fell about laughing. 'We nearly all fainted when he did that. For me, it was the last straw.'

'Well, you tried something new and were they all OK about it not running its course?'

'I think so. I returned all their money, and it has proved a good lesson. In future I shall stick to painting and concentrate on the gallery. I'm not a very good teacher.' She paused. 'That's Oliver's speciality.'

'Do you think you will try and reach him again?'

'I'm going to listen to his message, for sure.' Then Glanna heard herself blurting out, 'I love that man so much, Myles.'

'Tell me more about that.'

'I don't want to talk about Oliver any more, if you don't mind.' Glanna pushed her glasses back up her nose. 'What I do want to talk about is Mum and Dad. I am so happy they've actually seen sense. And for selfish reasons it takes the pressure off me as Dad now will be nursing her through her new hip.'

'How's she getting on, after the op?'

'Really good. Dad is running around after her like a little puppy dog. When she's not looking through every bridal magazine available, they are spending most of their time watching *Carry On* films, drinking tea and eating ham and cheese toasties. Acting like bloody schoolkids, in fact. She is even going to take his name and has already been on to *Country Lives* to ask if they would like to cover the wedding.'

'What does your dad think about that?' Myles enquired, his eyebrows raised.

'He has no choice.'

They laughed.

'So, it sounds like things are manageable?' Myles asked.

'Yes, I feel all right – much better, in fact. I just need some kind of resolution with both Isaac and Oliver; it's a gnawing pain in my tummy that won't go away.' Glanna made a wry face. 'Seeing my parents sort out their differences after so much heartache – and, I have to say, after some encouragement from me – has made me realise I need to confront this. They've left it so late though and I don't want that to happen to me.'

She groaned. 'I miss Isaac, as much as Oliver. He made me feel alive again.'

'Don't think he won't be thinking about you.'

'You mean that?'

'I know my normal mantra is that we don't know what other people are thinking, but it sounds as if you two have a deep connection.'

'And what if he never forgives me? What do I do then?'

'Give him some time, Glanna. Just give him some time.'

Chapter 41

Her session with Myles over, Glanna was just coming out of Ferry View Apartments when she saw Hayden getting off the *Happy Hart* and making his way back up Ferry Lane towards the market. She half ran to catch up with him. Banksy, enjoying this sudden surge of energy, raced ahead, tugging on the lead.

'Hi,' she said breathlessly.

'What do you want?' With his difficult upbringing, the boy had never suffered fools gladly.

'Hayden. I owe you a huge apology.'

'Yeah, well. Leopards can change their spots, you know. I learned my lesson in that hellhole of an institution – so why would I jeopardise my future any further? I also happen to like you, Glanna, so yeah, it bloody hurt what you said.'

'I just saw the black hoodie on the camera and well . . . I was wrong.'

'Oh, it's all right. Who am I to judge somebody else's mistake? Water under the bridge, eh,' the young lad offered. 'No harm done. Fact is, it's kind of made me and Sadie closer – so that can only be a good thing.' He grinned. 'She's a complete babe.'

'Yes, she is.' Relieved at his response, Glanna relaxed. 'I will talk to her too. She's angry at me for hurting you. Look, Hayden, you told me you've already got your Locals Pass to Tate St Ives and the Barbara Hepworth Museum and Sculpture Garden, but I wondered if you might like a year's membership – with guest – for all of the Tates? That means you and Sadie can go off together to see your favourite exhibitions for free in London and Liverpool if you want. It was going to be the prize for the best life drawing artist before I rudely shut the class, but between you and me, well . . . I know you would have won it hands down, anyway.'

'Really?' She could see the boy's face redden.

'You have a raw talent, Hayden Spargo. In fact, you remind me of a younger version of myself. Oh, to be that person again, knowing then what I know now.' She smiled.

'If you're sure, that would be amazing. Thank you and wow, I can't believe you said that.'

'Believe it – and I really am sure. It will be good for your studies – and who knows? Keep doing what you are doing, and you may be exhibiting in one of the Tates yourself one day in the future.'

'Like Isaac Benson.'

'Just like Isaac Benson,' Glanna nodded.

They reached the back of her gallery. 'I'll email you the details, OK?' she said, so happy to have repaired the relationship with Hayden. 'Have a good evening.'

'You too – and thanks, Glanna. I really appreciate your apology.'

Letting Banksy off his lead at the gate, she opened the stable door. Going through to the gallery she noticed how tidy Sadie had left everything as usual. The till was open and empty, aside from an envelope full of till receipts and the handwritten figure of that day's takings. She was just going through to check the front door was locked properly when her eyes fell on the answerphone. She had to listen to Oliver's voice, to hear exactly what he had said.

Pressing play, she leaned forward intently so as not to miss a single word. The first few messages were just people checking on opening hours, the price of works they had seen in the window, et cetera – and then there it was, the familiar deep, velvety voice of her ex-love. She put her hand to her heart at the uncharacteristic hesitation in his voice.

'*Glanna, hi. I hope this is the right number – anyway, it's Oliver here. You remember, Oliver Trueman, the tall, dark, handsome one from London? Draws a bit, chats a lot?*'

'Yes,' Glanna said aloud, pushing her bottom lip out. 'I remember him.'

'*Right, yeah. It was a shame we didn't get to talk a few weeks ago, and I'd still really like to do that. So, um . . . maybe next time you're in London, we could meet or er . . . I could come down to you. So – please call me, Glanna. I'd love to see your gallery and Hartmouth, your new/old hometown. The best number to get me on is this one.*'

Glanna sat down on the high stool behind the counter, deep in thought. Rightly, the message Sadie had sent her simply said, *Oliver Trueman called,* and gave her his mobile number, but this message said a whole lot more than that. This message said, *I really like you and I don't even mind if I have to come all the way down to Cornwall to see you.* This message meant that whatever was happening in his life, she was still important to him too.

Reaching for her mobile, she brought up his number and, after taking a deep breath to marshal her thoughts before she spoke to him, she was just about to press on his name when the words *Kevrinek Studio* flashed up on her screen. With a fast-beating heart, she picked up immediately and before she could utter a word, the broken voice of Isaac Benson could be heard saying, 'Lizzie is dead, and I don't know what to do.'

Chapter 42

Glanna tore out of Hartmouth and along the coastal road to Penrigan as if her life depended on it. The warm evening spoke of the joys of nature, bringing with it the delicious scents of wildflowers from the hedgerows flying past, and the sight of swallows darting gracefully over the fields in search of flying insects, their long tails tilted. Glanna was relieved that she had grabbed her glasses with the light-adaptive lenses that darkened like sunglasses whenever the light became over-bright. Finally, she pulled into the long narrow track to Kevrinek. As she attempted to mentally prepare herself for the difficult meeting ahead, she looked up and gasped, because appearing as a mirage ahead of her were two things that she adored: firstly, the magnificence of a rainbow, arching in all its glory over the imposing craggy cliffs beyond, and secondly, the figure of Isaac Benson waiting for her at his gate.

'Hi.' He leaned into her little Smart car. His eyes, she saw, were red from crying, and his voice softer than usual.

'Hi.' Glanna felt herself welling up at the sadness exuding through every inch of the man in front of her.

'There's a rainbow,' he said.

'I saw.'

'Follow me to the stables and hop in with me.'

♡

The short rattly drive to Patience's grave took place in silence. It wasn't until they were sitting close by it, side by side on a plastic sheet that Isaac had pulled from the back of his old Land Rover, that he spoke.

'She went in her sleep. Peacefully. Beethoven and I had said goodnight. I even read her a story that night – well, I made one up about Mum and Dad, and Patience and Beethoven, and how much we all loved her. Belle, that's one of Lizzie's nurses, called me at 2 a.m. to tell me she'd gone. I sat with her until the birds started singing, before I called a doctor. I needed a few hours alone before she had to leave me forever.'

'Oh Isaac, I am so sorry for your loss. What a lucky girl to have had you as a brother. You could not have done any more for her – you or your parents, by the sound of it.'

'Those words are kind; grief sadly is not.'

'When did it happen?'

'Three nights ago, now. I have already registered her death and she wanted to be buried in with Patience.'

'Can you do that?'

'Yes, I already enquired with the environmental agency

a long time ago as I want to be buried here too, under this grand old oak, looking out over the ocean. I can't think of a more peaceful resting place. I am conducting a little service right here, on Sunday. I'd like you to come, if you can.' Isaac's deep-set eyes were mirrors of sorrow. 'It will be just me and you.'

'Er, yes, of course. I'd be honoured.' Glanna reached for Isaac's hand. 'I am also truly heartbroken that I put you in that predicament with the press.'

'You are the first person I trusted in a long while,' Isaac said quietly.

'I know.' Glanna ran her hands through her hair. 'That is why it is unforgivable.'

'I got your letter, thank you. I could always have dealt with them writing about us; we knew the truth, so it didn't matter. It was the fact they had to bring my past and Lizzie into it, that is what broke me. I feared that they would start trying to snoop around the back of the house and frighten her.' Isaac was thoughtful for a second. 'It is only a weak man who can never forgive, Glanna. I look at it as cooling the sting.'

'Cooling the sting, wow, that's powerful.'

'You luckily missed my wrath. Belle showed me that pathetic article. I came up here, sat in the rain. Watched the ebb and flow of the water against the craggy rocks below. The skies changing from white to grey to black and back again, and from somewhere a quote from Van Gogh crossed my mind. He spoke of fishermen knowing that the sea is dangerous, yet this does not make them stay ashore. They throw themselves onto the mercy of the sea. What is this thing called life all about, Glanna? I don't know, but I agree with the sentiment of that great artist's words. We need to love, and we need to embrace risk. Sitting up here among the elements, I also realised that there is little place for anger in this life. We just need to live every single precious second that we are given.'

Glanna felt so emotional, to hear those words. She said shakily: 'I was so worried because you stopped painting before and I would hate that to ever happen to you again, and to have been the cause of it. I would never have been able to forgive myself.'

Isaac gripped her shoulder comfortingly. 'Who knows what grief will bring but strangely, once the private ambulance had taken my precious girl away, I went to my studio, hunted out the biggest blank canvas I could find, and I started to paint. I painted for hours without stopping, just sobbing and painting and sobbing and painting until I could do no more of either, then I fed Beethoven and went to bed.'

'You are an amazing man, Isaac Benson, in so many ways.'

'There is something else I need to say to you. Our hug the other day meant a lot. It felt lovely, close, and I really did need it at that moment in time. And don't get me wrong – that kiss was pretty lovely too and like I have said before, love *is* massive. But there are different sorts of love, and at the moment I can only offer you one sort and that is one of a trusting, deep friendship.'

'I understand,' Glanna said, and it was true. 'We talked about it before and it made so much sense. In such a short time, I have come to love you in that way too. I can't explain it, it's as if there has always been a piece of you in me and you have drawn it out and I feel stronger for it.'

'Love.' He held the word on his lips for a second. 'It comes in many guises.'

'Yes, it really does. Sibling love in your instance, parental love, friendship. Romantic love. I even feel some sort of love for my therapist. And I couldn't be without my Banksy.'

'So, when we lose it from any one of those areas, it's hard. Very hard. But with all that other love around us, we will be all right. They will hold us until we are ready to hold ourselves again. I have Beethoven and Beauty, and I hope that you will hang around for a bit too, dear Glanna.' Isaac's voice wobbled slightly.

'The feelings I have for you have also brought my feelings for my ex, Oliver, to the surface. I'm not over him yet, and in fact I don't want to be over him. I was just about to ring him when you called.'

Far from looking hurt, Isaac was visibly relieved. 'The last thing I would want to do is lead you on with anything more,' he said, 'and maybe our meeting has happened for a reason, then? Life and love is all about timing, after all.'

'Isaac, you are so wise and you have made me rethink so many things. Also just spending time in nature, with peace all around us. I haven't even thought to look at my phone when I've been with you. My life, my sobriety, Oliver, my parents . . . everything somehow feels clearer. Oliver was my world, but he wanted to marry me and have children and I couldn't deal with that level of love or commitment. To put it bluntly, I fucked everything up.'

'Can you turn it around?'

'If he's in a relationship, I'm not sure, but what I do know is that I want him to understand how I feel.'

'To be vulnerable.'

'Exactly.'

'So, if Oliver still stated that he would only stay with you if you had a child with him, would you consider it then?'

'This is all so hypothetical, but no. It is not what I want. Motherhood is not for me.' Glanna shrugged and looked out to sea. 'He has a baby now. And if he is with a partner, I don't ever want to be a home-wrecker. I've caused enough destruction during my unruly past. I want him to know that I still love him, and I want to thank him for helping me with my addiction to become the woman I am today.'

'Maybe he knows that already.'

'Maybe.' Glanna went quiet.

'Well, if it's worth anything from a man who hasn't exactly excelled in romantic liaisons, if you and Oliver are done, promise me that you won't give your heart too freely. Place it in the tender hands of a man who will accept every part of you. A man who will see past your imperfections to the point where they're blurred and no longer visible.'

Glanna swooned. 'Isaac Benson, you should be a poet as well as an artist. And what you've just said, you are literally describing Oliver – he is that man. I met him at Brightside House, which is a rehabilitation centre for addicts. He helped to pull me out of the mire. He still teaches art there for the pure love of it, on Sundays and Mondays. That's the kind of man he is.'

'Keats, Wordsworth, Byron, you can't beat the greats when it comes to romance. "Love will find a way through paths where wolves fear to prey." That was Byron, a genius of a wordsmith.'

'I love that.' Glanna felt herself welling up.

'Yes, and do you know, I feel inspired to do a painting based on that subject,' Isaac said. 'Do what you need to do. He'd be a fool not to love you back.'

'Thank you, Isaac, and I am so sorry again about Lizzie slipping away. What time would you like me here on Sunday?' she asked.

'As the sun is rising, please. If you can.'

Chapter 43

Fred Gribble greeted his waiting daughter with a huge smile as he moored up alongside Hartmouth quay in *Ups & Downs*. Banksy's ears pricked up at the familiar male voice's cry of, 'Ahoy me hearties.'

'What a gorgeous day.' Glanna followed him down on to the little boat.

'Yes, your mother could be right with her Indian Summer prediction. Anyway, how was market day, love?'

'It was good. Busier than usual. Now I have Isaac's painting back in the window, it attracts all sorts of people who may not have noticed the gallery before. All his signed prints have gone now, which is fantastic for the business. He does need the painting back though for his upcoming preview exhibition. They'll be wanting to hang it soon, so I was going to ask if I can borrow your van tomorrow to take it to him.'

'I can do that for you if you like, love.'

'No, I need to go to him at sunrise. For his sister's ceremony. So if it's OK with you, I'll drive the van back around the headland after dinner, as the ferry won't be running over here, and I can load up the dolphin picture from the gallery first thing.'

Fred lifted Banksy on board and steadied the little boat as Glanna stepped in and sat on the middle bench seat.

'Sure, that's fine, as long as you can manage on your own.'

'I'll be fine, Dad, the canvas isn't heavy, just awkward.'

'Good. So it won't take us long to get over to Crowsbridge. I think your mother wants to watch a film with you. I've made you both your old favourite. Salmon with a soy and ginger sauce and a big green salad.'

'I can't wait – thanks, Dad. And how's it all going with you two lovebirds?'

'Really well. I'm suggesting she has the other hip done, as she's much easier to manage when she can't move.'

Glanna laughed out loud. 'Dad! You can't say that.'

'I just did. It will be fantastic to go to my club tonight and catch up with everyone. I'm not the best of nurses.'

'I'm sure you are, but it's good that you're getting a break. Have you set a date for the wedding?'

'No, not yet. It'll probably be sometime next year now.'

'At least it's taken the heat off of my birthday.'

'Umm. Yes. Your birthday.'

'Dad, if you know anything, you will tell me what's going on, won't you?'

'Such a lovely evening, isn't it?' Fred steered towards Crowsbridge quay and started to whistle.

'Dad?'

'Having an allegiance to both Pascoe women is quite

a job, I tell you, but fret not, dear daughter. I have your back and that's all I am saying on the matter.'

The little white boat chugged across the estuary where other boat owners were making the most of the late evening sunshine. A couple of wet-suited teenagers on paddleboards screamed as a jet-ski making its way to the harbour from a yacht wobbled their watery path, nearly making them fall off.

'That awful night I took the painting, I put it on the boat,' Fred confessed. 'I turned into a proper criminal. Thought the police would find it harder to trace me if I went the water route.

'And when you told me about the tracker, I panicked so badly.'

'Luckily for you, I threw the tracker in the river.'

'Glanna, why?'

'Because I was mortified for him to find out it might be at my parents' house and I was scared he might show up and then Mum might get on her high horse and be rude. I don't know, it was a terrible time.'

'Does he know now that it was me?'

'No. He's had so much else going on he hasn't even asked about it and being honest, I've been stalling telling him.'

'Will you tell him it was me?'

'That's why I've been holding off.' Glanna sighed. 'But, yes, I will,' she added without hesitation. 'I have to, Dad. He trusts me and I want to be honest with him.'

'I was such a fool, I'm so sorry. What if he presses charges?'

'He won't. He really does hate intrusion of any kind.'

'And I hate all the trouble I've caused. How about you offer him my services if ever he needs them – DIY or anything I can do that he wants me to fix. He only has to call and I will be there. Give him my number. Promise me you will. And promise to say sorry.'

'I promise.'

'How did it go with Oliver? You were calling him last time I spoke to you.'

'He didn't pick up. I left a message, saying I really wanted to talk to him.'

'And?'

'He rang back, and I bloody missed his call, but he left a message saying that things were crazy at the moment, but he promised me he would be in touch and would see me before the month was out.'

'That's OK, isn't it?'

'It's a bit wishy-washy.'

'Well, man to man, that seems reasonable to me and it's not that far away now, is it darling?'

'Glanna, is that you?'

'Yes, Mother. I said goodbye to Dad at the club. Banksy was eager to be with him, so it's just me.' Glanna went through to the huge but cosy kitchen of Riversway. 'Look at you, making dinner *à la* crutch.'

'I know,' Penny said proudly. 'I've got the hang of using them now – positively speedy, I am. Anyhow, I can't claim the credit: your father organised everything for us tonight. He never could make a decent salad dressing though, could he? Carry it all through to the dining room, darling. I thought we'd eat now, and we can choose a film on Netflix when we're ready. Saying that, I'd quite like to watch the first Fifty Shades again if you're up for it? Just for the buns on Jamie Dornan, if nothing else.' She beamed.

Glanna laughed. 'Does my dear father realise what he's got himself back into here?'

'You know I'm only joshing, darling.'

'Good, as I haven't seen him, or you for that matter, this happy for ages.'

Penny Pascoe eased herself awkwardly into the special chair she had bought to use whilst she was recovering, positioned at the end of the long table in the dining room. Candles glowed along the marble mantelpiece and a beautiful display of fresh flowers stood on the table by the French doors. Glanna put the tray of food down and went off to the kitchen to get some plates and the bottle of zero Prosecco she had brought with her.

'It looks beautiful in here, and most importantly feels homely again,' she said, and poured them both a drink. 'Are you OK with no alcohol, Mum?'

'Yes, that's perfect, thank you. I need to be stable until this hip heals itself – and the truth is, I was drinking a bit too much before, and alcohol is so bloody wrinkle-inducing.'

'How are you feeling anyway, Mum?'

'Brilliant, dear. Physically – and more important, mentally. I realise now how much time I wasted chasing something that doesn't even exist. I'm not even sure what exactly I was looking for, when I dated all those younger men. Silly, when what I wanted was right here in front of me all the time.'

'Sometimes we all need a shake-up to wake up,' Glanna said diplomatically.

'True – but how vile that it had to be in the pasty-filled shape of Linda Harris,' Penelope said, then she laughed. 'But hey, whoever said that life was going to be perfect?'

'Well, like I said earlier, I am glad you are both happy now.'

'And what about you, Glanna? Are you happy?'

'I'm doing fine, thanks, Mum. The gallery is flying, and I have new friends in both Jen and Isaac. I'm meeting Oliver sometime this month too, I hope.'

'You hope?'

'Nothing's set in stone yet.'

'Bloody men. If you haven't heard from him in a week, make that date, I say. Men need a push, they don't feel things like we do. Get practical, darling. But he's got a kid and a girlfriend, you say, so don't be his mistress. And don't be wasting any more time, like I did. Such a shame. Oliver is a good man, darling.'

'Mum!' Glanna felt frustration rising within. 'Don't I know that – and even if Oliver suggested an affair, which he wouldn't as he *is* such a good man, I'm far too big to be a bit on the side.'

Penelope slow-clapped. 'Hal-le-bloody-lujah! Let's drink to that.' She raised her crystal champagne flute. 'To my little girl being too big to be a bit on the side.'

Glanna stuck her bottom lip out and sighed.

'How's Isaac Benson doing?' her mother went on. 'What a terrible business with regard to his sister. Do you still see him, after your own flesh and blood stole one of his precious paintings?'

'He's grieving, Mum, so he's sad. I'm going to Kevrinek to say goodbye to Lizzie with him tomorrow,' Glanna explained.

'Oh, a funeral on a Sunday.'

'He's buried her on his land.'

'Oh. Well, if it's good enough for Barbara Cartland.'

'What – *the* Barbara Cartland? Romance novelist extraordinaire, wearer of pink clothes in all shades and lover of honey and vitamin pills?' Glanna laughed.

'Yes. She was laid to rest in a cardboard coffin in the grounds of Camfield Place, her mansion home, under a four-hundred-year-old oak tree which was planted by Queen Elizabeth I herself.'

'How fitting for a romantic novelist.'

'Quite.'

Glanna instinctively looked up at *The End of the Land As We Know It* painting.

'That woman in the painting is Isaac's sister,' she told her mother. 'And you know we discussed the easel that was covered in black silk during the documentary about him, and wondered what was under there?'

'Yes, dear?'

'Well, he started a painting of Elizabeth before she had her terrible accident – and then just couldn't finish it. This figure on the cliff is her, and it's the only one he ever finished of her. What's more, there are no photographs of the painting, or prints, and he didn't even know where it had gone to. It was a great relief for him, to learn where it was.'

'That poor man,' Penelope said, genuinely moved. 'That poor, poor man.'

They ate in silence for a bit, aside from the noises of appreciation for Fred's tasty lasagne and his homemade crusty and buttery French garlic bread.

Penelope Pascoe refilled both their glasses. 'Another toast to you.' She paused for effect. 'I am so proud of you, darling.'

Glanna felt her eyes filling with tears at the words she had longed to hear from her mother her whole life.

'You hit rock bottom and look at you now – you bounced right back up to the top. With not a lot of help from me, might I add. I know I haven't been the best mother.' The woman sniffed loudly. 'And it's taken me this long to realise that money cannot buy happiness, contentment or love.' Tears slowly began to fall down Penelope's cheeks.

'Mum! It's OK.' Glanna rushed to sit by her side.

'It's not OK,' Penelope said. 'I lost my husband and

my parents, and in turn you gained an absent mother. This thing they talk of called love must be made of stronger stuff than I am because I don't think I'd have put up with me the way you and your father have.' She let out a little sob. 'But I'm here now and I'm not going anywhere.'

'Thank goodness for that.' Glanna managed a laugh as she put her arm around her mother. 'Because you're stuck with me and Daddy forever, by the look of it.'

Penelope Pascoe patted Glanna's leg as the screen credits came up for *Fifty Shades of Grey*. 'Now don't you be leaving too late as you've got to be up at some ridiculous hour in the morning.'

A relaxed Glanna stood up and stretched as her mother held her hand out to her. 'Help me up, will you, darling? I've got something for you. Come with me.'

Glanna followed her mother slowly as Penelope made her way on crutches from the cosy little TV room back to the dining room.

'Now, you know you asked me for a print of one of Isaac Benson's paintings for your birthday? Well, I haven't been able to find one yet – like hen's teeth they are, evidently.'

'Mum, my birthday is not for a while yet and I already knew it could be a long shot, asking for that, so honestly don't worr—'

'Shhh, Glanna. I haven't finished.'

Penelope lifted a crutch and pointed it at the magnificent Isaac Benson oil painting which had taken up half a wall of the Riversway grand dining room for so many years.

'*The End of the Land As We Know It*!' Penelope Pascoe announced dramatically. 'I want you to have it. Happy fortieth birthday, my precious Glanna.'

'But, Mum . . .' Glanna was deeply shocked. 'I couldn't possibly.'

'Oh yes you can – and you will.'

'I really don't know what to say.'

'You don't have to say anything.' A tingle of love flew through Glanna from head to toe as her mum then added meaningfully: 'And I want you to do whatever you see fit with it. You hear me?'

Noticing yet another rare glint of a tear in her mother's eye, Glanna nodded furiously. 'I hear you, Mum, loud and clear.'

Chapter 44

Five a.m. Sunday morning and Glanna groaned at the sound of her alarm in the flat above the gallery. Thankful to her parents for keeping Banksy overnight to save her walking him, she jumped in the shower, slurped down a coffee, then loaded her dad's van ready for her journey. Sunrise was at 6.42 a.m. precisely, and there was no way she could be late.

Swearing because she had forgotten the flowers that Kara had lovingly prepared for her, she ran back upstairs, grabbed them then, checking her watch for the tenth time, started the van and headed off down past Frank's Café and on to the coast road for her forty-minute drive to Penrigan Head.

It felt strange driving in the dark, even though it was clearly morning, the semi-light tricking her body into thinking she should still be in bed. Yawning loudly, she put on Bowie at full blast to keep her awake, then sang with him as she sped along the quiet lanes until she reached the gate of Kevrinek and saw Isaac waiting for her. Guarding the entrance as if his life depended on it, he looked surprised to see a van approaching then, on seeing a waving Glanna, he made the familiar gesture with his arm to follow until she reached the stable block and jumped into the old Land Rover beside him.

'Remind me I've got something for you in the back of the van, before I go.'

'My dolphin painting?' he asked, unsurprised.

'Yes.'

'I knew it would come home.'

She rested the huge bunch of brown-paper-wrapped flowers on her lap and kissed him on the cheek. Beethoven sat in the footwell and licked her hand.

They made their bumpy way across the fields towards Patience's and now Lizzie's resting place.

'I buried her myself,' Isaac said, 'so we are just saying a peaceful goodbye now.'

Glanna imagined how much physical and mental strength it must have taken for Isaac to dig the grave and lift his beloved sister into the earth to join her much-loved pony. She also felt relieved that she had not been asked to witness the whole burial. She had only ever been to two funerals in her life before, those of her dad's parents, but the grief had been easily managed on her side as the couple were both in their eighties, and had lived a long life. Their deaths had been in the right order of things, plus she had drunk herself into oblivion in the months that followed. Or in Isaac's words, 'the alcohol had tasted better than tears' and she had literally drowned her sorrows.

As they reached the fresh mound of earth, dawn and the rising sun awoke the birds, who began to sing rapturously. The branches of the big oak above swayed and rustled in the light morning breeze. Beethoven, sensing that something solemn was afoot, lay down at their feet. And as the fiery sun rose above the horizon, spreading its glory on the ocean below, Isaac cleared his throat and started to recite.

'My dear, darling Lizzie. You were a light shining bright in this natural landscape. A joy to behold for our parents, Elizabeth and Ernest. The best sister a brother could ask for. I come here today with my dear friend Glanna, not to say "farewell" but "see you later". And may your young and vibrant spirit fly as free as a bird, your twinkling laughter jump from cloud to cloud and your happiness continue as far as the mind can see.'

His voice cracked slightly. 'Run free, sweet Lizzie. Run free.'

Isaac knelt down and placed a bunch of sweet peas on the mound of earth, Glanna following suit with her flowers in this simple but profound message of love. Isaac then stood and reached for the wooden cross with its hand-engraved brass plate and, with a mallet, he knocked it into the ground beside the grave in one sure strike. This new cross, replacing the original one for Patience, now read: *Lizzie & Sweet P, a girl and her horse, together forever.*

Glanna instinctively put her arms around Isaac. They stood there, joined together for what seemed like forever. The sea breeze whipping around them, the sense of Isaac's loss stronger than the early morning sun. A shared action of compassion so great, confirming that their love may be platonic, but it was as deep as the sea swirling below.

♡

'Here, let me help you get the painting out. I know it's not heavy, but those canvases are awkward as they are so big.' Isaac opened the back of Fred Gribble's Transit van. Glanna leaped up inside the van and carefully shifted the painting towards the doors. Unwrapping it from the blanket protecting it, Isaac smiled and exclaimed, 'Here she is! Am I pleased to see you!'

'I thought you didn't care about it.' Glanna was surprised.

'I could sense how distressed you were, and didn't want to make you feel worse.' He ran his hands along the back of it. 'The blighters threw away the security tag. So much for my cunning plan to always be able to know where my paintings ended up.'

'Isaac, my dad stole the painting. And like you with me, I forgave him. It cooled *my* sting.' Glanna attempted a watery smile.

Isaac was taken aback, then said, 'It takes a desperate man to steal from his daughter, the poor fellow.'

'He did it for love.'

'Then I need know no more.'

'He is back with my mother, which is a blessing for

me too. He says to convey his apologies for the worry caused, and I am to give you his number as he wishes to make reparation. If there is anything at all that he can help you with, whether it be DIY or gardening, or maybe even creating something from wood, he is your man and at your service.' Glanna scribbled down Fred's number in the little pad she always carried in her bag, ripped off the page, and handed it to Isaac, who put it in his shorts pocket.

She then halted, and looked him in the eyes, saying, 'Um, Isaac, there is something else in the van for you too. It's quite big so you may want to get it out yourself.'

Isaac gazed at her quizzically, then climbed into the van to find another huge canvas wrapped in brown paper like *Safety in Numbers* had been when he had sent it to her. He carefully undid one corner, then seeing part of the girl in the white dress with her hair flowing behind her, he ripped open the rest and stood transfixed, gazing at his sister as she had once been. Stepping slowly down from the back of the van, his legs shook and he needed to hold Glanna's hand for support. Tears were streaming down the big man's face.

'I can't,' he wept.

'You must.' Glanna was near to tears now too. 'My mother giving this to me for my birthday, knowing I would give it to you, was the best thing she has ever done in both of our lives. This painting belongs here at Kevrinek, nowhere else.'

'I love you.' Isaac nodded furiously.

341

'And I love you too.'

At that point, Beethoven dashed out of the house barking in greeting, and started running around their legs, no doubt looking for his pal Banksy.

'And we both love you, mister.' Glanna fussed his ears. Then, looking at Isaac: 'Will you stay on here, do you think?'

Shrugging his shoulders, Isaac looked out to the cliffs beyond. 'Where else would I want to be?'

'Yes, what a stupid question that was.'

'And . . .' he paused and looked bashful, 'you know what I said about Lizzie's nurses being angels – well, Belle has asked if I could give her some painting lessons and . . . it's early days but she's very sweet.'

'Hearing that makes my heart happy,' Glanna said and she meant it. 'Right, let's get these paintings into your studio and I will leave you in peace with your thoughts.'

'Giving me back the painting with my precious Lizzie on it is the most wonderful thing that anyone has ever done for me. Thank you, and for coming today, Glanna. It meant the world.'

'And I wouldn't have missed it for the world.'

'And don't you be forgetting my little Tate Preview Exhibition at the Penrigan Arts Centre.'

Glanna laughed. 'Try keeping me away. I will be there with artistic bells on.'

Chapter 45

'So, Markus is moving down here already? That was some blow job, girl.' Glanna laughed, then sipped on her macchiato innocently.

'Well, I say he's moving down here . . .' Overhearing talk of fellatio and without catching their eyes, Mrs Harris put menus down on their window table in Monique's as Jen continued, 'The new Wimbledon pad fell through, and he has also been contemplating a seaside place for us to retire to, so he's going to buy somewhere up on Penrigan Head.'

'Nice.'

'Isn't it, just? Five bedrooms, large sea-facing terrace and a leafy garden. It will be lush, and obviously when he's not here, you – and Banksy, of course – can come and stay any time. It will be a great party house too. Happy me, happy families all round.'

'Great for Kara, Billy and the kids too. They are still in their estuary flat at the moment, aren't they?'

'Yeah, although they are thinking of moving soon, into Bee Cottage actually. Dad and Pearl want to go travelling so Kara and Billy are planning to rent out their Ferry View apartment and look after the cottage, whilst the olds spread their wings for a while.'

'What about Bob the Dog?'

'He comes with the cottage.'

'Ah, so sweet, and as compromises go that's a pretty good one for you and your dad. Joe can leave the cottage in good hands and he must be so pleased to know you'll be settling locally and buying a place in Penrigan, even if you and Markus aren't there together all the time.'

'Yes. Like I've said before, life isn't two point four kids, a mortgage and a gravel drive any more. People may not think it is a perfect scenario, but it is the perfect scenario for us. Markus can be a miserable old bastard sometimes, but he's my miserable old bastard and I wouldn't change him for the world.'

Jen changed tack. 'So, Glanna Pascoe, what's happening with you, then? I feel like I haven't seen you for ages.'

'All right, ladies, what can I get you?' Mrs Harris, still feeling a little guilty for cheating on Fred with Gideon, directed the question at Jen.

Glanna answered. 'A warm traditional Cornish pasty for me, please, and another coffee. Oh, and Dad's getting married, by the way.'

'Really? To whom? He doesn't mess about, your father, that's for sure.'

'Shock, horror – to my mother. You did them a favour by going off with Gideon, so you really don't have to ignore me. It's all good.'

Mrs Harris shuffled from foot to foot. 'Me, ignore? I'm happy he's happy. Jenifer, what about you?'

'I'm not getting married if that's what you mean.' They

all laughed as Jen handed the woman her menu. 'I'll have a traditional pasty too and a strawberry milkshake please. Now back to you,' Jen said to her friend as Linda plodded over to the counter.

'Isaac invited me to say goodbye to his sister on the clifftops. It was beautiful and sad all at the same time. Just me and him, up there in the elements at the end of Penrigan Head.'

'You must be really important to him.'

'Yes, and he to me.'

'I can't believe you didn't try to shag him, Glanna.'

'Nor me.' Glanna laughed. 'The old Glanna would have made an attempt at first sight, but no, we have a deeper connection than that. I think a lifelong friendship with him will be far more fulfilling than the twists and turns of a romantic rollercoaster.'

'I just got an invite through the door to his little preview exhibition, entitled: *Rainbows: A Sense of Porpoise* with a special guest artist.'

'Yes, me too,' Glanna nodded. 'It looks as though he painted the flyers himself – they really are beautiful. Bit miffed though, as he's nicked my rainbows theme.'

'I'd take it as a compliment if I were you. Maybe the actual Banksy is the special guest and is going to reveal himself, after all the joint press they got.'

'Not funny, Jenifer, not funny at all.'

On seeing Glanna approaching the gallery, Sadie ran to the front door to open it.

'Morning!' The young girl gave her a wide smile; she seemed out of breath.

'Everything OK?'

'Yes, yes. I've just been unpacking some boxes of ceramics from Sally Jefferson. I think she must have felt guilty as there's a note inside reducing the commission she wants from you. I locked the front door and forgot to open it again. Oops.'

Glanna noticed some obvious gaps on the whitewashed gallery walls. 'Wow, it looks as if you've been a busy girl selling already. A few of mine seem to have gone too, is that right?'

'Yes, yes. I was just going to tell you. Henry Hall, the general manager of the Dolphin, literally just came in and actually took six of them. I couldn't believe it, as he already bought five for the dining room at the hotel before, didn't he? He wants to position them first and see if they all fit in the lobby before he pays. I hope you don't mind,' Sadie said, looking nervously at Glanna. 'I said that was OK.'

'Of course, that's brilliant.' Glanna grinned. 'It'll be the Penrigan View Hotel next, if they'll have me. And when Henry comes back to pay, we must include a bulk discount.'

'Yes! That's what I thought.'

'And Sadie?'

'Yes?'

'Everything's been so crazy I haven't had the chance to properly apologise about the Hayden incident and for stopping the art group so suddenly.'

'It's fine,' the girl said. 'I know there was so much going on for you with the stolen painting and your parents and Isaac's sister. And to be honest the art group was fun but not exactly serious, was it? I'll need to keep going to the life classes at college where I'll learn more – oops, sorry, that's no slur on your teaching.'

Glanna laughed. 'I hear you. Maybe I should have just advertised it as a dating event. I don't think I will *ever* get over the sight of Gideon with those red crotchless knickers.'

It was Sadie's turn to laugh.

'And it's not fine,' Glanna went on. 'There was no excuse for me being so mean to Hayden and also, I've been putting on you so much lately. I hope you can make the most of the Tate visits with Hayden and I'm aware you'll be back to university soon but I'd also like to offer you a twenty-pound-a-day pay rise for all your hard work on the days you can fit in for me before Christmas.'

The young woman beamed. 'Aw, thanks, Glanna, you really don't have to do that.'

'Yes, I do. You are a great asset to the gallery and a gifted artist too. How's it going with Hayden anyway?'

Sadie blushed. 'Good. I really like him.'

'Excellent.' Glanna noticed a pile of flyers in the front window advertising Isaac's preview exhibition at the Penrigan Arts Centre. 'These are everywhere. I think it's really good that he is doing a local preview, so that his local fans can get to see his work, without having to travel to St Ives if they don't want to. I can't wait to see who his mystery guest is – so weird that he's keeping it a surprise and wouldn't tell me. Oh well.'

She turned to Sadie. 'Are you and Hayden going to come along?'

Sadie nodded brightly. 'Definitely. OK, I'd better get on and finish what I was doing out the back.'

Glanna looked around the gallery and felt a sense of clarity and zen. Sales were going well, her parents were at last happy together and Isaac was feeling well enough after Lizzie's death to carry on with his exhibition. Jen and Markus had sorted their lives out, meaning that Glanna had a lovely new friend close to hand, and she had secured her forgiveness with both Sadie and Hayden. By fixing her troubled mind and overcoming addiction without a man in sight, she had also found a deep peace, inner strength and the feeling that she could now tackle anything thrown at her. If she could now just find out where Oliver Trueman's heart lay, then (dare she say it?) her life would at last, after nearly forty years of living it, feel complete.

Chapter 46

Glanna waved from the *Hart*mouth Gallery window as she spotted her parents pulling up outside to collect her for the journey to the Penrigan Arts Centre.

'Good, good, she looks gorgeous. I knew she would,' Penelope Pascoe said under her breath from the passenger seat of the old family Bentley that had been gaining dust in its Riversway garage for the past forty years.

Fred opened the back door to his daughter as if he were a proper chauffeur. 'Your carriage awaits, modom.'

Glanna laughed. 'What's all this? We are only going to an art preview, not the bloody Ritz.'

'I love your trouser suit, darling,' Penelope Pascoe said to distract her. 'You look stunning.' Glanna had teamed her smart red two-piece with a crisp white shirt done up to the neck, and high black ankle boots. She had chosen her trendy thick-framed black spectacles and a small black clutch bag to finish off her outfit. 'I need to look the part for Isaac, it's a special day for him,' she explained.

'How's your hip, Mum?'

'So much better, thank you. I'm using just the one crutch now, but they said it'll be six weeks before I can run a marathon, so I'm nearly there.'

The three of them laughed.

The old Bentley sped along the coastal road to Penrigan with Glanna thinking how lovely it was to be a passenger for a change, allowing her to take in the beautiful scenery on this crisp and sunny September morning. She put her head back on the leather seat, breathing in the distinctive aroma of 'old car', and sighed contentedly. Here she was with her parents, now very much together, on her way to an exhibition by a person and artist she adored, and to top it all Oliver had texted her at 8 a.m. to say that he had one important event to attend in his diary that morning and he would be in touch later that day.

Penrigan seemed to have a buzz about it today. The high street was very busy for a Monday and as they turned the corner to the Arts Centre, Glanna let out a little gasp. For right in front of them, in big wording on a long white banner stretched across the whole of the brickwork, was a picture of a giant rainbow with the words:

Rainbows: A Sense of Porpoise by Isaac Benson with special guest artist, Glanna Pascoe.

A queue of at least seventy people were waiting outside for it to open.

'What the . . .?' Glanna was open-mouthed.

'We are so proud of you, darling,' Penelope Pascoe said emotionally. 'Now, remember: tits, eyes and teeth. There are photographers here and everything.'

'I'll go and park round the back with your mother,' Fred said. 'You go on in, pet.'

Taking a deep breath, Glanna got out of the car.

'That must be her,' a member of the waiting crowd whispered to her mate.

'Yeah, she looks like the one in the article.'

'A lot prettier in the flesh though.'

With a security guard ushering her to a side door, Glanna made her way to the exhibition room to be greeted not only by a beaming Isaac, dressed beautifully in a stylish tartan suit, waistcoat and bow tie included, but also by Jen and Markus, and Hayden and Sadie. Surrounding them were the six paintings that Sadie had told her had gone to the Dolphin but more importantly, in pride of place alongside *Safety in Numbers* on the stage where Isaac was to do a short talk, were two paintings that were very special to her; the one she had drawn in Isaac's cave, that he had insisted on keeping, plus the tiny sketch of him leading Lizzie along the clifftops on Patience. Glanna put her hand to her heart as she greeted him.

'Why?' was all she said.

'Because you have a gift and I want people to see it.'

'I do it for love, not the fuss.'

'As do I, but when one is lucky enough to possess a talent, as we do, Glanna, it would be selfish not to share it with others. And now that dear Lizzie has passed and it's just me to worry about, this whole side of things somehow is not so daunting.'

Penelope and Fred were now in the room. 'Three cheers for my beautiful daughter!' her mother cried out, lifting her crutch to reveal that it was faux-diamond-encrusted.

'Mum, not now – and Sadie, you little minx. I thought you were behaving a bit oddly the other day when you told me the paintings had been sold.'

'Your dad had literally just left with them and was sneaking out of the back door.'

'He's good at that.' Isaac winked and Fred looked like he wanted to fall through the floor.

Isaac noticed and went on: 'In fact, Glanna, your father has been amazing with his help in getting all this together in such a short time.' Fred's face reddened with the praise.

Rochelle, the smart-looking Arts Centre manager, arrived and took Glanna and Isaac to the side. 'So, the public will be let in at eleven, your talk is at twelve until twelve thirty, Isaac, and then I will take you two through for a press chat in a private room from twelve thirty until one thirty. Are you OK with that?'

Isaac nodded then looked to Glanna. 'Are you?'

'Yes, but what if they ask us about us – you know, that stupid newspaper gossip thing.'

'Then I will answer them,' Isaac replied firmly. He turned to Rochelle. 'You organised the VIP press pass for the guest I mentioned, I take it?' he enquired.

'Yes, it's all been done for you, Mr Benson. Now let's get this show on the road, shall we?'

The morning flew by in a haze of questions, answers, selfies and utter pride for Glanna and everyone who knew her. Even Myles had sneaked in without a fuss with his husband and winked at her as Glanna went up on the stage for a question-and-answer session with Rochelle right after Isaac had finished speaking.

Afterwards, as they both sat at a table waiting for the *Hartmouth Echo* reporter and a few national journalists to walk in the room, Isaac whispered to Glanna, 'Unlike me, you're a natural at this lark.'

'Hardly,' she giggled nervously, 'but I can't thank you enough. This whole thing is beyond my wildest dreams.'

A slightly harassed Rochelle appeared at the door. 'All set for the press?'

'Oh yes. Unleash the beasts,' Isaac said good-humouredly.

Relieved that all press present seemed to be generally interested in the exhibition and that all questions were art-related and not personal, Glanna began to relax into the event. Isaac was right – she found she was a natural.

'OK, time's nearly up, so let's make the next one the last question from the floor, please,' Rochelle announced. There was a shuffling of seats, so Glanna didn't hear the door at the back of the room opening or even notice a figure walking in. In fact, it wasn't until the tall, dark and handsome latecomer spoke that she looked up and gasped.

'My question to Miss Pascoe is that, following on from the dreadful scandal that she was apparently involved in with Mr Benson, is she in fact still single?'

'You don't have to answer that,' Isaac's agent, who was standing to the side of the room, said hastily. Glanna ignored her. Isaac was trying not to smirk.

'Yes, she very much is.' Glanna could feel her heart sing and her tummy do a somersault.

'Then I wonder if she would like to have dinner with me this evening?'

Glanna's face glowed. 'Yes, I do believe she would.'

A jubilant Oliver came up to shake Isaac's hand and to stand beside his beloved.

Everybody laughed at the similarity to the scenario from one of Glanna's favourite films, *Notting Hill*, starring the wonderful Hugh Grant and Julia Roberts.

Glanna and Oliver couldn't stop smiling as photographers jostled to get a shot of the happy couple to ensure a great feel-good follow-up story from the untruths that had been published before.

With Oliver and Isaac going off together to find them all a drink, Glanna was just about to go and look for her parents when a familiar face appeared in the doorway.

'Myles!' Her face lit up. 'I was so happy to see you in the audience.'

'Slightly unprofessional, I know, but I couldn't not come and support you or leave today without saying how proud I am of you.'

'Who'd have thought it, eh? Following my dreams in more ways than one.'

'It takes a lot of hard work to turn those dreams into reality. You should be proud of yourself. And, I take it from your description of him, that was Oliver who just passed me in the corridor.'

Glanna grinned. 'We are having dinner later.' Her eyes

suddenly filled with tears. 'Myles, I don't know how I can ever thank you enough. I wouldn't be here if it wasn't for you.'

'Like I've said, it takes courage to walk inside a therapist's door and you did this all by yourself.'

'Yeah right! This is so hard to say but I think it's time to break from our sessions now. I feel so much better. But if I do need to come and see you, I still can, can't I?'

Myles replied softly, 'I'm always here.' Coughing to hide his emotion, he put his arm on hers. 'Good luck, Glanna. You've done so so well.'

Isaac crossed Myles in the doorway on his way out.

'Who was that?'

'Oh. Just someone who knows me better than I know myself.'

Without question, Isaac handed her a glass of fake fizz and they chinked glasses.

'You thought of everything.' Glanna grinned. 'Where's Oliver?'

'Your mother has kidnapped him.'

They both laughed.

'Today really did have a sense of porpoise, didn't it?' Isaac Benson teased her.

'I don't know what to say.' Glanna suddenly felt humbled in this beautiful man's presence.

'If we could say it in words, there would be no reason to paint.'

'Edward Hopper?' Glanna replied, smiling.

Isaac put his finger on her nose. 'Edward Hopper.'

Chapter 47

Oliver had insisted that they get a taxi to the Penrigan View Hotel, where he immediately relayed the news about Clarence and his extended family to a relieved and happy Glanna.

'Is this OK for you?' Oliver asked tentatively as they sat down at the terrace restaurant.

'Dinner in a fancy hotel overlooking the sea with a handsome man – what's not to like?'

'I can't stop staring at you.' Oliver poured some water into her glass from the jug on the table. 'You look so different, and I don't mean in your appearance, as you always look great. It's the way you are holding yourself now, so confident, so self-assured. It's incredibly sexy. You blew me away at that exhibition. Your painting has improved so much too.'

'Oh my God, Oliver,' Glanna laughed. 'Really?'

'Really, on all counts.' He leaned across and took her hand. Glanna squeezed it.

'I am so happy you have a son, it's what you always wanted. But I can't believe I got it so wrong. Seeing you with one of Clarence's mums and Clarence is a prime example of "one must never assume". How ridiculous was I?'

'Not ridiculous at all. You saw us and your head told you everything you feared might happen and you believed it.'

Oliver added a little reproachfully, 'It was just a shame you didn't show up at the station the next morning and I could have explained.'

Glanna assumed an officious voice. '"We do what we do," said the therapist.' They both laughed.

'All this time we have wasted,' Glanna said sadly, then added, 'Actually, Isaac said that time is never wasted if you've learned from it.'

'And Isaac is a wise man. Have you learned from it, do you think?'

'Yes, and I'm so happy that Isaac is now in my life. He is a true friend.'

'Pretty handy as a sidekick too. What a dude for organising all that today, not only showing your work but filling me in on what was going on.'

'He contacted you?' Glanna was wide-eyed.

'Yep. How else would I have known that you were doing this today?'

'What did he say?'

'He said that if you started asking questions, to remember how private he is and that our conversation should remain that way.'

Glanna laughed out loud. 'He knows me so well. I'd have loved to have been a fly on the wall during *that* conversation.'

'When I left that first message for you, I honestly was

ready to tell you how I felt and then I saw that article in the papers and stupidly believed it, without hearing it from the horse's mouth. When you messaged me back, I was cool as a cucumber as I didn't want to put my heart on the line, nor your happiness.'

'Oh Oliver, I can't believe you are here.' Glanna buttered her bread roll. She said happily, 'Clarence looked such a cute and squidgy baby. And he looks so much like you.'

'He really is. I can't wait for you to meet him.'

'So do you see him much?'

'I see him a lot. That was part of the deal. Katie and Ellie are such great women and the whole situation is working out better than we could have imagined. They will have him living at theirs, but we have a rota that fits with us all. For example, when they go on their honeymoon for a week, I will take a week off and have him. Clarence is used to it – it's his "normal". He has two mums and a dad, and two bedrooms, one at theirs and one at mine. The common denominator is pure love, so it works perfectly for us all really.'

'I'm so pleased for you.'

'Let me show you him now, he's grown so much.'

Glanna oohed and aahed as Oliver showed her some photos of his little lad. Putting his phone back down on the table he said, 'Now come on, let's order some food, shall we?'

As they ate and fell into easy-going chatter, the sun started to sink as silently as it had risen. Pretty fairy lights now shone around the picturesque hotel terrace and a smartly uniformed waiter asked if they wanted the outside heater put on, to which they both nodded.

'I had a whole speech planned for when we did eventually meet.' Glanna sighed. 'It took me so long to rehearse it over and over in my head that I have to say it to you.'

'What – now?'

Glanna nodded earnestly and Oliver couldn't help but smile.

'Shhh.' Glanna closed her eyes for a moment to ready herself.

'Oliver Melvin Trueman,' she began, then cleared her throat to release the words that had been trapped for far too long. 'I made a huge,' she put her arms out wide to her sides, 'and I mean *huge* mistake in letting you go like that. And I am truly sorry.' She looked down. 'I said the most dreadful things, but I realise now it was fear talking, not fact. Everything inside of me was telling me to protect myself. Not let myself go back to you, because I felt *I* wasn't enough.'

Oliver leaned forward to kiss her forehead. He had prayed that his beloved girl would take stock and think about that awful day when she had cheated on him. He knew there was nothing he could say to make her realise that they should be together. He just had to wait it out and hope that, with help, her troubled mind would eventually work it out for herself.

The relief and love he was feeling for this woman now was so intense, he could feel the stinging of tears as his emotion took over his senses.

'The truth is, I have wanted to do this every day for the last two years. Oliver, I've never known love like I do when we are together. And, if you'll still have me, let's fill a blank canvas with love, light, colour and happiness.'

Oliver stood up, pulled her up towards him and crushed her in his arms. 'Oh Glanna, of course I'll have you. I've never stopped loving you, you know that. You're attractive, eccentric, kind, talented, troubled . . . well, actually no, not troubled any longer, because look at you! Right here is a new, emotionally available version of the woman I first met in the corridor at Brightside House, and I love her, just the same as the original.'

'Wait, don't say you'll have me yet, because this is the really hard bit.'

Glanna moved a little away from him, and her voice was wobbly when she spoke again.

'Oliver, I don't want to have children. I've thought about it a lot. I can't see myself as a mother to our own child now. We have to face it – I'm almost forty, so a dinosaur in this baby-making lark. And seeing you with Clarence made me feel a great sense of relief, that you have the child you've always wanted and I don't have to hold the responsibility for that part of your happiness any longer. If you'll let me, I'll do my best to be in his life, when it's your turn to look after him. And I want to do this, not just for you or for me but for us. The three of us.'

'That's fine.' Oliver held her closely.

'Are you sure?' Glanna cocked her head to the side and assumed her doe-eyed look. 'You really mean it – you're not just saying that?'

'Glanna, no games, never any games with me and you; from now on, just pure honesty. I've been thinking about it too. I said it was you I loved, and now I have Clarence, it's made me realise that life isn't so straightforward. It's how *you* feel about having our own little ready-made family with Clarence that is important now. We wouldn't have him all of the time, but he is a huge part of my life and I hope you can fall in love with him, like I have.'

'He's half of you, so how could I not?'

'That's perfect.' Oliver brushed his lips with hers.

'We will be a family of four as I have a baby of my own of sorts, Banksy. My little whippet. I can't wait for you to meet him. He's such a good boy.'

'Oliver, Glanna, Clarence and Banksy, I can see it on the Christmas cards already.'

They both laughed.

'I'm so happy things have turned out this way.' Glanna couldn't keep the grin from off her face.

'Me too. I wasn't sure how it was going to pan out, so I booked a room here, just in case you ran a mile.'

'Then what the hell are we doing standing out here in the bloody cold?'

Their lovemaking had been frantic at first, full of missing, of wanting. Then it changed to tender and caring, soft and considerate.

'If I had a paddle, like the judges do in *Strictly*, I'd be holding up a ten.' Glanna pushed her sweaty face into Oliver's neck and gave it a huge noisy kiss.

'God, I've missed you,' Oliver groaned.

Glanna put her arms around the firm naked torso of her beau, then pressing her cheek into his smooth chest, she inhaled the sweet smell of safety and peace. 'We need to discuss where we are going to live.' Her voice held a pang of concern.

'Together, we will work it all out,' Oliver said gently. 'Me.' He brushed her lips. 'And you.'

Glanna kissed him lovingly on the forehead. 'I'm so sorry I've caused you such pain.'

'What is it they say, whoever *they* are? "You can't have a rainbow without the rain." And how boring life would be if it was sunshine all of the time.'

Glanna rested up on one elbow and replied, 'And Dad telling me that rainbows end in Ferry Lane Market just isn't true. You are my happy ending, Oliver Trueman, and my rainbow ends with you.'

Epilogue

'Come on, Glanna, we're going to be late,' Oliver shouted up the stairs from the Hartmouth Gallery as he fixed his bow tie.

'I'm just putting Banksy's jewelled collar on,' she called back. 'He needs to look the part too.'

Glanna checked herself in the mirror. Forty today. She looked pretty good, if she said so herself. After not drinking for so long, her skin was clear and youthful, and now that she had Oliver back in her life, her brown eyes sparkled with happiness behind her trademark big spectacles.

She walked slowly down the stairs, her ankle-length dark green velvet dress accentuating her long and lean figure, and her high heels bringing her to eye level with her handsome boyfriend.

'Wowee.' Oliver kissed her on the cheek to avoid smudging her bright red lipstick. 'You look out of this world.'

'And you'd give Idris Elba a run for his money in that tux, I tell you.' She lovingly put her hand under his chin and gave it a little squeeze. 'I am so glad that Mum wasn't up for arranging a huge party at Riversway. Dinner at the Dolphin is far more manageable.'

As she locked the front door to the gallery, she heard music drifting up from the harbour front, but not any old music . . . if she was not mistaken, it was the undeniable din of a full-on Mexican mariachi band.

'Oh my God, no!' she exclaimed.

Oliver's shoulders were shaking with laughter. 'You didn't really think she'd let you off with some quiet affair, now did you?' He grabbed her hand. 'Don't worry, we've got this.'

'Surprise!' everybody shouted as Glanna, Oliver and Banksy arrived at the fairy-lit terrace of Frank's Café. Outdoor heaters were on full blast and the whole area had been decorated with bunting and lights of every colour. A rainbow-shaped banner with *Happy 40th Glanna* hung across the entrance to the cafe. The four-piece mariachi band were resplendent in their charro outfits: elegant, snugly tailored black suits and waistcoats, extravagantly trimmed with embroidery and silver buttons, and worn with a soft tie, and wide-brimmed sombrero. Playing with gusto, they were in full noisy flow, their positive energy lifting the already excitable crowd.

'Kara, so lovely to see you.' Glanna kissed the pretty redhead on the cheek.

Kara was grinning like a Cheshire cat. 'It's my first night to be out having fun. I wouldn't have missed it for the world. Dad and Pearl are babysitting, so hurrah for that.'

Billy came over and grabbed his wife around the waist. 'Come on, Mrs D, let's party – or maybe we should just go home and shag like rabbits.'

'Billy Dillon!' Kara blew a kiss back to Glanna as her exuberant and tipsy husband whisked her away for a dance.

Star came over to Glanna and handed her a card and a tiny crystal in a little gauze bag. She nodded her head towards Oliver. 'I told you it was the right time for you for a lot of things, didn't I?'

'All that mumbo jumbo,' Glanna joshed.

'Well, that little stone in there is a Blue Tiger's Eye. You don't even have to look up what it means, but it had your name on it. Put it by your bed, or in a pocket. Happy Birthday, Glanna, and I wish you all the happiness for the future. Cheers!'

'Thanks, Star, and I still love driving that car of yours. Best thing I ever did, buying it from you. What are you doing, just drinking water? There's plenty of champagne by the look of it.'

Star pointed down to a growing bump. 'Oops, we did it again.' They both laughed.

'Aw, congratulations. Where is Jack?'

'He was getting Matthew down to sleep, then Skye was going to take over the babysitting duties. Here he comes now.'

Sadie and Hayden appeared from nowhere, they were both already well on their way to being drunk. The young girl handed her a card. 'We love you, Glanna, we do,' she sang out of tune. 'Happy Birthday to you and thanks for getting us together.'

Oliver took Glanna to the side and embraced her, saying, 'How are you doing?'

'I'm fine. And you?'

'I couldn't be happier, and that's the truth.' He tenderly kissed her forehead.

'Sorry to break up the love-fest.' Penelope Pascoe appeared from nowhere.

'Mother! I was looking for you.'

'You know me, I was scurrying around being the hostess with the mostess.'

'Scurrying being the appropriate word,' her daughter noted. 'Your hip is obviously fixed.'

'Yes, I feel like a teenager again. Me and your father, well . . .'

Glanna put her hand up to stop her. 'Too much information. I'm just happy you are both getting on so well.'

Fred turned up and kissed his daughter on the cheek. 'I did try and stop her organising all this, but you know what she's like. Happy Birthday, darling.'

'Well, you did say you wanted a mariachi band down at Frank's, so that's what you got, darling, and I promise you, there's not a Penhaligon or St John-Davis in sight. They can all keep their pesky opinions to themselves, the lot of them, and if my daughter wants a cheap band and burgers in a harbourside cafe, then so be it.'

Penelope Pascoe took a sip from her plastic champagne flute and made a face. 'I was even persuaded to use these.'

'Did you invite Isaac?'

'Of course. I have a card at home for you. He sent his good wishes and apologies for his absence but he'd booked a holiday to the Shetland Isles with someone called Belle, I think he said.'

'Aw, that's made my day.'

'So darling, about your present?'

'Mum, the painting was the best present you could ever have given me.'

'But you had to give that away. So, I discussed it with your father, of course, but we've completely decorated the lodge, for you and Oliver.' She tapped the big man's arm firmly. 'Oof, those muscles.'

'Get off, he's all mine.' Oliver smirked as Glanna went on, 'That is so amazing, the surprise about the lodge. Thank you, Mum and Dad. So much.'

'And we've set up a nursery for Clarence there too.' She handed Fred her glass and reached for her phone. 'Look.' A photo of a little boy's bedroom with pictures of animals and trains on the walls, and a cot decorated with teddy bears, with a tiny bed close by for when he got older, was flashed in front of their eyes. 'Your father made the crib, Glanna, and I chose the colour scheme. That is your Cornwall house now, if you would like it.' Penelope handed over two keys with a rainbow ribbon on each.

Glanna reached for Oliver's hand and looked into his eyes for confirmation. He gently nodded.

'I am so touched that you included my son. Thank you, Penny and Fred. Your kindness overwhelms me,' Oliver said emotionally, then added: 'And it will fit perfectly with our plans.'

'Yes,' Glanna told her parents. 'We've had a heart to heart. I was intending to go to London with Oliver, but we agreed that I've worked too hard to let the H*art*mouth Gallery go. I've seen how split-living has worked so well for Jen and Markus, so we are going to see how it pans out. Sadie can take charge in the holidays and I will recruit somebody else who can fill in when I am not around.'

'I plan to get a teaching job down here in the future as I won't be with Clarence all of the time,' Oliver joined in. 'Long term, running a gallery with Glanna would be a dream.'

'For us both,' the birthday girl smiled.

'Brilliant. And there are four bedrooms at the lodge, so our grandson's mums would be welcome anytime down here too.' Penelope hiccupped. 'I decided if we don't embrace this modern world, then more fool us.'

'Thanks for that. It really does mean a lot.' Oliver felt as if his heart was bursting with their acceptance of him and his beloved son.

'Grandson, Mum?'

'Well, Clarence will be our grandson. Oh, you know what I mean. Oliver is family now.'

Just then, Pat and Charlie Dillon appeared in front of them, arm in arm.

'Happy Birthday, Glanna,' said Pat, on her best behaviour.

'Yeah, Happy Birthday, sweet'eart.' Charlie gave Glanna a smacking kiss and shook Oliver's hands with his own, work-hardened ones. 'We've got some news tonight. Me and me old treacle here are renewing our wedding vows.'

'We are?' Pat Dillon beamed.

'Yeah, you're not a bad sort, I thought I might keep ya.'

Penelope Pascoe faked a smile at the couple as she swiftly headed back to the main throng.

'Yeah. It's been quite a day for us,' Pat Dillon offered. 'My Daz, that's Billy's brother, and his fella Philip, well, they've got the approval to adopt a little girl. I can't wait. We are going to head down to Cockleberry Bay where they live for Christmas, aren't we, Chaz? Billy, Kara and the twins are coming too. Yeah, our Daz has just moved in next to a lovely couple, Rosa and Josh Smith. Two kids and a dachshund called Hot, they've got. We spoke to 'em all on Facetime, last night. They was in a cafe on the beachfront. It's gonna be a right old knees-up there in Devon, ain't it? I can't bloody wait.'

'Sure is. Now come on, woman, stop your nattering and let's get another drink.'

Glanna and Oliver, now blissfully alone, looked out across the estuary. There was a chill in the October night air and the sea was dark apart from the reflecting lights from the cafe and the lights on the boats moored in the now emptying harbour. The full moon did its part, creating a magical twinkling pathway right across the estuary.

'After all tonight's baby talk, are you 100 per cent sure

about us not having a baby together?' Glanna asked Oliver. She needed to know the truth.

'Glanna, yes. It was always you I loved. A little one made from you and me would have been the cherry on the cake, but now I have Clarence, I have all that I ever wanted. We make a good team, me and you, and that's what relationships are all about. Complementing each other. Bringing out the best in each other. Two parts that come together as one.'

'I thought about the eggs we froze too,' Glanna said hesitantly.

'And?' Oliver looked into her eyes.

'If possible, I would like to donate them to anyone who may not be able to conceive naturally. Is that OK with you?'

Oliver grasped her hand and kissed it. 'You, my darling, are one gorgeous woman and yes of course, if that's what you want, then you must do that.'

A seagull flew closely overhead, causing them both to look to the sky.

'Not a rainbow in sight,' Glanna murmured.

'But just look at all those stars.' Oliver held his glass aloft. 'Happy Birthday, Glanna Constance Pascoe, and cheers to filling that blank canvas.'

'Cheers to that,' she raised her champagne flute of fizzy water, 'partner.'

Read on for an extract from

WELCOME TO FERRY LANE MARKET

The first book in the
Ferry Lane Market series!

Chapter 1

'I bet even the real Sid Vicious didn't shit in his bathwater.'
Kara Moon stared down at the noxious poo in the terrapin's
tank.

'Ooh, I bet he did,' her boyfriend Jago murmured whilst
flattening down his dark-brown Beatles-style haircut and
patting his khaki jacket pockets in turn. 'Seen my keys, Moo
Moo?'

Kara cringed inwardly at her once much-adored nick-
name. Then, retrieving the keys from the orderly rack in the
kitchen, she came back through the open archway into their
compact living space.

A lone beam of golden sunlight made its jittery mark
across the wooden floor as it seeped through the open crack
of the balcony door. The sounds of mewing seagulls and
creaking yacht masts in the estuary harbour rose up from
below, comforting and familiar, yet they did not ease the
gnawing feeling in Kara Moon's stomach. Hoping for a
different answer to the one she was expecting, she asked
casually, 'Where are you going this early, anyway?'

As Jago reached for his battered Beatles key ring, Kara
caught a whiff of the Gucci aftershave she had given him
for Christmas. He looked at her with a perplexed expression.
'It's Jobcentre day. You know I always go over to Crowsbridge
on a Friday.'

'How could I possibly forget?' Kara said sarcastically. 'Oh yes, maybe because it's been eighteen months and you still haven't come back with a job.'

'Don't start.'

'It's just, James Bond needs his flea stuff and I'm not sure if there's enough money in the blue pot and—'

Ignoring her pitiful plea, Jago went to the open hallway, jumped down two stairs at a time, then looked back to say in a patronising tone, 'My little Ginger Princess. You look quite pretty when you forget to tie your hair up in that stupid ponytail.'

Fighting back tears, Kara put her hand to the back of her long, messy auburn waves as her errant beau of eight years stalled again to say nastily, 'And why aren't *you* at work? Or did you stupidly forget about that too?'

Kara sighed deeply and held her palm up to him. 'Just go, Jago. You mustn't be late now, must you.'

She loves you, yeah, yeah, yeah. The famous Lennon-McCartney lyrics that Kara had chosen for his special key ring followed after Jago as he hurried down the stairs, jumped down the last three and went out, slamming the door.

To try and regain a modicum of inner peace, Kara stood still for a minute and stared out of the window at nothing in particular. Here she was, at thirty-three years old, living with a jobless, feckless, twenty-nine-year-old youth, with no mention or hope of plans for the future. And despite her working her butt off to support the two of them, she seemed to barely make ends meet, let alone save any money. The more cash she put aside in the blue ceramic savings pot for unseen eventualities and 'nice things' like holidays or weekends away, the more excuses Jago Ellis found to dip into it. In fact, tragically, the only holiday they had ever been on together was a long weekend to Liverpool where she was dragged around every street and tourist attraction to satisfy his insatiable hunger for anything and everything relating to his precious obsession: the Beatles.

Deftly avoiding a bite from Sid Vicious, Kara swore loudly and continued to hold back the tears she had been gripping on to. Then, gagging as she pulled her pink rubber washing-up gloves up as far as they would go, she scooped up the offending smelly mess in the tiny net bought for the purpose.

It was five years ago when Jago had arrived home drunk, carrying a huge tank up the steep stairs, slopping water as he went. And five years ago when the job of looking after this poor little reptile, first seen by Kara hanging on to a rock for dear life, had become *her* responsibility. She lifted her head in thought. Had they been getting on then? She couldn't remember.

Their living room with a view offered an optical illusion of space but despite the long bay window seat and door out on to the balcony, there was barely room for their table/desk with a couple of dining chairs and a sagging, two-seater sofa. Jago had cack-handedly fixed a TV far too big for the room to the wall above the fireplace. And the glass shelf that was eventually put up for the tank to sit on was placed at such an angle that when poor Sid wanted to get out of the water and bask under his heat lamp, it took him several attempts to scrabble his way up the slope to his rock. A canvas of the iconic *Abbey Road* Beatles cover hung on the wall above him; it was as if the Fab Four were taunting the little terrapin with their ability to walk in a straight line.

Despite the lack of space in the two-bedroomed flat, when

Kara had caught sight of the Painted Turtle's cute little prehistoric face, she didn't have the heart to say he had to go back to the pet shop from whence he came. And by the time she had got around to googling 'How long do terrapins live' and realised it could be up to thirty years, it was too late: Sid Vicious, the most aggressive reptile in Cornwall, along with James Bond, the skinny twelve-year-old black-and-white rescue moggy, with his furry white tuxedo and 007 air of nonchalance, were now very much part of their dysfunctional little Ferry Lane family.

Grimacing, she emptied the terrapin's mess into one of the big terracotta flowerpots on the first-floor balcony. Then, taking in the fresh sea air, she looked down to see the welcome sight of her father opening the metal gates of the ferry float and Jago running across the road towards it at full pelt so as not to miss its prompt departure.

As if sensing his daughter's sad eyes on him, Joe Moon looked up, smiled, waved, then turned his attention to beckoning the queuing cars on to the beloved car and passenger ferry service – the thriving business that had been part of the Moon family's life for as long as Kara could remember.

Chapter 2

Kara scraped her hair back into its customary loose ponytail, pulled the one remaining ten-pound note out of the blue pot on the kitchen windowsill, took her own keys from their usual place on the rack and headed down the flight of stairs to the front door of their flat. As she reached it, James Bond screeched in through the cat flap, stopped briefly to scratch himself frantically and then, as if sensing that a vet's visit was due, he tore up the stairs straight past her without so much as an acknowledgement.

'You stay in now, you hear me? Or I'll be in a whole lot of trouble,' Kara warned her beloved feline in her faint Cornish accent. She paused. Then she did something she never did. She locked the cat flap shut. Feeling a surge of guilt, she quickly ran back upstairs, pulled an old baking tray out from under the oven and filled it with some compost from one of the flowerless pots on the balcony. 'Just in case,' she said aloud as she placed it under the cat flap and shut the door behind her. 'I won't be too long,' she warbled through the letter box.

The door to Number One, Ferry View Apartments opened out on to the bottom end of Ferry Lane. Kara tentatively looked left, then right, then scurried around to the front of the Victorian block and began to walk along the crazy-paved promenade to work.

Up at the top of the hill, Ferry Lane Market was bursting into life. Every Friday and Saturday since she could remember, all market dwellers would set up outside their fixed, covered premises and sell their wares to not only the inhabitants of Hartmouth and its plethora of second homers, but also to the many seasonal visitors to the small, historic town. With the market having a reputation for being the best in the area, tourists would make the short journey across from Crowsbridge, some by foot, but most by car on her dad's ferry.

Nobody could deny that there was something magical about the community feel on open-air market days. Stallholders and customers alike would mingle and chat. Fresh, locally grown produce and original handmade items and gifts were beautifully displayed and sold. And despite Kara having worked her stall for the past fifteen years, she had never tired of the theatre of it all.

The late-spring breeze today was carrying the regular sales banter from the Dillons' fruit and vegetable stall. 'Come on, ladies, here's your early rhubarb, two quid a kilo. Make the old man a nice crumble with that; put a smile on his face. Give him a bit – no madam, I don't mean that bit. Here, feel my asparagus. Plump and juicy. Have a little squeeze if you like – I won't tell if you don't. Bananas, as long as you need 'em, madam.' And so on.

Despite the miserable start to her morning, Kara managed a smile, then turned to look at Nigel's Catch fish stall – which was so colourful that local artists would often paint pictures of it to sell to visitors. Squid, spider crabs, scallops and clams were arranged in glittering beds of ice, next to the most recent catch of fish; and when she closed her eyes and focused, above the fishy aroma Kara could smell tempting wafts of savoury Cornish pasties coming from a stall up the hill.

Ferry Lane Market was her life. She had started working at Passion Flowers, the florist shop and stall run by Lydia Twist, on her eighteenth birthday. But before that, from just twelve years old, she had worked on other stalls at many open Saturday market days. Joe Moon, Kara's dad, was Hartmouth born and bred, as were his parents before him, and with the ferry crossing being essential to everyone, he knew most of the locals. So, he had put the word around that his younger daughter would like some work and if anyone needed an extra pair of hands, then Kara Moon was their girl.

She had been happy then. With her sister Jenifer already away studying business and finance at Leeds University, for a while Kara felt like an only child. She didn't miss the bolshie, forthright Jenifer Moon one bit. With a seven-year age gap, the siblings had never been close. Kara had always been made to feel like an inconvenience, with Jen's bedroom door being slammed shut on her on many occasions and their mother rarely bothering to react to their shouting matches. In fact, if it didn't involve her directly, Doryty Moon had rarely reacted to anything.

At least with her mother walking out long before she had received her A-Level results, Kara didn't have to face the disappointment of her non-reaction. And with the little study she had put in, she had not only been elated to get such good results for all three of her exams, but with the cash that her dad had given her for doing so well, she was also at last brave enough to get her teeth fixed.

With an infinite fear of the dentist and after years of being called Bugs Bunny, she had finally allowed her father to gently persuade her to see an orthodontist. Oh God, how she had hated those painful restorative sessions! But the result had been worth it. Thanks to her hair colouring, she continued to get the odd 'Ginger' labelling, but she could just about cope with that now that she had a set of Hollywood veneers to beam back at the perpetrator. So it had been with a renewed feeling of confidence that she had turned up for her first day of work at Passion Flowers at the tender age of eighteen – until she saw the bright pink top she was expected to wear, and knew at once that it would clash dreadfully with her colouring. She also realised in that moment that she was as green about floristry as her sparkling emerald eyes.

Today was another first – the first time in fifteen years that Kara had ever taken some last-minute time off work. When Kara had asked Lydia, her boss, the inflexible florist had huffed, 'I cannot *believe* you are asking me this on the day before market day too. Really, Kara, can't you rearrange the vet appointment? And a *whole* day? Surely you can come back when the cat has had its bloody injections!'

Lydia's furious reaction was thoroughly predictable, as it meant that she herself had to get up at 4.30 a.m. to drive over to the flower market in Penrigan, the place where they were certain to purchase the finest and freshest flowers for the shop and stall. For the past five years, this weekly task had been entrusted to Kara, who quite enjoyed doing it and wasn't afraid of the responsibility – not that she got any thanks. Since handing over the keys of the company van for

Kara to use at her leisure, Lydia felt justified in demanding that she work ridiculous hours. And Kara, used to the many unreasonable requests from her uptight fifty-year-old employer, just complied for the sake of a quiet life.

But today, for once, Kara had held her ground. Taking James Bond to the vet wasn't a full-on lie, as he did need his annual cat flu injection. The fact that she had told Lydia he always got a weird reaction afterwards was, on the other hand, a downright stinker. But as Kara didn't know how she'd feel once she'd done what she needed to do, rather than take the chance of getting upset at work, she had decided that the best tactic was to just not be there.

With funds so tight, she couldn't afford to take James Bond to the vet any more unless it was an emergency. Her old family cat, Bawcock, had lived to the venerable age of twenty-two and he'd never had an injection in his life. The one and only time he'd had to go to the vet was when his ear was hanging off after a fight with the next door's tabby. Kara's mother had insisted he be treated right away, but Kara's grandad Harry had been round and said that the battered moggy was as brave as old Tom Bawcock, his name-sake, and that animals healed themselves quite ably. Grandad Harry would have been quite happy to clean up the raw bits with disinfectant and put a plaster over them. But Doryty Moon had got her way, as she always did. The beloved pet was patched up and to this day Kara still hadn't found out who the old tom's namesake was and what he had done that was so great.

Chapter 3

Frank's was a stand-alone oblong brick building located right on the estuary-wall edge. It had a gaily striped awning and a pink neon sign saying plainly, Frank's Café. To the right of the building there was a roped-off concrete area housing fixed wooden table benches with red and white sunshades for use in the summer months. Now that the weather was warming up, the side hatch where you'd queue for delicious home-made Cornish ice creams would soon be opening up, too. At the end of the day, seven days a week, market stall-holders and visitors alike would companionably unwind at Frank's and watch the sun go down over the sea as boats of all shapes and sizes plied the busy waterway.

Kara loved looking down to the estuary mouth, where the left point of Crowsbridge, scattered with its white dots of houses and open green fields, stared almost belligerently across at the rugged cliffs and big posh houses of Hartmouth Head. From Frank's, the gap out to sea appeared just a few metres across. Up close, it became a wide window to the infinite ocean stretching ahead.

The café wasn't licensed, but Big Frank Brady, the muscly tattooed Irishman who ran the place, brewed his own magnificent dark ale, serving it in iced-tea bottles straight from the under-counter fridge. His sloe-infused gin also passed perfectly as a blackcurrant cordial; poured on ice with refreshing tonic water, it made for a perfect illegal summer cocktail. Inside the café was an old-fashioned jukebox, where hits mainly from the 1950s and 1960s blared inside and out, rain or shine, in an attempt to encourage customers to come in. In fact, Big Frank had been known to turn the volume up full blast if he suspected anyone of even daring to walk past and across the road to the Ferryboat, the white-painted pub on the corner.

Frank's was set out in the style of an old-school American diner, sporting red leather booths, white Formica tables and a jazzily tiled floor. There were six high metal stools where you could prop yourself up at the bar and, if not wanting some hooky booze, you could choose one of the milkshakes, hot drinks, or plentiful juices on offer. As for the snack menu, everything on it was freshly made and moreish. The walls were adorned with black-and-white prints of the Hollywood stars of yesteryear. Kara particularly loved the one of Audrey Hepburn in *Breakfast at Tiffany's* – the famous one in which she is wearing a gorgeous, tight black dress and seductively holding a cigarette holder. Kara sadly acknowledged that even if she signed up a personal trainer of great ability for the rest of her life, she could never look like that. Her double D-cup boobs would not fit on such a tiny frame, for instead of being blessed with Audrey's waif-like figure, her own body sported ample thighs that led up to a large, round bottom. With a slim waist, she was in perfect hourglass proportion – just not the proportions she'd have chosen. The older locals of the estuary town of Hartmouth didn't much care for change, so when Big Frank Brady and his long-term partner Monique had arrived in a flurry of paint tins and extravagant interiors, there had been a bit of a to-do. But as with anything, time is not only a healer but a leveller as well, and despite the completely random concept of a Hollywood-themed café in a Cornish town, pretty soon Frank's and its renowned all-day breakfasts and frothy coffees were as much a visitor pull as the stalls and stores of Ferry Lane Market.

The owner of Frank's took up a lot of space. Six-feet four of it, in fact. Big Frank Brady had a brooding gypsy-type look about him, with black collar-length hair and brown eyes so dark they were impossible to read. His full lips were the envy of many of the young girls who insisted on paying fortunes for false fillers. His tattoo sleeve was a work of art, displaying angels, birds, and at the top a young, naked Monique with one arm in the air and pouting red lips of her own.

Kara found something very sexy about good tattoos on a man. Her boyfriend, Jago, hated any kind of body art. 'Tramp stamps' he would call them. With her love of flowers, she had always wanted a tiny rose tattoo, somewhere discreet, but he had been drunk when she had mentioned it and, slamming his hand down on to the table, he had labelled her a slut for even thinking about it.

The early morning rush had subsided, and Big Frank greeted Kara with his lopsided grin. 'If it isn't the lovely Kara Moon. It's not like you to be down here at this time on a market day.' He carried on wiping the glass counter.

'I've taken a day off.'

'Have you, now. Bet that's got old Twisty Knickers' knickers in a bigger twist than usual.' He laughed. 'And try saying that after a Guinness or three.'

'Yes,' was all Kara could manage, her face falling instead of smiling.

'Who or what else has been upsetting you now, then?'

'I don't want to talk about it.' She sighed deeply, then looked away quickly to stop tears from falling.

Seeing this, Frank reached his big hand over the counter and gently stroked Kara's cheek.

'I've got your back, Kara Moon, you know that, don't you?'

Kara's throat began to burn. She nodded. When her mother had abruptly decided to up and leave her family when Kara was just thirteen years old, Frank had only just arrived in Hartmouth – but on finding out what had happened, he had been a silent helper. The best kind. Additions to his orders from the big cash-and-carry place had been delivered straight to her dad. And many a lasagne or bag of cakes would be handed to the distraught man to take home to his family after a long day working on the ferry. Both her dad, Joe, and her Grandad Harry had a lot of time for Big Frank Brady. A mutual respect.

'Coffee?'

'Yes, to take away please. One for Dad and I'd better get Billy one, or I'll never hear the end of it. Oh, and a couple of bottles of water too, please. And, um, two of those custard doughnuts.'

'Coming up.'

Frank quickly returned with takeout cups in a cardboard holder. 'So, that's one white, no sugar, and one extra milky with three sugars for the lad. Two chilled waters and the cakes are in here.' He balanced a bag between the cups.

'Memory of an elephant you've got, Frank Brady.'

He then gestured at his flat wide nose. 'Not quite the trunk though. Too much boxing.' He winked.

Kara reached for her purse and paid. 'No Monique today, then?' she asked.

'She's gone to Paris to see her sister. Got to let her have a break sometimes.'

They both laughed. Half-French, half-English, Monique rarely spent much time at the café. In fact, she rarely spent much time in Cornwall. Rumour had it, Monique had been working in Las Vegas when she had met bad boy Frank there on a gambling weekend. She had subsequently saved him from a violent lifestyle by moving him to Cornwall, where her great-aunt from the Cornish side of her family had just left her a wonderful large and sprawling four-bedroomed house on the edge of the town.

A formidable woman, Monique still did the odd bit of directing dance shows around the world, and if not doing that she would be either relaxing in their beautiful home or visiting family and friends. The couple spent little time together but when they did, they made it count and for them, the arrangement somehow worked.

Kara picked the cardboard tray up from the counter. Just as she was about to leave, Frank turned from the customer he was serving and said in her ear, 'I had a young lad in here earlier. Gutted he was. Been dumped by his girl.'

Kara wasn't quite sure where Frank was going with this.

He finished up with: 'I told him to get over it. That some break-ups are meant for wake-ups.'

A watery smile was all she could manage in return.

**Welcome to Ferry Lane Market
is available to order now!**

Looking for more from Nicola May?

Sign up to the Nicola May newsletter for exclusive updates, extracts, competitions and news at www.hodder.co.uk/landing-page/nicola-may/

Or scan the QR code below

Stay Social and Follow Nicola:

@NicolaMay1

@author_Nicola

@NicolaMayAuthor

www.nicolamay.com

Bookends

When one book ends, another begins...

Bookends is a vibrant new reading community to help you ensure you're never without a good book.

You'll find exclusive previews of the brilliant new books from your favourite authors as well as exciting debuts and past classics. Read our blog, check out our recommendations for your reading group, enter great competitions and much more!

Visit our website to see which great books we're recommending this month.

Join the Bookends community:
www.welcometobookends.co.uk

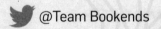 @Team Bookends   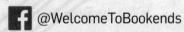 @WelcomeToBookends